THE PRISONER OF CASTILLAC

Molly Sutton Mysteries 3

NELL GODDIN

Beignet Books

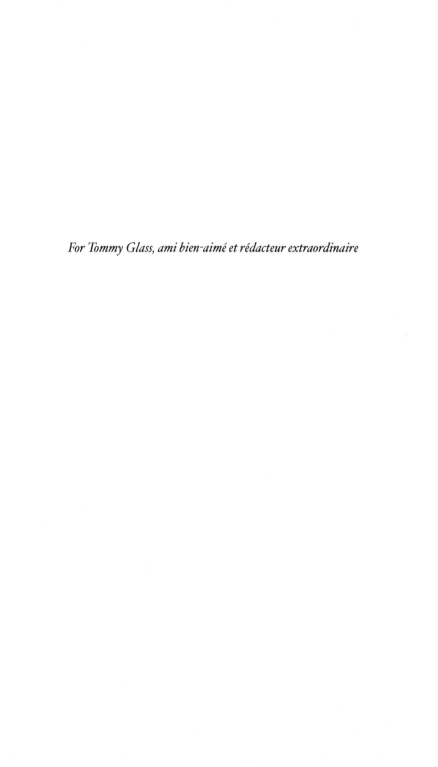

For Tommy Glass, ami bien-aimé et rédacteur extraordinaire

CONTENTS

PART I

Chapter One

2006

His girls were anxious in the morning, nosing up to the fence, mooing.

"You think I'd forget about you?" Achille Labiche said to the one with a black patch over her right eye. He reached over to scratch behind her ear. "I'm here every morning like clockwork. You know I'd never abandon you, no matter what."

He had thirty-two cows in his herd, all Holsteins. It was not large, as herds go, but it was enough for Achille and all he could handle by himself. Any more and he'd need to hire help, which was out of the question.

He whistled to Bourbon and the dog scampered around behind the cows and pushed them through the gate. They clopped up onto the concrete floor, into the barn. The smell of manure was deep and sweet, mixing with the scent of spring mud and all the plants in the pastures and woods coming back to life. Before going inside to do the milking, Achille tipped his head back and inhaled, and a smile broke over his face. He was the kind of man who most of the time had a rather affectless expression—not angry, not upset, but implacable—and the smile looked awkward on him, as though his facial muscles were confused.

Bourbon knew what to do and the girls did too. They jostled along, each cow wanting to get to the stations first, and Achille went down the row with the milking claws and hooked their teats into the teat cups. He had taken out a monstrous loan to pay for the machine and the barn that housed it, but that's what farming was like nowadays, and he felt he had to do his best to stay up with the latest dairy technologies, even if in his heart he wished he still milked all his girls by hand and plowed the fields by driving a plough-horse.

Achille lived alone in the small farmhouse he had grown up in. His parents had died almost ten years ago, when he was in his early twenties. Both of them gone the same year, both buried under an oak in the middle of the back hayfield. After their deaths, the central problem of Achille's life, as he saw it, was a terrible, aching loneliness. And yet he would not venture into the village of Castillac, which was nearest to his farm, and seek the company of others. He was far too timid. He imagined that strangers were talking about him unkindly, or making faces behind his back. He was certain he would never be able to think of anything to say if he dared go to the market on Saturday mornings and someone greeted him or even simply asked which artichokes he would prefer.

No, Achille guarded his privacy above all else. And he loved his cows and his dog and they gave him a great deal of solace. Just walking through the herd and bumping up against their big bodies and smelling their earthy cow smell—that went a long way towards assuaging his loneliness.

But it was not enough. Wouldn't anyone say the same?

MAY WAS LOOKING FAR BETTER than winter, with bookings for

Molly Sutton's *gîte* business at her place, *La Baraque,* finally starting to pick up. During the slow winter months, her fear of being carted off to a French poorhouse had been vivid even though she was pretty sure poorhouses no longer existed. At the moment she had an Australian couple and their baby staying in the cottage for ten days, and a single older man coming on the day the Australians were leaving. Her bank account was lean but not empty, and before long the rebuilt *pigeonnier* would be ready to rent as well.

True, there was more to running a *gîte* business than she had anticipated—more paperwork, mostly, and the necessity for nerves of steel when the cottage sat empty for months on end during the cold winter—but on the whole, it was turning out to be almost ridiculously fun. She loved meeting her guests and figuring out what she could do to make their vacations perfect. She adored not going to an office every day for eight hours or longer. She didn't even mind doing repairs, although it would be nice if things didn't break down quite so frequently.

And here it was, glorious springtime, and at long last Molly could throw herself into the making of the garden she had dreamed about ever since first seeing the photographs of *La Baraque* online over a year ago.

She was having a third cup of coffee while checking her email and corresponding with potential guests when she heard someone banging on the door.

"Bonjour Constance! I thought it must be you," she said, smiling and opening the door.

Constance fell into Molly's arms sobbing.

"What's wrong?" said Molly, putting her arms around her.

Constance lifted her head and started to speak, and then dropped it heavily on Molly's shoulder and kept crying. Molly stood and held her, thinking it was probably boyfriend trouble. She was not wrong.

"I thought he was *different!*" Constance got out between sobs.

"Didn't you, Molly? Didn't Thomas seem...." and then she was off again, bawling so hard her whole body shook.

Constance was Molly's occasional house-cleaner, a young woman not terribly talented at her job but of whom Molly was very fond. Molly led her over to the sofa and sat her down. "Tell me what happened," she said.

"Well, you know Simone Guyanet? We've never liked each other, she's like my arch-nemesis, you know? Even back in first grade. She's the type who's always got to win at everything, you know what I mean?"

Molly nodded.

"And I swear she snatched Thomas away just to beat me again! I've got the same sick feeling in my stomach I used to get on the playground when I was nine years old!" A gust of crying hit her and Molly squeezed her arm and got up to find some tissues.

"Here," she said, giving one to Constance. "Now come on, settle down a moment. Tell me the story."

"Well, a few weeks ago, Thomas started acting kinda funny. You know, not answering my texts and not saying a whole lot when we were together. And I'll tell ya, one of the things that makes Thomas and me get along so well is that he's a talker. I can't stand that silent type, you know? And Thomas isn't like that. He'll talk about anything too, it's practically like having a girl-friend. But with benefits," she added, and then burst into tears again.

Eventually, after a cup of tea and sandwiches and quite a few more outbursts, Molly got the story out of her. An old story, to be sure: her boyfriend Thomas had begun to be less attentive and less available, and eventually Constance found out that he had been seeing Simone Guyanet on the side.

"But why didn't he just break up with you and then go out with Simone?" asked Molly.

"Guys hardly ever do that, do they. Not the guys I end up

with. Instead of just coming out with it, they start acting like jerks so *I'll* break up with *them*."

"Chicken-hearted weasel-pigs," said Molly in English.

"Huh?" said Constance, who had taken English in school but knew only about six words.

"Not sure what the translation would be," said Molly, continuing in French. "This situation, Constance—that's how my marriage ended, more or less. I don't know why it's such a shock, finding out people are not who you thought they were. I mean, it happens all the time, yet we're never prepared for it. At least I'm not."

"That's exactly it, Molls," said Constance, her voice dejected. "Thomas is not who I thought he was. It's like he was wearing a nice-guy mask, and now the mask has slipped and he's nothing but a jerk underneath."

"That's verging on profound."

"That's me, Molly, your philosopher-housecleaner. I do it all. Just not windows, if you please!" She was trying to joke but her shoulders were so slumped they no longer looked like shoulders, and her usually open and smiling face was mournful.

"I wish there was something I could say to make you feel better, but I know from experience there isn't really anything. But —I do have a bag of almond croissants, fresh this morning from *Pâtisserie* Bujold...."

"Hand 'em over," said Constance. "*All* of them."

Chapter Two

Benjamin Dufort, late of the *gendarmerie*, was up at five in the morning for a run before heading off to his temporary job at a nearby farm. Another man might have been satisfied with the physically demanding work and not pushed himself to run in addition to it, but running was a habit Ben was unwilling to give up, no matter how inconvenient and unnecessary it was.

He allowed himself one cup of coffee before heading out, then laced up his tattered sneakers, put on a wind jacket, and hit the road.

It had been no small thing, giving up his work at the *gendarmerie*. Years of police training and experience tossed away in one impulsive moment. But he didn't regret it. No, there was no regret—and yet his mind was still not at ease.

The story he was telling himself was that he was really not good at delving into the minds of criminals. He didn't understand what made them tick. He believed that made him a poor detective, because no matter how diligent a person was about following procedure, a great detective or even just an adequate one has got to be able to put himself in the perpetrator's shoes, to take the imaginative leap so that he can anticipate what the criminal will do next, and have insight into where the bad guy might have tripped up.

But Dufort was made of sunnier stuff; he naturally avoided darkness, and when he had been in charge of cases where slipping into the dismal and dangerous state of mind of a potential criminal was necessary, he had not been able to do it. At least, this was the reason he assigned to his failures.

And he did not see how he could continue living a life doing a mediocre job when people were depending on him, and more than that, desperate for him to succeed.

The farmer he was working for was Rémy, an old friend. He depended on Dufort's help, and it was a real pleasure to Dufort to show up every day on time or early, ready to exert himself fully in the bracing spring air, and then go home pleasurably exhausted. It was strenuous work but he could handle it easily. At the end of the day, he felt, for the first time in years, as though the workday had been a complete success. No loose threads, no one disappointed.

No missing girls.

After his run, he changed clothes without showering since he would be sweating the minute he started work—and Rémy wouldn't give sweat a second thought. Then he drove over in his battered Renault, leaving the tiny apartment which was all he could afford after quitting the gendarmerie and being out of work for several months.

"*Salut!*" he called to Rémy, who was taking some heavy bags of chicken feed out of the back of his truck.

"Get over here, you lazy sod!" shouted Rémy.

Dufort grabbed two of the bags and the two men walked towards the chicken house. "So tell me," said Rémy, "what's next for you? I'm happy to have your help for as long as you want, but let's be honest my friend: farming is not the life for you."

"Why do you say that?" asked Dufort, surprised.

Rémy shrugged. "I know you like the physical labor because it calms your mind. Right?"

Dufort nodded.

"But if that is what farming is to you, a way to lower stress, and a workout—like going to a gym but in a prettier place? Then you're not...See, I enjoy the labor too, most of it. But I also get a genuine thrill when I see the lettuce sprout. It's a chore to collect eggs but I notice how warm they are in my hands—and I think nothing is funnier than a chicken. And beyond that, it matters to me to grow the highest quality food I possibly can. It's like I have a calling in a way, you understand?

"But you, Dufort—this is not your mission." Rémy pulled on a straw hat, the sun already bright.

"What if I don't have a calling," answered Dufort.

"Sure you do. Everybody does. It's just that some people fight against it."

"You and your New Age hippie talk," laughed Dufort.

"*Bon*," said Rémy, "let's get to work. I'm putting you in the asparagus bed today. I want you to apply a bit of compost, and then a thick layer of mulch."

Rémy got his friend organized with a large fork and a wheelbarrow, and showed him where the compost and mulch were before taking off in his truck.

My calling, thought Dufort, rolling his eyes. And then he got to work, shoveling a load of compost into the wheelbarrow with a wide shovel, and then making another trip to fork in a load of mulch. He managed to apply the compost and mulch as Rémy had directed him, but his mind was somewhere far away. He did not notice the lovely asparagus shoots, poking their purple heads up through the dark crumbly soil, or the clouds that rolled in, threatening rain.

Instead he was thinking about Valerie Boutillier and Elizabeth

Martin, two young women who went missing right after he first came to the gendarmerie of Castillac. Their files were always open on the desk in his mind, and as he worked, he leafed through the pages, becoming so absorbed that by accident he completely covered the spinach with mulch too.

Chapter Three

The first thing was a note, stuck with a bit of tape to the front door of the station. No envelope. The paper just a torn scrap of graph paper like that used by schoolchildren. Like a clichéd ransom note, the letters had been messily clipped from newspaper headlines and formed in a sentence: *I saw VB*.

That was it. No signature, of course, and no further elaboration.

Gilles Maron removed the paper from the door of the station with tweezers and sent it to the forensics lab along with the tape for fingerprinting. Others may have called him overly meticulous at times, but to Maron's mind, there was really no such thing. The way you gathered enough evidence for arrests was by being careful at every opportunity, doing your very best not to let anything slip past—not a bit of thread, a hair, a phone tip, a fingerprint.

Perhaps he would have been tempted to be less meticulous in this instance if the initials had been something else. But "VB," he immediately realized, could be Valerie Boutillier, a young woman who had disappeared before he came to Castillac and never been found. A stone cold case, and a cloud over the village that many had not forgotten.

"VB" could mean Valerie Boutillier, or something else altogether. The note could be insignificant, the initials just a random coincidence, a childish prank. Or it might be a mean sort of joke, someone trying to lure the gendarmes on the Castillac force into opening up the case only to waste resources on a case with no new evidence or leads.

Maron did not mention the note to Perrault, the other officer. He wanted to wait to see what the lab had to say first.

Maron was extremely pleased to have been promoted to Chief, even if it was only an interim appointment while the gendarmerie found someone to replace Benjamin Dufort, who had surprised everyone (except perhaps the herbalist who prescribed his anti-anxiety tinctures) by resigning his post just before Christmas. Unlike Dufort, Maron was not from Castillac. He was from the north of France and had not made many friends in the village. Which was how the gendarmerie liked it, believing officers did more objective work if they lacked deep ties to the people in their jurisdiction.

He was mostly skeptical about the note. It was very likely meaningless. But what if someone really had seen Valerie? Why not simply call the gendarmerie and report it? Did something about the circumstances—who she was with, or where she was seen—make the witness wary?

Or frightened?

MOLLY SPENT most of the day in the *potager*, weeding and turning over the soil in the raised beds. No one had lifted a finger there in some time, and it had taken days of clearing vines and even small bushes before the raised beds were clearly visible. Six of them, about half a foot high—or eight centimeters she should say, in an effort to practice the switch to metric—surrounded by deep blue porcelain tiles. The tiles were more for decoration than anything else, as they weren't very stable and dirt spilled through the cracks onto the path. But Molly decided to keep them because she liked looking at them, and wondered about the former inhabitant of La Baraque who had put them there.

Growing vegetables wasn't her favorite part of gardening. It was practical, yes, but for Molly practicality wasn't at the top of her list. What she liked most was abundant, fragrant blooms, disorderly and lush, and her plan for this vegetable bed was to make it as ornamental as possible. So far she was thinking artichokes, so glorious with their grand thistly heads, and she had started five plants indoors under a light. It was time to get their home in the garden ready.

After all that labor, her back feeling it, she texted her friend Lawrence Weebly to see if he'd like to meet her for a drink, and when he immediately answered OF COURSE, she went inside, showered, and was on *rue des Chênes* on the way to Chez Papa in record time.

"Hello, my dear!" said Weebly in a posh English accent when she came in.

"*Salut*, old chap! Bonjour, Nico!" Molly kissed cheeks with Lawrence and Nico, the bartender, and settled herself on a stool at the bar. "I'm so happy to be here. My guests are out on a long hike—I haven't seen them all day—and much as I love gardening, I was starting to talk to myself even more than usual."

Lawrence smiled and sipped his Negroni. "I do love this time of year in Castillac. When winter is over, everyone in the village comes out of their burrows, blinking in the sun, ready to socialize again after a long winter huddled next to the woodstove."

"Long winter, are you kidding me?" said Molly, who was from Boston and knew a thing or two about long winters. "It's practically tropical here. But yes, I admit I did spend plenty of time in front of my woodstove over the last months. So good for a nap, aren't they? But maybe I'd have had more fun if certain people hadn't extended their holiday in Morocco for months and let me get bored and lonely!"

"Well, you did have Frances," said Nico, almost shyly.

"Until you stole her!" said Molly. Her best friend from the States had come for a visit, but once Molly started having paying guests again, Frances happily moved in with Nico, never being one to resist romantic impulses.

"She should be showing up any minute. Then we can fight over her. She'll like that."

Molly laughed. "Wait. Lawrence, I'm not done telling you how forlorn I was without you. How could you end up staying in Morocco for three whole months?"

Lawrence smiled. "Ah Molly, you wouldn't want to stand in the way of love, would you?"

She paused. "I have no idea what to say to that," she said wryly. "Love is…not my area of expertise."

"Oh poor poor you," said Nico, walking along the bar as he wiped it down.

"I'm not feeling sorry for myself," she said. "It's just true. But so anyway…Lawrence, tell the story, please. You found love in Morocco? And if so, where is he now?"

"Well, you know how it is," said Lawrence, and Molly thought she saw a fleeting expression of pain on Lawrence's usually cheerful face. "I actually did fall in love, embarrassing as that is to admit. He was a little younger than me, but not much. Beautiful beyond words, and tremendously amusing." Lawrence took a big swallow of his drink and did not continue.

Molly put her elbows on the bar and looked at her friend. "That's the thing," she said. "It's all just impossible. You meet somebody, your heart says *yes yes yes*, but most of the time it turns out to be *no no no*."

She waited to see if Lawrence wanted to talk any more about the man in Morocco. When she saw that he didn't, Molly continued, "I'm sorry it didn't work out." There was a long silence as all three of them got lost in their own memories for a moment.

Molly said, "I'm not still messed up from my divorce—really, that's the past and I'm over it. But I admit, I miss living with someone. I'm not a solitary kind of person and even though I appreciate the luxury of always being able to do exactly as I please and never having to compromise, living alone can be sort of sad sometimes, especially at night, you know? But I just don't see romance working out for me, if that makes any sense."

"It does not," said Lawrence. "You talk about love as though it's something you can schedule, or see coming down the track. But it's not like that at all. I went to Morocco to get a little sun and avoid the dreary weather around here in winter, that was all. I had no idea I would go into a coffeehouse and Julio would be waiting for me." Again Molly saw a quick pang cross her friend's face. "Well, Molly, shall we eat a proper dinner for once? Nico, what's good tonight?"

"Rémy brought in some early asparagus, and there's a chicken in cream sauce with mushrooms that will make you cry from happiness."

"Well then," said Lawrence, mustering a smile. "Let's have it! Molly?"

"Yes, that sounds perfect. And Lawrence, for what it's worth, I'm very glad you're back. You missed all the excitement with Josephine Desrosiers, and the village has been totally placid since then. We've needed you back here to liven things up a little."

"Oh, I doubt that," said Lawrence. "I'm sure something will come along for you to stick your nose into. It always seems to."

Molly put her arm around him and gave him a squeeze. "No more murders are on the docket at least," she said with a laugh, and Lawrence thought perhaps he could detect a slight air of disappointment in Molly's tone.

Chapter Four

Frances had borrowed Nico's car so that she and Molly could drive to Périgueux where there was a flea market that afternoon.

"Are you ever going to get your own wheels?" she asked, as Molly climbed in.

"Stay, Bobo!" Molly said to the big speckled dog, who had shown up just before Christmas and quickly become part of the household. "I know you hate to miss out but I'll take you on a long walk when I get home. Promise!"

Bobo's head drooped. Then she turned and loped back to the house and curled up on the doorstep, the picture of dejection.

"You know, 'Bobo' is a very undignified name for that dog. I think she deserves better," said Frances, just managing to turn around without running the car into the flower border.

"Says the woman who tried to name her 'Dingleberry'."

"It just came to me. Sometimes you have to go with inspiration."

"Right," said Molly, looking out the window and rolling her eyes. "And about the car—I know, I have to do something. Actually I was thinking about getting a scooter."

"Whoa, that would be be awesome! I say go for it!"

"It would be cheap, but otherwise completely impractical. What if I need to pick up guests at the train station or something? But anyway, that's a decision for another day. Today is just about getting some furniture for the *pigeonnier*. Once that's done, all that remains is getting the plumbing hooked up, and it's ready to rent."

On the half hour drive to Périgueux, Molly and Frances chattered about how good the chicken had been at Chez Papa the night before, and about Lawrence's fizzled romance. They argued about whether iron bed frames or wood were preferable. And before long Frances was pulling into an underground parking lot in the center of town, making the tires squeal as she rounded the tight corners.

"Frances, I'm not in any hurry," said Molly, gripping the armrest. "Has Nico ever seen you drive?"

"He loves how I drive," said Frances smugly. "Says it's hot."

"Oh, my eyes are hurting, they're rolled back up in my head so far."

"Well, roll them back down, silly. Nico and I—we understand each other."

"I'm happy for you both."

"Your eyes are still rolling."

"Never. Now let's get to the flea market before all the good stuff is snapped up."

They wandered into the old section of Périgueux, swiveling their heads all around so as not to miss anything. The streets were narrow, most likely former cow-paths as the streets were very old, and the buildings close together. Molly didn't understand why old buildings made her so happy to look at, but they did. They had stood there so long, seen so much history, held so many mysteries....

The flea market surrounded the old cathedral, an unusual Byzantine and Romanesque building with large domes. Sellers were clustered all around it, with small items on tables or spread on blankets, and furniture of all shapes and sizes was on offer.

"So what's on our shopping list?" asked Frances. "Beds? Tables? Chairs?"

"The pigeonnier only has one bedroom. So let's see, a full-sized bed, and a kitchen table, which'll double as a dining room table. Maybe three chairs? And a bedside table if we find one, or something that would do for one. And I guess keep your eye out for a sofa, though I'll probably have to shell out for a new one."

"Used sofas give me the creeps, ever since the one I bought at a used furniture store, remember? Right after college for my first apartment? I was so proud of it. It was bright green. But when the weather got warm it smelled of cat pee. Burned your eyes it was so bad."

Molly was laughing, remembering. "I recall that air freshener did not work."

"Just made for flowery-smelling cat pee," agreed Frances.

"*La bombe!*" a man said, almost in Molly's ear. She turned to find Lapin standing with his arms open, grinning. Awkwardly they kissed cheeks.

"Bonjour, Lapin. I suppose I shouldn't be surprised to find you here. See anything good?"

"Today is a total bust so far. Nothing but junk. Allow me to introduce myself, since Molly appears to have forgotten her manners," he said to Frances, with a bow. "I am Laurent Broussard, but the world calls me Lapin."

"Translate?" asked Frances.

"She doesn't speak French," said Molly.

"No problem," said Lapin in English, introducing himself again.

"Very nice to meet you," said Frances, giggling. Molly wanted to elbow her in the ribs but restrained herself.

"All right, we have much to do—I'm trying to outfit my pigeonnier. *À bientôt*," said Molly, beginning to walk away.

"Wait, why didn't you come to me? You know I can get you the best deals, and tell you who to go to. I'm afraid I don't keep much furniture of that size, not unless it's a very special piece. But I can introduce you to a fellow on the other side of the cathedral who most likely has the sort of thing you're looking for."

Molly and Frances followed Lapin as he nimbly moved his big self through the maze of sellers and their furniture. Molly was torn. She needed his help but didn't especially want it. Lapin made such a pest of himself most of the time, although she had to admit he had toned down his ogling and suggestive remarks after the Amy Bennett case.

"You know, I'm planning to open my own shop in Castillac soon," Lapin told them. "I just signed a rental agreement and will be spiffing the place up a bit before moving in all my valuables. You might find all sorts of things that would be perfect to decorate your gîtes."

"The cottage could use a little jazzing up," agreed Frances, and Molly shrugged, though she thought maybe her friend had a point.

Several hours passed as the three of them argued the merits of each piece and then haggled with the merchants, but by noon the purchasing was complete, the deliveries arranged, and all that remained to do in Périgueux was find the place where they sold the most delicious prunes stuffed with *foie gras*, and then eat lunch.

Molly considered inviting Lapin as a thank-you for his time and help, which had been substantial. Then she talked herself out of it. Then back into it, then out, then in...and finally Frances asked him to join them and her fate was sealed.

Back in the fall if she had been told that in a few months she would feel grateful to Lapin and willingly sit down to lunch with him—and even pay for it—she would never have believed it. But then, looking into the future had never been one of Molly's talents.

❧

MARON STUCK his head out of what he still thought of as Dufort's office, and called for Thérèse Perrault. She wasn't exactly thrilled about having Maron as her boss, but told herself it was a test of both her flexibility and ability to hide her feelings at work, which were skills she knew she needed to develop if she wanted to succeed in the gendarmerie.

"What's up?" she said evenly.

"Take a look. It was taped to the front door." The note was sitting on his desk and he pushed it towards Perrault.

She read it, looked up quickly at Maron, and then studied it more closely.

"Valerie Boutillier," she said.

"Right. My first thought as well. So what do you think? Does it look genuine to you? Like a prank? What?"

Perrault considered. "I doubt it's random. The chances seem pretty slim that someone would happen to choose the same initials as one of our cold cases, with V and B not being the most commonly used letters. And not just any case—a girl who disappeared without a trace right before going off to university, her dream school where she had worked so hard to get in. A girl many of us knew and loved."

Maron just nodded. Then he said, "I sent the note to the lab, but there were no usable fingerprints."

"What? When did you find it?"

"The day before yesterday."

"And you didn't tell me?" Perrault's face was blazing.

"I wanted to have a fuller picture before I—"

"Listen, Gilles, I know you're probably loving every minute of being my boss, but let me tell you first of all that I am absolutely dead clear that you are my superior and I have no problem with that whatsoever. But I would ask you, respectfully, not to keep me in the dark when new evidence falls out of the sky like this apparently did. And about a case this important."

Maron froze when Perrault began to speak. The truth was, he was uncomfortable being in charge of anyone, and spent much of his energy trying to hide that embarrassing fact. He had a grudging respect for Perrault, which she returned, but they were not friends, and they had not worked together all that happily in the past.

"Look, Perrault, no need to take offense. Of course you will be notified when we have new evidence." Maron stood up and then sat down again. "Tell me what you know about Valerie. I was not yet in Castillac when Dufort was working that case and all I know is that she disappeared and was never found. No suspects, and no idea what happened to her, have I got it right?"

Perrault got control of herself and took a deep breath. "All right. Valerie is older than me. I was sixteen when she disappeared, she must have been...eighteen? I wasn't a close friend—but everyone in the village knew her, or knew who she was. She was that kind of girl—charismatic, you know? Fun-loving and smart as a whip. She used to play practical jokes on people all over the village, and sometimes she would go too far and people would get mad. I remember once she got into Madame Luthier's house —you know, she lives in that rat-hole over on rue Saterne—and while Mme Luthier was out, she took everything in the living room and put it in the kitchen, and everything in the kitchen and put it in the living room. So when Luthier came home, there was nothing to sit on in the living room but a bunch of saucepans."

Maron lifted the corners of his mouth in the direction of a smile, but not quite far enough to actually be a smile. "And did the village think that was amusing?" he asked.

"Oh, some people did. Mme Luthier is not exactly known for being able to take a joke, so for some people, that made it funnier."

"Seems like a lot of trouble to go to."

"One of the things that made Valerie so attractive was her limitless energy. She always had a lot going on at once, with a lot of different people."

"And what is this 'dream school' you mentioned?"

"*École Normale Supérieure,* in Paris," said Perrault, her eyes wide. "About the toughest school to get into in the whole world. Valerie had a serious side too, and she worked super hard at school. She wanted to be a journalist, the kind who digs up dirt on powerful people."

"Hmm," said Maron, thinking that Valerie Boutillier did sound like an interesting and accomplished person, even if one with an odd sense of humor. "Do you know anything about the investigation?"

"It was before my time too, obviously. We should ask Dufort to brief us."

"Of course. If we get any other indication that Boutillier is alive, I'll call him in."

"What do you mean, 'any other'? This is a *lead*, Gilles! Sitting right there on your desk!"

Maron shrugged. "I don't think that's likely. The girl has been gone for seven years. Would anyone in Castillac even recognize her now?"

"Of course! I would!"

Maron looked out of the window. He would never have guessed that he would be far more comfortable taking orders than giving them, but that was precisely how things were turning out.

"Just bring me one piece of additional evidence, something solid, and I will formally open the case again," he said. "In the meantime, if you would like to ask around, see if you can find out who put the note on the door? Go ahead, as long as your other duties are taken care of first," he said.

"Yes, sir," said Perrault, with not quite enough sarcasm for Maron to chew her out for it.

Chapter Five

Molly's current guests, a lively Australian couple, wanted to drive over to Rocamadour, an ancient village built right into a rock face high above the river Dordogne. The morning they were to leave, they rapped on Molly's door.

"Bonjour, Ned and Leslie! Are you all set for your excursion? The drive isn't bad from here, though I admit I haven't done it myself." Then Molly paused, seeing something was wrong.

"Bonjour Molly," said Leslie. "Here's the thing. Little Oscar isn't feeling well. He's not really sick, we don't need a doctor or anything like that. But I think a day trip like we have planned wouldn't be very fun for him, you know?"

Molly nodded. Bobo came up behind Molly and stuck her head between Molly's legs.

"So...we know it's short notice...well, no notice I guess. But we were wondering whether you knew of anyone who could look after him just for the day, so we could go on ahead and see Rocamadour, and he could stay here and rest."

"Hmm," said Molly. "Come on in, let me pour myself another cup of coffee while I think about it. You want a cup?"

"We don't drink coffee," said Ned, grinning. "Got too much energy already!"

Molly laughed, although she considered non-coffee-drinkers to be a species of human she could not comprehend.

She thought of Constance, but wasn't sure if she had any experience with kids, especially sick ones. She thought her neighbor Madame Sabourin might know of someone, but that might take time.

"Oh hell, I can do it," she blurted out before she could stop herself.

"All right!" said Ned, pumping his fist. "You know, I think he's already quite taken with you, so I think it should be easy enough."

"Of course he's taken with me. I'm the chocolate lady," laughed Molly. When the family had first arrived, Molly had brought Oscar a small chocolate bell—the French version of Easter candy.

Leslie took Molly to the cottage and showed her where the diapers were and told her Oscar's general schedule while Ned packed up the car. Within ten minutes they were gone, and Molly was alone in the cottage with a sick eleven-month-old. Who was thankfully having a morning nap.

Molly crept into the bedroom and over to the crib, glad she had found a sturdy one at the flea market a few months earlier. The little boy was asleep on his stomach, his arms sticking straight up over his head, and one knee bent up. His face was flushed and his brow sweaty. Molly wanted to stroke his cheek but was afraid to wake him.

Quietly she went back to the small kitchen, and steamed some vegetables for his lunch. The orange cat appeared from nowhere and rubbed up along her leg.

"I'm not fooled," she told it. "And leave that baby alone."

Bobo scratched, wanting to get in on whatever was happening. Molly went over and spoke to her through the door. "I'm looking after the baby, Bobo. And none too confident about it, since I haven't actually touched a baby since I was in high school and used to babysit for Mrs. Stout who lived two doors down. So just stand guard outside, okay? And no scratching on the door."

Molly heard a low grumble but then the sound of the dog flopping down on the doorstep.

"See that?" Molly said to the cat. "Obedient. Helpful."

The cat streaked into the bedroom and jumped into the crib. Molly cursed under her breath and ran after it.

Oscar was sitting up, rubbing his eyes. The orange cat was rubbing along his back, its tail wrapping around into Oscar's face, making him giggle.

"Hello!" said Molly. "Do you like cats, Oscar?"

"Mum?" said Oscar.

"Mum is...uh, Mum and Dad went on a short trip, they'll be back later. In the meantime we can play, how about that?"

Oscar reached his arms up for her to pick him up and the gesture made tears spring to Molly's eyes. He was so trusting! So willing to adapt to what was happening, even if that meant an almost complete stranger mysteriously replacing his parents. Molly reached into the crib and lifted his small body, pulling it into hers. She smelled his hair and let her cheek touch his.

"I don't know about you, but I love to play," she said to him, and with a pang realized that there was not a single toy anywhere at La Baraque. She carried Oscar into the other room but saw nothing in the open kitchen/living room either. Ned and Leslie must have driven off with everything except for the stuffed animal in the crib, or possibly they thought toys were bad for some reason?

If there was one thing Molly understood at the age of thirty-eight, it was that people were nutters. She didn't follow the latest trends in parenting, as it only reminded her of what she wished for but did not have, and so if there were a robust anti-toy movement she wouldn't know about it—but wouldn't have been surprised either.

She put Oscar down on the wood floor. He crawled a short way and then sat, looking at her. He rubbed his eyes again.

"You don't feel well, do you?" she said, squatting down beside him. "Are you hungry?"

"Mum?"

"Right. Mum. She'll be back before long," said Molly, knowing it was at least a two hours' drive each way, and a lot of walking and sightseeing once you were there. She and Oscar had many hours to kill before Mum was going to show up. So Molly played peek-a-boo. She made up a long story about goats and a mean orange cat, successfully changed a diaper, and served him lunch on the front step, in the sunshine.

She delighted in Oscar's company and simultaneously felt trapped and desperate to get free. When her cell phone rang Molly was relieved to make contact with the outside world.

"It's Thérèse," said Perrault.

Molly could hear a horn honking in the background. "Hey Thérèse, how are you?" The two had been friendly since Molly had helped with a couple of murder investigations.

"I've got something I want to pass along. But...you've got to keep it on the down-low."

Molly handed Oscar a wooden spoon to bang on the floor. She felt a familiar tingle of anticipation. "All right," said Molly. "I'm all ears."

❧

VALERIE BOUTILLIER. A beautiful name, thought Molly. And now, maybe, just maybe...still alive, against all odds. Valerie had disappeared years before Molly moved to Castillac, but she was not forgotten there, and Molly had heard enough stories about her to feel as though she was not a total stranger.

And now someone had seen her.

Molly did not spend any time doubting the note. She reasoned that if it turned out to be a joke of some kind, there was no harm in having done whatever they could in the way of investigation. Far worse to disbelieve it, do nothing, and never know if the note had been true or not. It *might* be true. And for Molly—and Thérèse Perrault—"might" was good enough.

It was one o'clock. When Thérèse called, Molly had been about to put Oscar down for a nap (which they both needed). He was fussy and hadn't eaten much, mostly just slurped a lot of water. "So Oscar," she said, picking him up. "How would you like to go on a walk? Get a little fresh air, see the sights? And if you're not in the mood for sights, just go ahead and close your little eyes. How's that sound?"

Molly's plan was to take Oscar into the village and see whom she could find to talk to about Valerie. She had no stroller and certainly no baby carrier, so she took him to her house. In the foyer she found a very wide and long heavy cotton scarf, wrapped it around them both leaving spaces for his legs to hang down, and knotted the ends. With a little adjusting, her improvised sling seemed to be working perfectly, the baby secure against her chest. She bent her knees quickly and stood up, and Oscar gurgled happily.

"You like it?" she asked him, her voice all high and cooing and unrecognizable to herself.

"Mum," said Oscar. By this point Molly understood that he was not calling his mother so much as saying the one intelligible word he could say.

"Mum indeed," she answered. She kissed his cheek, which was astonishingly soft, and set out for the village. The walk was still new because Molly had yet to walk it in every season. The weather was lovely. Birds were making a racket, trees were leafing out, and the world was bright and green and sweet-smelling.

And was Valerie outside, somewhere, seeing this blue sky? wondered Molly. If she's alive, why hasn't she come back? If someone has seen her, why has Valerie not reached out, called for help, somehow made her presence known?

Molly figured the most likely explanation was that Valerie was imprisoned somewhere—everyone had seen reports every so often of that happening: girls snatched up and kept in some bunker or basement, sometimes for years on end. Is that what had happened to Valerie? And yet somehow, someone had seen her?

As she walked, Molly thought of a long list of questions for Thérèse, but Thérèse had been quite clear that she was violating all kinds of regulations by telling Molly about the note, and it was better if they did not meet. Molly thought that perhaps a chance encounter in the village would be all right, if they didn't linger. So she walked towards the station, one hand on Oscar's deliciously fat little leg, talking to him about what they saw along the way...a red squirrel, a car with a dent in one side, some late tulips not yet in bloom.

It was one o'clock and all of Castillac was sitting down to lunch. Not a soul on the streets. Molly kept walking, aware that she was carrying something defenseless and precious. She wondered if mothers got used to that, or whether they continued to worry constantly that something dreadful might happen—she could fall and land on him, or a car could jump up on the sidewalk and run them over; there was no end to the catastrophes lurking around every corner.

When she reached the station, she walked to the front door, studying it. She closed her eyes for a moment and tried to imagine someone approaching it, not wanting to be seen, note in hand with a piece of tape already attached. She stepped back and looked at every detail of the door—the big hinges, the decorative molding, the glossy green color.

Oscar's head had lolled to one side when he fell asleep. Molly had a sudden idea and startled, nearly waking him up. She ran her fingers over the wood, trying to feel where the adhesive had been. After moving her fingers lightly over much of the door, she found a small patch, maybe about a square centimeter, just lower than chest height. Looking at it closely, she could see it was relatively fresh—not completely covered in dust and pollen as it would be if it had been there long. Maybe at some point (if she was ever allowed to talk openly about the case) she would have an opportunity to ask Maron whether he remembered where on the door the note was taped, just for added verification, but she trusted she had the answer. Molly was a little on the short side.

Which meant that whoever taped the note on the station door was not tall.

It was the first step towards finding Valerie. A small one, Molly had no illusions about that.

But you have to start somewhere.

Chapter Six

Molly was giving Bobo her breakfast when she saw the delivery truck pull into her driveway with the furniture for the pigeonnier, followed by Dufort's green Renault. Quickly she ran into her bedroom and whipped off her nightgown and robe, and put on a clean pair of jeans and a shirt.

"Coming!" she called out, leaving by the French doors and walking around the side of the house to greet them. Bobo ran frantically back and forth, unsure what her job was.

"Bobo! Down!" said Molly, before the dog flattened the truck driver with her excitable leaping. Bobo stopped on a dime and dropped to the ground.

"Impressive," said Dufort, walking up to kiss cheeks.

"Bonjour, Ben! And bonjour, Monsieur," she said to the driver. "Can I ask you to drive a little farther? The furniture is going in there," she said, pointing to the meadow where the pigeonnier stood, its walls no longer crumbling thanks to the exertions of the mason, Pierre Gault.

"Looks like I came just in time to help," said Ben.

Molly grinned. "Well, I won't say no. I can carry some of it but honestly I wasn't sure I could hold up my end of the bed going upstairs—there wasn't room in there for anything but a ladder."

"It has a loft bedroom?"

"Exactly," said Molly. "It's very romantic. Pierre Gault left all the little nestboxes or perches intact, and made some of them into tiny windows. It looks amazing! I'm desperate to get photos up on my website, but I've been waiting to get the furniture in."

The driver knew his business and with Dufort's help, all the furniture was unloaded and roughly in place in half an hour.

All through the unloading and the talk of furniture and dogs, Molly had been wondering whether to tell Ben about the note. Thérèse had only said not to say a word to Maron. Perhaps Thérèse was actually hoping she would tell Ben?

"I'm sorry, I got distracted. What were you saying about asparagus?" said Molly.

"Oh, it doesn't matter. I was just telling you about a typical day at Rémy's."

Molly cocked her head, then lifted the bedside table and put it next to the bed. "Want a coffee?" she asked. "Or maybe lemonade?"

"Sounds good." Dufort and Molly climbed down the wooden ladder to the bottom floor of the pigeonnier. "The place turned out well," said Dufort, looking around the cozy downstairs room with its tiny kitchen.

"Yes, I think so too. I should find interesting things to put in the rest of the little nestboxes. Or maybe my guests will leave mementos in them, if I hint enough."

"Come, Bobo!" Molly called, wanting to make sure the dog was out of the way as the delivery truck backed up to the driveway and turned around. Bobo popped out of the forest and streaked to Molly's side.

"How did you train your dog so well?" asked Ben.

"I can't take any credit at all," answered Molly. "She just

showed up one day acting like she lived here. Already trained. I swear you can talk to her like a person and she understands."

"I would guess someone is looking for her."

"Yes. Well, I'll give her back if I have to. But in the meantime, we are pals. Isn't that right, Bobo?" she said, scratching behind Bobo's ears. "So, Ben. Do you miss the gendarmerie?"

Dufort thought a moment. "That's hard to answer. I suppose the fairest thing to say is that quitting the job has not given me all the freedom I was looking for."

Molly looked at Ben questioningly but he shrugged and looked away. His rampant anxiety had disappeared once he gave up the gendarmerie, but nonetheless, he did not have peace. They walked back to the house in silence. Molly was still trying to decide whether she would be causing trouble for Thérèse if she told Ben about the note. And Ben was thinking, as he so often did, about Elizabeth Martin and Valerie Boutillier, because he was not free from his responsibility to them, and never would be, until they were found.

The day had turned hot, the way spring days sometimes do, as though suddenly opening a window onto summer. Molly got out two tall glasses and filled them with lemonade. While Frances had stayed with her, she had gotten into the habit of making it fresh every morning, because Frances said it gave her inspiration for jingle-writing. And Molly had been happy to oblige, because of course fresh lemonade is one of life's most sublime pleasures, especially with a splash of fizzy mineral water.

"Oh, I'm just going to tell you," she finally said.

Dufort raised his eyebrows and smiled.

"I probably shouldn't. Or I should ask first. But you're here, and I know this matters to you deeply, so...but listen, I don't want you to think I can't keep a secret. I'm actually quite good at it. Then again—"

"Molly, just tell me!"

"Yes. Well, all right. Perrault called yesterday to tell me that someone had taped a note to the station door that said 'I saw VB'." She waited to see Ben's reaction.

He narrowed his eyes slightly but was otherwise completely still. Like a hunter who has just spied a sign left by his prey.

"Interesting," he said at last. "Is that a direct quote—'I saw VB'? Did it say anything else?"

"I don't think so."

"Unsigned of course?"

"I assume so. We didn't get a chance to talk long. I gather Maron isn't going to pursue it and that was why Thérèse called me. She's hoping I'll…I don't know, follow up somehow."

Dufort took his glass of lemonade and slowly sat down on the sofa.

"Let's go on the terrace," said Molly, and watched as Bobo sailed through the French doors and disappeared in the tall grass of the meadow.

They sat in the shade on the rusty chairs and drank their lemonade. It was a full moment, a pause before something they couldn't yet imagine started to happen, and they both understood this.

"We'll do it together," said Dufort softly.

Molly nodded, her face turning a light shade of pink because she was so pleased he put it that way. "I've got a little something so far," she said, and told him about the adhesive on the station door.

"So the note-leaver is someone short. Could be a kid just messing around," cautioned Ben.

"Oh, sure," she said, "could be. But would a kid that short even have heard of Valerie? Or okay, maybe. I know her story— she's part of Castillac mythology. But it's not like she disappeared yesterday and people are talking about it all the time. I have a hard time believing that if a kid wanted to play a joke, he'd choose something that happened so long ago, maybe even before he was born. That's like ancient history to a kid, you know? Might as well be an event from the Middle Ages."

Dufort nodded. "Good point, Molly. Good point."

"So," said Molly, almost shyly, "if we're really going to be working together, will you tell me everything you know about the case? Do you need to get files—do you even have access to them anymore?"

"Not officially, of course. But I think Thérèse might be persuaded to sneak it to me. I'll warn you—the file is thin. I can tell you much of it from memory. May I have another lemonade? And then we'll get started."

Molly jumped up to get a notebook and pen, feeling a wild mixture of excitement, happiness, and gravity. "Yes," she said, taking a big gulp of lemonade and cracking open the notebook. "Start with everything you know, and I mean everything!"

❧

CONSTANCE CAME to clean in the morning and afterwards climbed back on her bike and rode off, her glum mood almost leaving a trail of gray behind her. Molly had learned from sore experience not to meddle in the love affairs of her friends, so as much as she wanted to call Thomas up and give him a piece of her mind, she resisted the impulse. She had a real soft spot for Constance and was outraged on her behalf, incredulous that Thomas could have cheated on her. And Molly was curious about this Simone Guyanet, who she remembered had a small part in the Amy Bennett case.

Meanwhile, Lawrence, Nico, and Frances were coming to dinner and she had cooking to do. In honor of spring, she was making an asparagus soup followed by grilled lamb and a huge heap of tiny buttered potatoes she'd snagged at the market that morning. Dessert was posing a problem, however. She was stuck at the first fork in the decision-making road: chocolate or not? And so far had not been inspired to go either way.

Then Ned had appeared and reported that Leslie was throwing up like crazy—had perhaps eaten a bad cream puff—and would Molly mind terribly looking after Oscar to keep him out of the way?

Well, the cottage was small, and way smaller if one inhabitant was upchucking every fifteen minutes. Molly said yes.

And in approximately three minutes, before she knew what had hit her, little Oscar was in her arms and she was smelling the sweet smell of his hair and squeezing a chubby thigh in one hand.

"Not sure how I keep ending up with you," she murmured to him. "But of course I'm very happy to see you."

"Mum," said Oscar.

"You like chocolate, don't you?" She hitched Oscar higher on her hip and opened up the refrigerator and peered inside. "I've got cream. Cream makes everything better, have you learned that yet?"

Oscar stuck his hand in her hair and yanked.

"Yowch!" she said. "Whoa!" Molly moved out of the kitchen and put Oscar down on the sofa. "That really hurt. Don't pull my hair." Oscar looked at her uncertainly. "But look, I've got the best thing ever right here. Check this out." She reached down to the woodbox and pulled out a stick and handed it to him.

Oscar's eyes lit up as though she had given him his heart's desire. "Mum mum mum mum!" he said.

"Right. I have a feeling Mum might not approve. Don't eat it, okay?" She put him down and watched as he immediately put the stick in his mouth. "Okay, listen, we're both going to get in trouble if you end up with a mouth full of splinters. Tell me this," she said, wiggling the end of the stick to keep it out of his mouth, "how am I supposed to get ready for this dinner party if you're going to be munching sticks the minute my back is turned?"

Oscar smiled at her. Molly felt a kind of melting happiness

surge up in her body that she wasn't used to. She leaned over and kissed the top of his head, picked him up, and went to find the scarf she'd used for a sling the day before. Distracting him with another chocolate bell, she managed to get him strapped onto her back with minimal complaint, and went back in the kitchen.

The presence of Oscar somehow allowed her to stop dilly-dallying over dessert, and she decided to make a *coeur à la crème*, which had the advantage of requiring a special mold that she would need to go into the village to buy. She had given enough dinner parties to know that shopping for kitchen equipment on the day of wasn't the best idea, but it would give her an excuse to go into the village for the second time that day, and this time maybe she could get someone to talk about Valerie.

Plus she had a secret desire to have a kitchen so well outfitted it could make meals for the President of France, so it was the perfect two birds with one stone situation.

Chapter Seven

The dinner went better than she expected. Ben had come a little early and brought some asparagus from Rémy, and the resulting soup was absolute perfection, like putting a spoonful of delicate springtime in your mouth. Frances had managed not to spill anything important, and Molly was highly amused to see Nico watching everything Frances did with an utterly besotted expression.

"It's good to have you back, Larry," Nico was saying, although his eyes were on Frances. "Chez Papa has definitely not been the same without you."

"I expected Molly to hold the fort until I got back. I am shocked and disappointed to hear that was not the case."

"Oh, I did my best," she answered, bringing a pot of coffee to the table. "But deep down, I'm really a placid sort of person—"

The whole table guffawed at that. "Yup, that's you, Molls. Tranquil as a cow, just happy to chomp a little grass."

"Well, maybe 'placid' wasn't the right word. Anyway, I'm glad you're back, too, Lawrence. To long vacations! And coming home!" she said, raising her glass of red from the Sallière vineyard just outside the village. "And now I've got what I hope is a stunning dessert." She went back to the kitchen and took the coeur à la crème from the counter. A mixture of goat cheese, cream cheese, honey, and cream—shaped like a heart thanks to the ridiculously expensive mold she had bought that morning—and surrounded by a sauce of strawberries and vanilla. With a *soupçon* of peppercorns, cinnamon and cloves tossed in just to make things interesting.

"That," said Frances, "looks amazing. Out of my way, people!" She stood up and waved her fork around.

"All right, old timers of Castillac," said Molly, as she passed out dessert plates. She was hoping her guests would be so involved with dessert they didn't notice the awkward transition, or sense her intense interest in what she was about to bring up. "I've been wondering about Valerie Boutillier. I know, it happened ages ago, but you know I'm a gal who likes to dig in to a mystery. And what could be more mysterious than a popular, clever girl disappearing without a trace?"

Dufort shot her a glance and then a sly smile when no one else was looking; they had not told anyone about their plans to investigate. And Molly had been right about the coeur à la crème: Nico and Lawrence were digging in with rapturous expressions and apparently enjoying the dessert so much it made them deaf. Molly ate a spoonful of the delicious cheese and struggled to be patient. Finally Lawrence took the bait.

"Valerie Boutillier. Hmm. That all happened not long after I moved to Castillac," said Lawrence. "How long ago, eight or nine years, was it?"

"Seven," Molly said quickly.

Nico said nothing. Molly saw him reach for Frances's hand underneath the table.

"And so?" Molly said, trying to sound nonchalant. "What do you remember, Lawrence?"

"Not a whole lot, I'm afraid. She was apparently quite a firecracker. People liked her. A bit of a troublemaker, but not in an annoying way."

"What kind of trouble?"

"Oh, I can't remember now." He ate some of the strawberry sauce and closed his eyes, savoring it.

"Ben, you got anything?" Molly asked. They wanted to maintain their privacy, but it would look odd not to ask the chief investigator to comment.

Dufort sighed. "The case was one of my biggest failures. And one of the reasons I quit the gendarmerie." He had drunk more wine than usual, and the effect was that he said things that normally he would have kept to himself.

"Can't win 'em all," said Frances.

"But I want to," said Dufort, with a hard sort of smile.

"Nico?" prodded Molly. "Anything?"

Nico slowly dragged his gaze from Frances. "I was in school, in the U.S, when Valerie disappeared. I did know her though. She was younger than me by a few years, but she was the sort of girl who had older friends. Younger ones too, for that matter. Anyway." He ate more dessert and then smiled at Frances.

This was getting annoying. "Well come on, what are your guesses, then? What do you think happened to her?"

"She's not a parlor game, Molly," Ben said in a low voice.

"Of course not," she said, almost snapping at him. "I'm just curious about how people deal with something like this. What kind of explanations do they come up with, so that they can live with the unexplainable and possibly incomprehensible?"

"Is it totally impossible that she just ran away?" asked Frances. "She was eighteen, right? I'm sure when I was that age, I wanted to get lost. That whole adulthood thing wasn't looking so good to be honest. Bills, work, all that studying...."

"Not totally impossible, no," said Dufort. "But we were not able to find a single indication that she felt that way, Frances. She had been a bit wild, but it was more pulling pranks than rebelling out of dissatisfaction or unhappiness. She was very interested in journalism and some of her teachers told me she couldn't wait to start nosing around where she didn't belong so she could uncover corruption and bad behavior on the part of the rich and powerful."

"Now that could get you killed," said Nico, finally alert to something besides Frances. "I completely believe some corporations kill people who threaten them too much. But I guess that wouldn't apply in this case—Valerie might have ended up making some powerful enemies, but she hadn't even started her career yet."

"Exactly what I was thinking," said Molly.

Everyone at the table startled when a cry pierced the air.

"Oscar!" said Molly, jumping up and running to her bedroom, where she had made a makeshift bed for him by putting boxes around some bedding on the floor, trapping him in so he couldn't crawl into any mischief. He was sitting up and rubbing his eyes.

"Are you wondering where everybody is?" Molly said to him, her voice soft. "I'm just in the next room, having dinner with some friends. Your Mum and Dad are back in the cottage and will be here soon. Can you go back to sleep? Do you need a fresh diaper?"

Oscar raised his fat arms up and made fussy noises.

"All right," said Molly, feeling that melty happiness again. She reached down and lifted him into her arms, holding his small body close. "I don't have a rocking chair, I'm afraid. I'll have to get right on that." Instead of rocking the boy, she walked back and forth in her bedroom, singing gently, old nursery rhymes and snatches of songs she half-remembered from childhood. He continued to fuss and she kept walking, and before long she felt his body start to relax, and his head dropped to her chest.

She loved this little Australian child. Just two days of being around him and Molly felt as though his safety and well-being and happiness were more important to her than anything. But the joy she felt holding him—she couldn't help wondering—how did mothers stand the possibility of something terrible happening? Your popular daughter just disappearing one day, without a trace? How do the mothers *bear* it?

Spending an evening with her friends around the table, eating wonderful food and drinking good (and cheap) wine—that was one of the deep pleasures of life. And so was this time with Oscar, holding him and rocking him in her arms as his little body let go and sailed into sleep.

Molly let go too, and she wept. Her tears bounced off Oscar's head and onto his playsuit. And then he was asleep and she laid him down on the makeshift bed and crept out of the room, glancing back to make sure he stayed asleep before returning to her guests.

❧

MOLLY WAS A MODERATE DRINKER, except on the rare occasions when she let herself get swept up into a festive mood and ended up drinking something like Lawrence's lethal Negronis. At dinner parties, she didn't get drunk, or even tipsy, usually...but still, over the long course of the evening, she had ended up drinking enough wine that the next morning she felt a little foggy.

The night had ended late. After the coeur à la crème, she had made coffee, and then they polished off her cognac while arguing about politics, and it was nearly 2 a.m. when they said their goodbyes.

Molly was not about to clean up at 2 a.m., but of course that meant that when she staggered into the kitchen the next morning intent on making coffee, the destruction of the party was there to greet her.

"Oh my," she said, reaching for the can of coffee beans. She washed a few pots while waiting for the coffee to drip through, added a big splash of cream, and went out to the terrace. It was shady that early, being on the north side of the house, and too chilly, but Molly didn't feel like going inside to find a sweater and so sat on the edge of the metal chair shivering and enjoying the cool spring morning.

"Molly!"

It was Ned. He had come to collect Oscar around midnight, saying that Leslie was finally asleep and the worst appeared to be over.

"On the terrace!" she answered, and Ned came around the side of the house, holding a cup of coffee.

"Bonjour!" he said. "Thanks again for keeping Oscar last night."

"I hope Leslie is doing better?"

"Oh yes, she's fit and ready to go. Nothing keeps her down for long. Say, we're loving the Dordogne so much. Never been here before and there's just so much to do."

Molly nodded and sipped her coffee. Was he about to ask her to watch Oscar again? She hoped so.

"Anyway, we'd like to stay longer, if we could. I know you've probably got bookings and everything, but I just thought I'd ask. Or maybe you know of another place we could stay? Though I'd be sad to leave La Baraque," he said with a smile.

"Well, I do have someone coming. The day you leave actually, so there's no space for even an extra day."

"Ah. Well then."

"But listen. The new guest is a single, and I have plenty of room in my house. Let me email him to ask if that suits him—I can lower his rate since he wouldn't be getting his own cottage—and I'll let you know when I hear from him?"

"That's awesome, Molly, thanks!" They chatted about which local castles to see, and where to get the best ice cream, and then Ned went back to the cottage. Molly considered going with him so she could say good morning to Oscar, but instead neglected the kitchen clean-up to wander through the garden.

She had expected surprises when spring came, and she was not disappointed. Clumps of daffodils popped up next to the front door and along the stone wall that bordered rue des Chênes. Snowdrops had appeared in February under some viburnums in the yard. And now she spotted tulips coming up beside the wall of the potager. It was like little pieces of the people who had lived at La Baraque were still there, sprouting up in springtime, even though of course Molly couldn't know why they had chosen the color of tulip, or snowdrops over crocus, or that particular cultivar of daffodil.

But she felt as though she was getting to know those former inhabitants, very slowly, as their flowers showed up in spring and she uncovered the beautiful tiles in the potager.

Chapter Eight

Monday morning dawned sunny and bright. Molly took her camera over to the newly-furnished pigeonnier to take some photos for her website before the light got too harsh. Bobo bounded along at her side holding a stick in her mouth, hoping for a little tug-of-war, but Molly was thinking about the photos and didn't take the hint.

Wiping her feet on the new doormat, Molly looked around the bottom floor, pleased at how appealing it looked. Ridiculously cozy and comfortable. Unusual sunbeams coming through the tiny windows Pierre Gault had made. He was an artist, really—his mark was on the place and the feeling he had created was all good: original, but not for novelty's sake, and stylish without trying too hard.

She ran her hand over the smooth plaster wall, pleased that the old mortar would not be weeping dust all day and night and forcing Constance to clean more often and then Molly to clean up after Constance. Lifting the camera to her eye, she started snapping pictures, getting the sunbeams, the polished wood, the pretty jug she'd found at the flea market. And upstairs, the old carved bed with luxurious bedding—a real splurge—with more sunbeams and the rows of little plaster-lined nest-boxes.

She was planning to charge a lot for it. Even though she hadn't gone anywhere or bought anything remotely extravagant, her expenses were higher than she liked. She was just barely breaking even this month—although since the Australians were staying longer, that might be enough to push her accounts more comfortably into the black.

So what kind of stories will play out here, she wondered. Will a couple have the final fight from which there's no reconciling? Will someone propose? Have an idea that will change her life?

Or even—because Molly was a little bit stuck on the idea—plot a murder?

She closed the door and locked it, even though she gathered that door-locking wasn't quite the custom in Castillac. But she knew herself as a teenager, and thought the pigeonnier would have made the most awesome hideout imaginable for doing all those teenage things parents don't want them to do. And then she hurried back to the house to get the photos online, hoping for a quick couple of bookings.

Bobo flew along beside her in the meadow and then with a yip disappeared into the forest after something Molly couldn't see.

She wondered why she had not heard from Ben since the dinner party—shouldn't they be making plans, going over evidence, something? Because although she was able to take care of her daily tasks, make meals, and run her business, she was always thinking about Valerie in the back of her mind. But so far, there was not much concrete to think about.

A note on a door was all they had.

NOT WANTING TO BE OVERHEARD, Molly and Ben decided to have their first unofficial meeting about Valerie Boutillier at La

Baraque. Molly had of course laid in a supply of pastry and made some strong coffee. Ben brought her a bag of spinach from Rémy and the Boutillier file Thérèse Perrault had passed to him on the sly. Without wasting a moment, they went out to the terrace and set to work.

"First, I'd like to say that I don't want to be acting like a gendarme, now that I'm no longer in uniform," said Ben. "What I mean is, I don't want you to think you're my subordinate, or that I'm going to be insisting on any protocol out of the gendarmerie."

"Ha! Well, that's a relief, because no doubt I'd drive you crazy," Molly said, grinning. She reached for a *croissant aux amandes* and noticed she had a big muddy paw-print on her shirt.

"I have been doing some thinking about how to handle our investigation though. Let me lay it out and then tell me what you think."

Molly nodded and sipped her coffee.

"Setting aside the note for the moment, there are only three possibilities I believe for what happened. Number one, Valerie left the village, willingly or not, and is living somewhere else, freely or not." Ben laughed. "I see already I have more than three possibilities and I have just begun. *Bon.*

"The second is that she was killed not long after the abduction, and the body is still hidden somewhere locally. And the third is that whoever took her still has her, holding her prisoner all this time. Which honestly—it's hard for me to believe that's what happened."

"Or maybe just hard to stomach. Those kinds of cases do come up. I was just reading about one in Los Angeles—"

"I know cases exist, Molly," said Dufort quietly. "Though my brain seems to revolt against the idea. Which is exactly why I wasn't much of a detective."

Molly gave Dufort a long look. She decided he was not speaking from self-pity but from trying to be objective about himself, although she thought he blamed himself for things that were not his fault. "You know, nobody gets it right all the time."

Dufort nodded and drank his coffee.

"All right," said Molly. "Three possibilities altogether, or three-plus. But if we bring the note to bear on those possibilities, it seems to me like number three—that she's being held captive somewhere around here—is the most likely."

"Unfortunately, the most likely is that she was killed soon after being taken. It's the high percentage outcome. But as you say, that means the note is a fake, or a joke."

"And—correct me since I have no idea what I'm talking about —but it would seem like, if Valerie got taken and killed right away —if the criminal is local, why did he stop with Valerie, you know?"

"Could have been a tourist. Could have been someone who lives in the next département who travels around to do his evil business. Or it could have just been a one-off."

Molly nodded. "That's a lot of 'could have's.'"

"Yes. It was without doubt the most difficult case of my time at the gendarmerie. Much worse than the other unsolved case of Elizabeth Martin. Not because it was complicated but quite the opposite—I never had even the smallest shred of a lead. As you'll see, the file is nearly empty. All we could do was interview her friends and family, look at her phone messages, her computer... there was not a single moment during the entire investigation when I thought, 'aha! now we've got something!'"

"That must have been miserable."

Dufort's face was stony. He just nodded, then reached down and petted Bobo's speckled head.

"But now we have the note!" said Molly.

"Yes. I admit I felt almost gleeful when you told me about it the other day. Since then, less so. Perhaps I'm just reluctant to get my hopes up. But hopes are beside the point, really—I'm willing to work together and do whatever we can think of to find out whether Valerie is still alive."

"I'm totally in," said Molly, finishing the last of her croissant, the wonderful tip that was a little bit dry and crunchy, but in a delicious, buttery way. "Obviously I don't know how they do things at the gendarmerie, but how about this. We work together, but you concentrate on what you say is the most likely scenario—that she was killed quickly and her body is still somewhere nearby. And I concentrate on finding out who wrote the note and who might be keeping her captive."

Dufort considered. "Works for me. I might be able to borrow a cadaver dog from a friend in Toulouse. He's in the gendarmerie there and has developed quite a kennel of dogs trained in police work."

"Will they let you have one if you're not in the gendarmerie anymore?"

Dufort smiled. "Well, one of the benefits of no longer being on the force is that I can break some rules. My friend is sort of a secret renegade," he said, chuckling. "I think he'll be able to sneak me a dog—and enjoy himself mightily."

"I just...if there's a body? I want you to find it, not me," said Molly.

"Got it," said Dufort. They shook hands, and grinned at each other, filled with the pleasure of a shared mission and with optimism, at least for the moment.

Chapter Nine

I t's gotten stale.

That's the sentence that kept going through Achille's mind all day as he did the milking, lifted hay-bales onto the tractor trailer and drove into the front field, and ate his solitary lunch in the farmhouse kitchen. The small windows had not been cleaned since his father died, and the spring light did not penetrate beyond a vague glow. Achille was frugal and avoided using electricity if it could possibly be avoided, so he ate his lunch by candlelight.

The candle was made of tallow. He had to butcher his girls once they got too old, but he did his best to make use of everything he could. He rendered the tallow and then poured it into a glass jar with a piece of waxed string for a wick. The flame cast a flickering light in the drafty room.

It's gotten stale.

Maybe he should attempt a trip to Castillac. Or Salliac, the village in the other direction. Salliac was smaller, and Achille considered whether that was better or worse. Better because not crowded. But worse because he might stand out, might attract dreaded attention. It had been months since his last try out in public, which had not gone well.

Even though he did not yet know what he was going to do, there was no doubt he was going to do something. That's how it always was. He would begin to hear a sentence in his head, over and over, and the words would not leave him alone. The pressure would build and build until he took action. It was the rhythm of life for Achille and had been that way ever since he could remember.

When he was quite young, perhaps six years old? Squatting by the pond in the west field. He had watched the tadpoles hatch out of the egg masses along the bank, and then seen them develop over days into tiny frogs. It was spring and he was in school, so every day when he got home he would run down to the pond to see their progress. In his head, over and over like the refrain of a song, he heard "take the frog." Take the frog. *Take the frog.* The phrase beat itself into him, drumming insistently, so that finally he had stolen a jar from the kitchen, driven a nail through the lid several times so the little thing would be able to breathe, and gone down to the pond when his parents were busy with other things.

Catching one of the baby frogs was easy enough. He hid the jar in his room, bringing it out only after going to bed at night, and talking softly to the tiny creature. He didn't hide it because he thought his parents would object to his having a pet—it was that he liked the secret. Liked having the baby frog all to himself.

When it looked sick the next day, Achille was heartbroken, partly because he realized it was his own fault for failing to give it proper food. He had changed the water in the jar and given the frog a stick to climb on, but somehow in his fascination with his secret he had forgotten that the animal needed to eat. So once again he waited until his parents were occupied, and then took the jar to the pond and let the little frog go.

He had missed it, sometimes painfully so. But he no longer heard *take the frog* every waking moment, which was at least some compensation.

‌ ❦

HIS LEGS WERE SO PLUMP that she couldn't help giving them a squeeze now and then as though she were a very particular shopper looking for exactly the right chicken for Sunday dinner. Oscar was once again wrapped in her scarf-sling, bumping against her as Molly walked into the village. Ned and Leslie hadn't come knocking on her door this time; Molly had simply missed the little boy and asked if she could have his company while she ran a few errands.

Oscar had clapped his hands and beamed at her, and her heart swelled even more than before. She even had fantasies—ridiculously morbid fantasies, she knew very well—that Ned and Leslie died in a car crash and they had no family whatsoever and it turned out she got to keep Oscar and raise him.

She knew she was being silly, and she didn't actually want that to happen. But more for Oscar's sake than Ned and Leslie's, if she was entirely honest.

Now what did I come into the village for, she thought. I need a couple of potatoes from the *épicerie*, and a light bulb. I wonder when the strawberries will come in? And the big question: could Valerie be hidden right in the village somewhere?

And if she is, how am I going to get inside people's houses to find her?

She got the potatoes, greeting the woman at the *épicerie* but as usual avoiding any other conversation because Molly couldn't understand her accent. She introduced Oscar to a few people that she knew to say bonjour to, and he babbled charmingly at them, leaving everyone smiling.

Molly stood on the sidewalk in front of the épicerie, looking around at the houses on the street. Many of the ground floor spaces were shops, with apartments on upper floors. No way could anyone be hidden for seven years in a building like that, she reasoned. No way to keep Valerie from screaming, or banging on the floor or the walls.

So making that assumption narrowed her search at least a little. She would focus on free-standing houses. And probably the bigger the lot they were on, the easier it would be to hide someone. It was time to pay her friend at the *mairie* a visit—there must be maps showing all the houses in and around Castillac, and she supposed until she had a better idea, she could begin somehow checking them out one by one.

Somehow, indeed. Castillac was not huge, around four thousand people, but that was still a daunting number of habitations to get through. Even if half of those four thousand lived with someone else, and a quarter of those lived in apartments, that was still fifteen hundred houses to inspect. That would take years.

Not to mention—just how exactly did she think she was going to get inside these houses? And even once inside, she couldn't run around looking for trap doors and hidden compartments behind trick bookshelves without people thinking she'd lost her mind. She started home, walking slowly.

"Oscar, how am I going to pull this off?" she murmured into his soft hair. He beat his little feet against her belly, his eyes half-closed.

Molly stopped short. Parked on the sidewalk (probably illegally) was a scooter. The swankiest, most delicious scooter Molly had ever seen. Its lines swooped and curved, the paint almost glowed, even the instrument panel was adorable. "I want that," she said to Oscar, and he opened his eyes and kicked harder.

I can't afford it, she told herself. But...

She checked the beautiful machine out more closely, getting

the make and model, then glanced around the street to see if anyone was headed towards it. She wanted to know where such things were for sale, and how much they cost. Because dammit, if she couldn't have a baby, she was going to have a scooter. And that was that.

PART II

Chapter Ten

That night Molly was at loose ends. With Constance's help, she had prepared a room upstairs in her house for the new guest who had agreed to take the upstairs room—she called it the "haunted room" although nothing had ever happened to make it deserve the name. It was a small room with a low ceiling and something about it gave her the creeps, so the name had stuck. Probably it was nothing more than the faded wallpaper, which was vaguely pink in a pattern of roses. She remembered wallpaper like that in a scary movie she had seen as an eleven or twelve year old, in which an old lady had been murdered by a handsome stranger to whom she rented a room.

Maybe, now that she thought about it, running a gîte business as a single woman wasn't the best idea she ever had? Why hadn't she remembered that movie before now?

But Molly brushed that worry off, knowing that despite the small risk of renting to a very bad egg, the business suited her perfectly. She had liked every single one of her guests; some of them she had no doubt would keep up contact, and return to visit for years to come. She put away the cleaning supplies, took a shower, and walked to Chez Papa, picturing how stylish she was going to be when she cruised in on her new scooter.

"Should I get red, or maybe a snazzy green?" she asked Lawrence, once she was on her stool at the bar with a kir on the way.

Lawrence sipped his Negroni. "How about black? You can never go wrong with black."

"Too tasteful."

"Ah. Then perhaps the pink?"

"There's a pink?"

"I would imagine you can get any color you want, if you want it badly enough. Its not like the scooter is very big. You could probably hire someone to paint it neon pink with glitter if that's what you have in mind."

"Now that would be tacky," said Molly, laughing. "Why's Nico looking so morose?" she said, low enough that he wouldn't be able to hear.

"Trouble in paradise, apparently," said Lawrence.

"Uh oh. I was afraid of that. Have you seen Frances?"

"Nico just told me she's gone off to the coast with someone she met the day before. He looked inconsolable."

"Someone male or female?"

"Female."

"Eh, he may not have anything to worry about. Though with Frances...she's left a trail of romantic wreckage behind her since we were thirteen. You know I love her. But constant in love she is not."

Lawrence nodded. "I know the type."

"Your Moroccan Julio?"

"*Oui*," said Lawrence, and turned so that Molly could not see his face.

Chez Papa was quiet for a moment. The sun was dropping towards dusk but sunlight still poured in through the plate-glass windows, so bright it made the place look dusty, and put an unflattering light on everyone's faces. Then two men at the other end of the bar started arguing about politics, and a young woman came in holding a young boy on her hip, calling for Nico, and the rhythm of the restaurant picked back up.

"I'm sorry," Molly said to Lawrence, wishing she had something more useful to say.

Lawrence turned back to her and shrugged. "So tell me, Miss Molly—don't you have any interesting irons in the fire? Any curious deaths in the village this week? Any mysterious strangers come to town?"

She smiled. "No, not that I've heard. I do have a question for you though, since you know everybody. The Dordogne was important for the Resistance, back in World War II, am I right?"

"You are," he said, interested in why she was asking.

"I was wondering if there was anyone I could talk to about that—I mean, anyone who might have been around then?"

"Have you met Madame Gervais? She's 102, I believe, something like that. Lives on...what's that street that has the shop with the lamps?"

"Rue Baudelaire," said Nico, as he walked over. "Another?"

"By all means," said Lawrence. "I love that lamp shop. I could buy lamps all day."

"Mme Gervais's house is the teeny one right next door," said Nico.

"What's got you all interested in history all of a sudden?" asked Lawrence, eyeing her closely.

"Oh, nothing," said Molly. "Nico, bring us some frites, will you? And a salad for me. Lawrence, did I tell you I'm having a guest stay in my house, since the Australians are staying longer?"

"Is it so you can talk to your guests about the history of the region, is that what you're after?"

"Exactly," said Molly, feeling slightly bad for not coming clean with Lawrence, but on the other hand, not quite sure how good he was at keeping anything under his hat. "Guests do like to know interesting stories about history, you know? And what's more interesting than the Resistance?"

Lawrence nodded and sipped his drink, but he was not fooled. She was up to something, but apparently he was not going to find out what just yet.

§.

MOLLY WALKED ONCE around the yard with Bobo before locking up and going to bed. She had wanted to dive into the Boutillier file the minute Dufort had left the day before, but then found herself delaying and finding other things to do, perhaps to delay the disappointment at facing how little they had to go on.

Now it was time. She washed up and came to bed, telling Bobo firmly that her paws were muddy and she had to sleep on her own bed, which was a pile of moth-eaten blankets in the corner of the room. Molly climbed into bed and fluffed the pillows up behind her, opened the file, and began to read.

First the transcript of an interview with Mme Boutillier. Painful to read, as of course her agony was apparent in every word she said.

Valerie was an excellent student and got top marks in her class.

She was going to *École Normale Superieure*, an extremely competitive university in Paris. Was beginning to pack for her departure, the date only two weeks after her disappearance. No boyfriend. Never a serious boyfriend. Had mostly hung out with a large group of schoolmates.

Wanted to be an investigative reporter. Strong sense of social justice.

Molly looked up and rubbed her eyes. It was just so wrong for this ambitious, vibrant young woman to be wiped away like this, disappeared, lost. It was an atrocity—small scale for the world, perhaps, but immense for her family and friends, and the village where she had grown up.

Valerie was something of a tomboy, in jeans most of the time.

She wore her light brown hair in a braid down her back.

She was allergic to wool.

Her favorite food was *aligot*. (Molly had to look this up. *Aligot* is a dish from Alsace, in which cheese, Cantal or Tomme, is slowly melted into mashed potatoes, creating a wonderfully comforting and delicious stretchy, cheesy, potatoey mess.)

She wore a necklace with a charm in the shape of a star, which her brother had given her.

On the day of her disappearance, Valerie had been wearing a green sweater, blue jeans, sneakers, and a checkered scarf made out of silk. Hair in a braid down her back, no ribbon; the star necklace around her neck.

No rings, no bracelets, no coat. Her mother said she despaired of Valerie wearing coats when the weather got cold—she was always running around without one.

She had no visible birthmarks, moles, warts, or scars.

She liked pulling pranks. She laughed a lot.

The last time her mother—or anyone else—had seen her was October 29, 1999.

Chapter Eleven

L *a li lala lo.*
No one home. No one home anymore.

It was dark and she lay on the filthy mattress squinting up at a tiny crack of light that had recently appeared between two of the logs that formed part of the ceiling. It was not enough of a crack to give her ideas about enlarging it and somehow making an escape, because she no longer thought of escape. It was a concept that had gotten away from her. It wasn't that she didn't think it was possible, it was that *escape*, the idea, did not exist anymore.

He barely came now. He would open the door and push in a bowl of lentils and a jug of milk, he would take out the bucket that served as a toilet and empty it, then bring it back. But he no longer talked, not like he used to.

He avoided looking her in the eye.

It was bad before, unimaginably horrible. She was not suited for captivity, not that anyone is. She spent almost all of her time underground, in a root cellar he had made over many months, dug into a slope next to the barn. And all of that time, the long days— it was endless. Her old life, her old self, just a fleeting dream.

It was bad before, but now, with him not talking to her

anymore and not looking her in the eye—now it was worse. Valerie felt herself beginning to lose any hold she still had on what was real; the hold was already frayed, already tenuous, and now it threatened to snap altogether. But Valerie was not afraid. It was as though over the years the fear had been so profound and so constant that it had worn itself out.

La li la, la li lo.

She sang to herself as though she were a baby that she was taking care of. *La li la.* Her voice was rough and cracked, as were her her lips, and the skin on her hands and behind her knees.

Sometimes the man still opened the door wide and let her come out into the sunshine. He would tie a rope around her waist and around his own waist, and walk around the back field with her, out of sight of the road. In the beginning, he had tied her legs together so that she could only walk with short steps, but eventually he had trusted that she would not run. And he had been correct, because eventually the hope that would have fueled her running had been all but extinguished. She believed that her friends and her family had forsaken her. Stopped looking, left her to stay in the root cellar with this man forever.

Forever is a long time for anywhere, but even longer, unsurprisingly, trapped underground, in the dark, alone.

Chapter Twelve

At the farm next door to Achille Labiche's, nine-year-old Gilbert wished for his mother to hurry up and finish dinner, but oh, she was so very slow about everything. So methodical, so plodding. He felt as though he might burst into flames from impatience.

"Maman, is there anything outside you'd like to me do to before I start my homework?" he asked, thinking that even doing chores would be an improvement over sitting at the table for one more minute.

Madame Renaud tilted her head. Then she pushed some peas onto her knife and ate them, chewing slowly. She took a sip of wine. "Gilbert, you know I don't like you going outside at night. Do you want to be snatched up like poor Valerie Boutillier?"

Gilbert jerked his head up, and then looked down at his plate. Before today, he would have moaned inwardly at his mother's fears, sick of hearing her endless warnings about something that had happened practically before he was born. Madame Renaud had pinned some of her boundless anxieties onto the Boutillier case—a newspaper clipping, now seven years old, was taped on the refrigerator, so that Gilbert had grown up looking into the missing girl's cheerful face—and when her mother mentioned Valerie, it was always in order to prevent him from doing something he wanted to do.

You mustn't go out after dark. You cannot go to the market without me. You must be aware, Gilbert, of people around you and the horrible things they might be capable of.

But despite his mother's anxieties, Gilbert was not a scared child but rather fearless, wanting to be out in the world exploring instead of cooped up inside the farmhouse. And while Gilbert loved his mother, he resented her nervousness, and thought of Valerie as someone more mythical than real, like a character from a fairy tale.

But that was before last Sunday.

What had happened was: Gilbert was an avid reader, and he had read an article in the local paper about how the price of truffles was expected to go through the roof next season. He was alert to the mention of anything that he might be able to do to make some money, since he and his mother had little of it, and there were plenty of things he desperately wanted: a microscope and a remote-control helicopter were on his list that particular week. The article on truffles got him thinking about the oak trees on the back of their property. He wondered whether there might just be a treasure there, hiding in the leaves, if only he could figure out a way to find the precious little nuggets.

Dogs are almost universally used to find truffles these days, and Gilbert knew this. And he also knew that a dog would need special training—he couldn't simply borrow a friend's pet for an afternoon and expect it to find truffles right away. He figured the old-fashioned way of truffle-hunting with a pig, would do the trick. A pig can smell the truffle and will want to eat it, so the trick is to let the pig find it and then jump in and snatch the truffle before the pig can gobble it up.

Gilbert walked among the oaks for a few days, going there straight after school and daydreaming about presenting his mother with a stack of euros he had earned at the truffle market, and setting up his shiny new microscope on the kitchen table. He only needed to borrow the neighbor's hog and he would be in business. He understood that it was May, and truffle season was in winter, but figured that only gave him more months to collect them.

The neighbor was a dairy farmer, a quiet sort of fellow, not very approachable. So Gilbert thought it over and decided that he would borrow the hog on the sly—just slip a rope around its neck, lead it to the oaks at the back of the property, and get rich.

He was only nine years old. To his optimistic mind, the plan seemed solid.

So on Sunday, he fed and watered the chickens and brought in the eggs, swept his room, and helped his mother in the garden for what felt like an endless hour, until finally she told him he could go and play. He put on a pair of green pants and a green T-shirt, thinking it approximated camouflage. He took off for the grove of oaks first, and then through a bit of woods to the edge of the Monsieur Labiche's property.

The neighbor and his mother got along well enough, though they managed this by having as little contact as possible. Madame Renaud thought Monsieur Labiche was difficult to talk to. For a few years they had traded eggs for milk, but that arrangement had ended over eight years ago when Madame Renaud's husband died, since he had taken care of dealing with Labiche, and Madame Renaud did not want to, even though the trade was in her favor.

Gilbert saw Labiche's barn come into view though the trees. He crouched down as he made his way closer, stopping every now and then to listen, and hearing nothing but the sounds of springtime in the woods: birds making a racket, and the buzzing of insects, a random croak of a frog.

Since he had never visited the neighbor's farm, Gilbert wasn't sure where the hogs were kept. He stood behind an oak and peered around it, lifting a branch to see under the new green foliage.

He heard something...a woman singing. Gilbert was at the very edge of the woods and he lay down in the leaves, thinking someone was about to come around the side of the barn.

And someone did. *Two* someones.

Monsieur Labiche was walking ahead of a woman, and they were tied together at the waist. She was very thin, and Gilbert saw even from a distance that she was very pale.

"But why do you not come anymore?" the woman cried out, her voice rasping like sandpaper. "I'm your Valerie! Look at me!"

Gilbert did look. He wriggled forward in the leaves and squinted at the woman's face. With awe, he saw without a doubt that she was Valerie Boutillier. He was looking right at her, her face having the same blurry quality as the newspaper clipping he had grown up with.

The woman who had been missing for seven years was not lost —she was living right next door.

Gilbert was a clever boy. He noticed the rope, and even though she had said *I'm your Valerie*, he did not forget the rope, or misunderstand what it was for.

ACHILLE RINSED out the can that had contained his early lunch and put it in the garbage under the sink. He considered lying down for a nap. But then, with an unusual burst of confidence— or maybe it was simply giving way to the inevitable—he went outside and started up the tractor and turned left on the road towards Salliac.

It's gotten stale.

The village was six kilometers away and the tractor was slow. Luckily there was no traffic so he was spared having to decide whether to pull over and let someone by. Achille had plenty of time to change his mind, and knowing that was helpful to him. It was as though he could put himself on the road towards the small village but tell himself he had not yet committed to going, even as he got closer and closer.

Salliac had four streets that criss-crossed each other at either end. Achille parked his tractor on the wide shoulder just before the streets joined up, and walked towards the center. It was market day, though if he remembered correctly, that did not amount to much in Salliac, and he did not expect much activity.

And in fact, there were only a handful of vendors. A rosy-cheeked woman was there with a display of vegetables that had not been locally grown, Achille noticed right away. He walked hurriedly by, trying to hide himself behind a few of the sparse customers. Next he saw an older woman, about the age his mother would be if she were alive, selling homemade *cannelés*.

Achille loved *cannelés*, and they reminded him of his mother since she had once made them for him. They were an odd sort of cake, almost a cross between cake and custard, baked in fluted molds with a caramelized and slightly waxy crust. He closed his eyes for a moment, savoring the memory of his mother's allowing him to eat several when they were warm from the oven, and he could practically taste the vanilla and exotic flavoring of rum.

He flicked his eyes at the old woman, trying to see if she was approachable. She looked almost asleep, her face turned up to the sun, her eyes half-closed.

That could be a good sign. Or she could be like a snake, poised to strike.

Then he looked at the cannelés again, and his hunger for a taste of his childhood overcame his resistance. "Bonjour, Madame," he said, his voice surprising him by sounding confident. "May I have six?"

She opened her eyes, nodding, and slowly collected six of the cakes into a small paper bag while Achille dug into his pocket for some money.

"Merci, Madame," he said, the manners taught him by his

parents coming automatically, as though a button had been pushed.

He walked away, thinking that his father would have wanted him to take the cannelés home and eat them after a meal. But with effort Achille pushed that thought away and looked for some privacy in which to enjoy his treat. And then, in an unexpected moment when he wasn't even looking, he saw her: a teenage girl, standing next to a bike, chatting on a mobile phone.

Achille stood rooted to the spot, his eyes on her. The girl was wearing a T-shirt and jeans, and some high-top sneakers that looked strange to Achille since he was hardly up on the latest fashion trends. He walked a few steps closer, reaching into the paper bag and eating a cannelé without realizing it. He stood chewing and watching, but the girl was focused on her phone conversation and did not notice him.

He saw the way her shirt was wrinkled around the bottom as though she had picked it out of a laundry basket to wear instead of from a bureau drawer with neatly folded items. It was dark red with something written on it that Achille could not make out. He saw her greenish eyes widen and then almost close as she threw her head back laughing.

Finally she said goodbye and slipped the phone into her knapsack. Achille walked nearer, standing up tall, looking more assured than at any other moment since getting off his tractor at the edge of the village.

She was a lovely girl. Fresh-faced and not yet old enough to think being jaded was attractive. A scattering of freckles across her nose, and light brown hair tumbling down to her shoulders. He could see something in her expression that drew him in; he could tell she was trying to look brave when she did not feel that way. It was Monday, right around lunchtime, and doubtless she should have been in school.

When he offered her a cannelé, she smiled and said thank you.

"Let me guess your name," said Achille with a shy smile.

The girl laughed and shook her head as he ran through all the girl's names he could think of. Achille was laughing too and hiding his frustration at not being able to guess.

"I'm Aimée," she said finally, and Achille beamed at her, because her name was perfection itself: *Loved.*

Achille prided himself on having an exquisite sense of timing. So before any of the people at the market noticed him talking to her, he smiled and said goodbye, and was rewarded with a big grin, which he thought about during the whole trip home.

The beginning...the beginning was the best part, and he hoped to prolong it as long as he possibly could.

Loved.

Yes.

Chapter Thirteen

Gilbert had tried to think it all through before he took action. After he saw Valerie, his first thought was to tear home and tell his mother, so she could call the gendarmes immediately.

But as he ran home through the field he hesitated. His mother thought he was a daydreamer, always lost in the world of a book. She continually told him his head was full of cotton and outlandish ideas. She would accuse him of reading too many detective novels and fancying himself Inspector Maigret or some such.

It made Gilbert sad to realize it, but his mother was not someone he could go to and be believed.

All right, he had said to himself, I need to make a Plan B. And quickly he had come up with the idea of leaving an anonymous note for the gendarmes. It was only luck that his mother had needed to drive into Castillac later that day and allowed him to come with her, and even more luck that he had managed to get away from her long enough to sprint down the street to the station, the note carefully folded in his jacket pocket. And luck beyond all imagining that when he stood at the door and looked around, there was no one nearby, no one watching—and he could affix the tape to the green door and walk nonchalantly away, his heart pounding.

He had been tempted to go in and talk to the gendarmes himself. Perhaps if Chief Dufort had still been there, he would have. But the new man who was in charge—whenever Gilbert had seen him, he was glowering and looked unfriendly. The kind of grown-up you wanted to avoid, not go to with any sort of problem.

No, it was better to deliver the big news anonymously. It was the only way the grown-ups would listen.

On the way home, Gilbert had realized with horror that despite enjoying what had seemed like all the luck in the world, he had done something really, really dumb: he had failed to say in the note where Valerie *was*.

That was last Monday, over a week ago. Another whole week that Valerie had to live tied up, with her family and friends probably thinking she was dead. He didn't know how he could have been such a complete idiot. The whole point of the note was to alert the gendarmes that Valerie was actually still alive so they could save her! But he had gotten so carried away with the process of finding the right letters and cutting them out of the newspaper and gluing them—all without his mother discovering what he was doing—that he had left out the most important piece of information. Part of the trouble was that once he had the idea of cutting out letters rather than simply writing the note with a pencil, he got committed to doing it that way, even though all he could find to use was a four-page local newspaper his mother sometimes picked up for free at the supermarket.

There hadn't been enough headlines for him to spell Valerie's whole name, or even just "Valerie", so he had compromised by putting her initials, just glad that he had managed to find a "V" and a "B".

If he had written the note, he told himself, everyone would

have thought it was just a kid's prank. That angry-looking gendarme would have balled it up and tossed it in the trash.

But now, stuck on the farm away from the village, with no resources—how could he correct his error?

He considered calling the station and leaving a message, deepening his voice as much as possible, maybe putting something over the receiver to make his voice sound funny. But again—*they'll think I'm just a kid fooling around.* He considered trying to copy a grown-up's handwriting, but his own handwriting was so horrible —by far his worst marks in school—that he gave up that idea quickly.

Not for the first time, Gilbert wished for his father. If he was sure of anything at all, it was that his father would be someone he could tell something like this, and he would know exactly what to do. He had a quick flash of riding on his father's shoulders and watching a parade, with Valerie riding on a float and waving to everyone, and the whole village cheering.

All he could think to do was make another note and tell the gendarmes that way. But he wasn't so lucky this time around. His mother did not bring home the newspaper. She made no mention of needing to go into the village for anything—and if he had ridden his bicycle, the trouble he would be in would be so terrible he wasn't sure he would ever come out the other side.

So here it was the second week, and he had no way to make the note, no way to deliver the note, and no idea what to do next.

NOW THAT THE NEW GUEST, a Mr. Wesley Addison from Cincinnati, was due to arrive, Molly wondered if she had made a mistake. The Australians were staying an extra week, and she was thrilled about that since she dreaded having to say goodbye to little Oscar. They were all settled in the cottage, and when Addison's arrival was over a week away, it had seemed the easiest thing simply to move him into her house and leave Ned and Leslie where they were.

The pigeonnier was all ready, but she had Dutch newlyweds coming the next day. The woman who had made the reservation made it clear that what sold her were the beams of sunlight coming through Pierre Gault's artful little windows, so Molly was unwilling to try to foist an upstairs bedroom with faded wallpaper on her. The haunted room wasn't hideous, but it was hardly the place for a romantic getaway. Molly knew a mistake like that would end any hope of repeat business or good word of mouth.

So Addison was coming around lunchtime, and he would be staying in the haunted room. Molly had only exchanged a few mails with him. He was paid up; he had accepted the proposed switch from cottage to bedroom in the house without argument; she had no reason at all to have any misgivings.

Yet she had them.

The idea of having a strange man upstairs in her house, while she slept...it was, now that it was about to happen, a little unnerving. Though she thought it was unfair of her to feel so skittish. It was certainly going to be fine, she said to herself, as though saying it would make it so.

She spent the morning tidying up as she always did when a new guest was about to arrive. No time to eat apart from a hurried lunch of crackers and some Camembert that was about to be too old. As she was putting a load of wet laundry into a basket to take outside to hang, she heard someone pull up in the driveway—Castillac apparently had a taxi once again, and in the back seat was the imposing figure of Wesley Addison.

"Bonjour!" said Molly, coming outside and wiping her laundry-wet hands on her jeans.

"Hello, Miss Sutton," said Addison, paying the driver and getting his small bag from the backseat. "I am Wesley Addison."

Molly didn't like him. Yes, okay, it was a snap judgment, but the feeling was strong and immediate.

"Come on inside!" she said, with forced jollity that made her cringe.

He was large man, very tall, with a build like a former football player. He had broad shoulders and his neck wasn't visible. And when he smiled, Molly could see he was missing a tooth along the side.

"All right then! Let me show you your room—and thank you so much for being willing to switch. As you can imagine, sometimes the life of an innkeeper is one of moving pieces on a chessboard!"

Addison looked at Molly quizzically. "'Innkeeper'?" he said. "I thought you had gîtes."

"Yes! Well, sometimes French and English don't have the same exact words, you know? So if I'm speaking French I say gîte, and for English I say B&B, and call myself an innkeeper. It's all more or less the same thing."

"Does that mean you'll be serving breakfast?" asked Addison, looking confused. "And I understand that I will be staying in your house, but it is not an inn, am I correct?"

Molly took a long, deep breath. "That is all correct, Mr. Addison. Sorry for my imprecision."

They went up the winding staircase to the second floor, and Molly showed him his room, which looked pleasant now that she and Constance had given it a good scrubbing and the bed had a fresh duvet. "Here you are," said Molly, wanting to be done with Mr. Addison as soon as possible. "I'll be around La Baraque most of the time, so if you have any questions, or need anything, just give me a holler."

"A holler?" said Addison. "Curious, I'd have said you were from Boston."

Molly made a fake chuckle. "Yes, I'm afraid the accent gives me away every time."

"But 'holler' is a Southern Appalachian usage. Why would a person from Boston choose that particular word?"

Molly raised her eyebrows way up high and shrugged. "Can't say, Mr. Addison. I'm afraid sometimes I open my mouth and who knows what might come out. Maybe somewhere along the way I had a friend who said 'holler'. Maybe I heard it on TV."

"Television," spat Mr. Addison, rolling his eyes.

"Not a fan?"

"It has done more to confuse and muddle linguistics than any other influence. I abhor it. I'm quite glad to see my room does not have one, as most hotels rooms do. Now, would you be so kind as to bring me some mineral water? I would like Vittel. And then after I have rehydrated, I am going to rest. Traveling, as I'm sure you are aware, can be extremely fatiguing, especially when one crosses the ocean."

"Yes, Mr. Addison. I'll bring you some mineral water shortly."

Molly walked slowly downstairs, thinking this was going to be the longest week of her entire life.

Chapter Fourteen

All day at school Gilbert was distracted by thoughts of Valerie. He looked for extra newspapers lying around that he could pilfer, an old magazine, anything—but people didn't read the way they used to. They got their news online, read their magazines online, and loose newspapers for making anonymous notes were hard to come by.

Gilbert wondered what the old-school kidnappers were going to do now that their main stationery source had disappeared. During science class he cooked up a long story in his head about two hapless would-be criminals who snatch a little girl from the playground while her mother is talking to a friend, but when they cannot find enough newspapers to spell out their ransom note, they give up and let the girl go.

Amusing, at least for the duration of science, which Gilbert found acutely boring. But when the made-up story was done he was left with the reality of Valerie tied to Monsieur Labiche, and no way that Gilbert could think of to tell anyone about it.

He was herded onto the bus at the end of the day, as usual, and let off at the end of the Renaud farm driveway, also as usual.

He ran inside at top speed to get out of the rain and kissed his mother hello. She was sitting at the kitchen table cutting up vegetables for soup.

"Maman, do we have any old newspapers anywhere? I need one for school."

"I don't believe so. It's a fire hazard, letting things like that pile up. I try to read them and get rid of them as quickly as possible. We don't want to go up in flames, now do we? Sit down and have your baguette with chocolate."

Gilbert sighed. It was always that way with Maman: they were always one step from a conflagration that would burn the farm to the ground, taking the two of them right along with it, or one step from being knifed, poisoned, abducted. Gilbert suddenly could not bear to be in the house one second longer. He grabbed a rain slicker from the coatrack by the door and said over his shoulder as he went back out, "I'm going to check on the chickens. Be back later!" and slammed the door before his mother had time to draw a breath.

First he went to the chicken house in case his mother was watching out the window. He went inside, murmuring to the hens, who were quiet and mostly up on perches, asleep. The rainclouds darkened the sky, which made them nap. He waited long enough that he figured his mother had sat back down, and then went back into the rain and ran across the field towards the Labiche farm.

It was raining hard. Everything was brown and green, streaked and blurry, as though he were living inside a watercolor. The slicker had a visor but it didn't work very well, and he had to keep wiping water out of his eyes so he could see where he was going.

Why he wanted to see where Valerie was he couldn't say. He knew there was nothing he could do for her. But maybe, just maybe, he thought, with the optimism of the young—maybe Monsieur Labiche has left the door unlocked, wherever he's keeping her. Maybe he, Gilbert Renaud, could find out her hiding place and free her, all by himself.

It was awesome to think about. Once again a parade figured in his thoughts, and he sat astride the strong shoulders of his father until he realized that no, he would be *in* the parade, just like Valerie. On the float, waving to all his classmates as he rode by.

It ended up that he stood in the woods looking at the Labiche farm but saw nothing except cows. He was afraid to get close because the slicker was orange and so bright he figured a blind person could see it. So in the end Gilbert trudged back home, thinking about Inspector Maigret, Hercule Poirot, and even Madame Sutton, who was famous in Castillac for solving the Desrosiers murder—how would any of them be handling the situation, if they were nine years old and had no one to talk to?

"Gilbert!" his mother shrieked when he came inside, water sluicing down and causing a minor flood on the floor of the kitchen. "What were you thinking, running about in this weather? Don't you know you could catch your death of cold?"

"Oui, Maman," he answered robotically, knowing not to argue. "Maman!" he said, getting struck by an idea. "You know what happens after a rain this time of year?"

"Many things, Gilbert dear. Sometimes the lettuce rots right in the ground. The stream overflows—"

"No, I mean something good! Wild greens, Maman. Our fields will be filled with them. I want to pick baskets and baskets, and take them to the market this Saturday and sell them. I'm going to make us rich, Maman!"

"Oh, my boy, will you ever get out of your daydreams and into real life? You think you'll make us rich foraging in the mud with a basket on your arm?" Mme Renaud laughed and went back to chopping carrots.

Well, thought Gilbert, shivering from his wet clothes. She didn't say I couldn't.

❧

BEN HAD PAVED the way by calling Mme Gervais and asking if she would mind talking to Molly about Castillac during the war. She had readily agreed, always pleased when a younger person (and to Mme Gervais, absolutely everyone was a younger person) took an interest in the past. Molly swung by Pâtisserie Bujold on the way and picked up a couple of croissants and two chocolate *réligieuses*, the pastry named after nuns because the two custard-filled puffs one on top of the other looked vaguely like a sister. Very vaguely, but Molly was not going to get literal about it. They were breathtakingly delicious and her current favorite.

She found her way to rue Baudelaire without any trouble, stopping to look in the window of the lamp shop next door to Mme Gervais's little house, admiring the silk shades and astounding variety jammed into the area for window display. She had never really given lamps any thought, but now saw several that she hoped were not as expensive as they looked, since she immediately had the perfect spot picked out for them at La Baraque. Reluctantly she tore herself away from the lamps and knocked on Mme Gervais's door.

"Bonjour, Madame Sutton!" said the old lady, opening the door almost immediately.

Molly was relieved to hear that the Mme Gervais's accent was one she could easily understand. They went in to the sitting room —Mme Gervais seeming much younger than her 102 years—and made themselves comfortable.

"Now, tell me," Mme Gervais said as she bustled in the kitchen, getting the pot on the stove. "Ben was a little cagey when he called. Is there something in particular you want to know about the war years? Or do you want me to speak more generally? I can give you something of my own experience, or more of an overview."

Molly thought for a moment. "I'm not going to be cagey," she said. "I am interested in both your experience *and* your overview. Now that I live in Castillac, the history is important to me for all the reasons I don't have to explain to you. But this morning I am after something specific. You can keep a secret?" she asked, with a half smile.

Mme Gervais laughed. "Funny you should ask, because of course in wartime, the secrets were coming fast and furious. And they were often a matter of life or death."

"So is this one, possibly," said Molly. "I'm sure you remember Valerie Boutillier?"

Mme Gervais nodded slowly, surprised.

"There's been an indication that she may still be alive, somewhere in or near Castillac. The authorities, for whatever reason, are not going to do anything about it. So I am taking up the search."

"With Ben?"

"Yes."

Mme Gervais gave Molly a long look. "And why does this matter to you, an American who never knew Valerie?"

"Anyone who thinks about a woman being missing for seven years would try to help if they could, wouldn't they? Most people, I mean. And also—I suppose it's a common enough thing that newcomers might be more protective of their new home than some people who grew up there and take it for granted? My feelings about Castillac are deep. And Valerie is part of this village. She made a strong impression before she went missing, and of course she is now a source of collective sorrow, and even fear.

"I don't mean to sound grandiose, Mme Gervais. It's not that I think I have any special abilities or anything like that. But if Valerie is still alive I would like to find her. I would at least like to try."

"First, I'm going to make us some tea. Now, what else can we do?" said Mme Gervais, shrugging. "And how do you think I can help?"

Molly looked into the old lady's face. It was heavily wrinkled but her cheeks had color and her eyes were bright; she was vital and sharp and ready to join in. "You can be a big help, as I'll explain. I am making the assumption that when Valerie was abducted back in 1999 she was not killed, but hidden somewhere. And then a further assumption that the abductor is someone local, and she is still nearby."

"Held prisoner?"

"Yes."

The two women thought the proposition over.

"Sometimes I think there is no end to the horror we humans will visit on one another," said Mme Gervais.

"Yes," said Molly. "I think that too." They both sighed together. "So what I am wondering is whether you might have some stories about wartime that might be relevant. I've heard it mentioned that here in the Dordogne, people—Jews, mostly— were hidden for long periods, to escape both the Nazis and the *Milice* who got their orders from Vichy. How did they escape capture? What sort of hiding places were used?"

"You are thinking that if the abductor is local, he might know of these stories too, and have tried something similar?"

"Yes, exactly."

Mme Gervais finished putting cups and the teapot on a tray, and then poured hot water into the pot and carried the tray to the small living room.

"I am thinking, Molly. You know the forest called *La Double?*"

"Yes, Madame. I have taken some walks there."

"Many of the Resistance hid there. The local men had hunted in the forest before the war and they knew it intimately—they could give the Nazis the slip easily enough, and there were plenty of stories back then which ended with our fighters harrassing the

Nazis in some way and then disappearing into the sheltering arms of the forest.

"But I don't believe that is the kind of thing you are looking for. I will have to give this some more thought. Of course I knew of people who hid Jewish families—the Dordogne was thankfully one of the least oppressive départements in that regard, and we had Jewish children going to school openly in Périgueux for quite some time. It was only later that the Milice got so out of control and began executing French citizens right and left and going from house to house searching for Jews.

"One thing I can tell you—I might look harder at farms. Obviously it is more difficult to hide someone in town, where any stray noise might be noticed and in general there is less space. Doubtless you have considered these things."

Molly nodded.

"Additionally," continued Mme Gervais, "a farm might be able to provide some of the food for a long-time captive. Of course, during the war there were food shortages continuously and even the farmers struggled to eat. But if you have a village house, maybe you could provide a bit of lettuce to the captive, if you are lucky enough to have any sort of garden. But cheese and meat you would have to buy. There is the expense, of course, but also—it might be noticed. If a single man—and I don't think we need to bother about any politically correct idea that women would be equally capable of such a thing, just between us—if he were to buy enough food for two, it might, *might*, eventually be noticed.

"Though people are generally not very observant, wouldn't you agree?"

Molly nodded again. "I'm afraid so. Myself included much of the time."

"As for specific hiding places, I'm afraid I cannot think of anything especially unusual that you wouldn't have thought of. Attics, cellars, and barns, that is what I remember. The poor people would have to stay inside almost all the time, entirely dependent on whoever had taken them in, and all of them knowing that discovery was likely to mean execution or deportation for everyone involved and maybe even the entire community."

Mme Gervais bowed her head, lost in memories, and Molly sat with her quietly and did not interrupt.

Chapter Fifteen

It had rained during the night and the area by the barn was muddy. Bourbon looked as though she were wearing brown socks. After the morning milking, the cows lumbered into the west field where it was shady during the first part of the day, since it was already very warm.

"Bourbon!" called Achille, and the dog turned and looked at him questioningly. Usually she followed the cows to the field to make sure they got there in an orderly group. "We're going to check the fencing," he said, and he thought Bourbon nodded before trotting back to his side.

When they passed a small copse Achille cut a branch to walk with. Not to lean on, because he was strong and had no need for that, but only a stick to poke in the mud or swat through the air if he felt like it. The fencing on the farm was not in the best shape. Some stretches were wood, with a few sections of barbed wire. Several rotting posts needed replacing. Achille sighed as he found one that was so far gone it really couldn't be put off any longer. When he pushed at the post, it nearly broke off. His father had tried to teach him to dispose of the worst chores first thing in the day, but Achille had never managed to form that habit. Instead, anything he disliked doing, he put off and avoided and forgot about, until it was no longer possible to ignore.

"If I don't fix it, the cows will get out," he said to Bourbon. "And I wouldn't be surprised at all if some of the neighbors took the opportunity to steal one of them. Or even more," he said, working himself into a snit. "All right, let's walk the rest of this line and see if there's anything else I have to do today, and then we'll go back for tools."

Achille set off following the fence line, checking each post as he got to it, but before long his eyes were looking at the fence but he did not see it. Instead he was seeing the young girl from the market in Salliac last Monday. He guessed she was around twelve or thirteen. He thought about the way she had grinned at him when he offered her the cannelé. About her innocent expression. Her scuffed-up sneakers.

The more he thought about her, the more he was convinced she would do nicely. It would be much better, he reasoned, to have someone younger. That was a mistake he would correct this time, getting the age right. Younger would mean less fighting back, he reasoned. She would be more willing, more adaptable. More controllable.

He needed to see her again. And once he had that thought, Achille felt a sort of frantic pressure deep inside that he knew would stay with him uncomfortably until next week's market day when he could try to find her again.

What if she isn't there? What if she never comes back?

The fence post forgotten, Achille turned back towards the house, whistling for Bourbon. His face was contorted and one hand was balled up in a fist, while the other switched the branch against the ground, over and over.

It's gotten stale.

He had to act. It was not a choice but an imperative, and it had to happen soon.

❧

RUNNING a gîte business turned out to be like a lot of other jobs —you're just juggling one catastrophe after another. Molly went to give the pigeonnier one last check before the Dutch couple, the De Groots, arrived in the afternoon, and found that the dramatic rainstorm the night before had caused an equally dramatic leak in the new roof. She put in an emergency call to Pierre Gault and put her headphones in so she could listen to the blues while she spent the rest of the morning mopping up water, washing throw rugs and hanging them out to dry.

Thinking of what Mme Gervais had said the other day, she noticed that the pigeonnier would make a perfect place to hide someone. It was well off the road, for one thing. Even though it was bright enough inside, the windows were far too small for anyone to squeeze through, and too high up to see through. She made a mental note to look for more pigeonniers on the outskirts of the village and in the countryside nearby. Valerie could be like Rapunzel, being shut up in a miniature tower all those years. Molly shivered as a wave of claustrophobia passed through at the idea of being locked away for so long.

The hard physical work of cleaning up put her in a better mood, so that by the time Pierre arrived, she was no longer cursing but feeling optimistic that the De Groots would love the place—if Pierre could fix the roof before the next rain.

"Molly, I cannot imagine how this happened," he said, from up on the roof. "It must have been a terrific gust of wind—you see, this tile right here has broken right off. Are you sure no one has been up here?"

"Why would anyone have gone on the roof? No, it's been quiet around here as usual, and no one asking for a ladder to climb any roofs."

"I will mend it today," he said. "It is no problem. But I will need to remove the tiles above it, you see, before I can replace the one that broke. Perhaps something fell on it?"

"What could possibly have fallen from the sky heavy enough to break one of those tiles?" asked Molly, skeptically. "Come on, Pierre—you were napping when you put that one on. It must have been already cracked when you used it."

Molly honestly had no problem with the mistake; she accepted perfectly well that stuff happens. But come on, when you screw up, just admit it, she thought, after saying goodbye to Pierre and heading back to her house to change for the arrival of the De Groots.

And it was a good thing she hurried, because the village taxi pulled into La Baraque not fifteen minutes later, just as Molly was trying to run a comb through her hair and giving it up as a lost cause.

"Bonjour!" she called out, genuinely happy to meet the new guests.

"Hello, Molly!" said Herman De Groot. "I hope it is all right to call you by your first name? I feel I know you after our exchange of emails."

"Of course," said Molly with a smile. "I'm very glad to see you," she said to Christophe, the new taxi driver. "It would be a little crowded bringing guests here on my scooter."

Christophe grinned. The De Groots had taken their bags out of the taxi and were standing with their arms around each other, gazing into each other's eyes.

Ah, young love, thought Molly, with a manageably small pang of envy.

Herman smoothed his wife's hair off her face and leaned down to kiss her. Christophe chuckled and climbed back into his spiffy green Citroen and backed out of the driveway.

An awkward moment while Molly stood waiting for the kiss to end.

"Um, well then!" she said, trying to hold on to feeling of

graciousness when at a certain point she felt like giving them a kick.

The De Groots broke apart and Anika had the good manners to blush a little, and Molly led them to their lodging in the spick-and-span pigeonnier, nearly tripping over the orange cat who had suddenly appeared and gotten underfoot. They oohed and ahhed over the design, mentioning the glossy wood and the tiny windows, and after she got them settled Molly walked back to her house feeling a little less irritated with Pierre Gault.

But the worst of it was, she felt as though all of the tasks of her daily life—the cleaning and greeting of guests, fixing what was broken, making La Baraque a lovely and friendly place to stay—all these tasks were getting in the way of what really mattered, which was coming up with some kind of workable plan to find Valerie.

Who had left the note? And why, if he or she really had seen Valerie Boutillier, why not simply say where she was?

Chapter Sixteen

Of course Molly hoped all her guests enjoyed their stay at La Baraque, but she really wanted Ned and Leslie to leave feeling as though they couldn't wait to come back. Mostly—well, entirely—because she hoped they would return with Oscar. The parents had indulged Molly by letting Oscar stay with her a few nights, since it was obvious how much joy Oscar gave her. And it didn't hurt for them to get a little break from the little guy themselves.

They had made several more childless excursions and had a wonderful time, coming home to a happy child and a radiant babysitter. It was like having a grandmother who loved children right at hand, someone who was always ready to put any chores aside and scramble around on the floor to the delight of the crawling baby.

Not that Molly would have been pleased with being thought of as a grandmother; she was only thirty-eight and hadn't completely given up on having her own family, not all the way deep down. But the part about putting off work and being ready to play? Yes, a thousand times yes, and she was going miss the baby terribly when the family finally had to go.

They were leaving on Tuesday. Molly wanted to do something a little festive, so she invited some of her Castillac friends as well as Wesley Addison from upstairs (because how could you have a party and not invite a guest from *inside* your house?). Not dinner, just cocktails, or *apéros* as the French called them, along with "heavy apps", as they called decent hors d'oeuvres back in the U.S.

Molly spent a good couple of hours in the kitchen making those hors d'oeuvres: *gougères*, little cheesy puffballs; *pissaladière*, an onion tart; and *brandade au morue*, which was salt cod whipped with cheese and potatoes, ready to be scooped up with slices of toasted baguette. None of the dishes were difficult or demanded any particular precision, but still, an ambitious menu for one person to pull together in a few hours. Just when the first guests were due to arrive, Molly was sliding the last tray of *brandade* into the oven and running to shower and change. Luckily she knew no one would actually show up on the dot of the appointed hour.

She forgot about Wesley Addison.

As she was stepping into the shower, she heard him walking heavily down the stairs. It gave her pause, being naked with a strange man in her house, just down the hallway, but there was a lock on the bathroom door and she used it. Surely he could look at old gardening magazines for the few moments it would take her to finish getting ready.

"HELLO!" Mr. Addison shouted.

Molly rolled her eyes and put shampoo on her head, massaging it in, and trying to let irritation rinse off like the suds in her hair.

"MISS SUTTON!" he shouted again.

For God's sake.

"COMING!" Molly shouted back. Bobo watched intently as she hopped out of the shower, dried off, and put some product in her hair, making sure it got to the ends. If she skipped that step—actually let her hair do its natural thing, unaided by humankind—it would tangle up into the frizziest ball of crazy and no comb or brush would be able to tame it. But she suspected the delay was going to cost her.

Quickly she threw on a short spring dress, wiggled her feet into a pair of sandals, and left her bedroom, hoping to settle Addison down and put a little makeup on later.

"Miss Sutton! I was under the impression that you had invited me to a social gathering this evening?" He looked pointedly at his watch.

"Yes!" she said, with a false tone of gaiety that she was only glad Lawrence wasn't there to hear, because she'd never hear the end of it. "I'm afraid—oh! Let me—" The brandade smelled ready and she moved quickly to the kitchen and took it out of the oven. "I hope you're hungry!" she said, coming back around the counter while putting on an apron. "The others should be here soon. I'm afraid here in Castillac, the time given for something like this is more of a vague suggestion than a train departure time." She laughed.

Addison stared at her. "Train departure time?" he said, looking utterly confused.

"I just meant...oh, never mind. What can I get you to drink? Kirs are very popular, or I've got wine, and a bottle of vodka somewhere..."

Addison kept staring but didn't answer. Bobo growled at him —softly, as though wanting to be subtle about it.

"Or if you'd like something without alcohol, I've got mineral water and lemon?"

Molly thought she saw him nod at this, so she got a glass and made him a drink of cold Perrier, and added a chunk of lemon. "So, tell me how you ended up in Castillac," she asked him. "We do get some Americans visiting, but not all that often. I'm always curious about how people find their way here."

"I've been here before," said Mr. Addison. He lifted the glass to his lips and drank half of it. "I was here seven years ago," he said. "And I've always had the desire to return, and see how things had changed."

"So...back then, were you here for a long stay? What time of year was it?"

"Three months, July through September. I was meeting with a group of British people who had moved here, studying the progress of their language acquisition."

"Interesting! And how did they do?"

"Poorly. Too old. You do know that after a certain age, fluency in a non-native language is no longer possible?"

Molly nodded. "I'm not surprised to hear that. Although I feel quite comfortable speaking French now. Comfortable making embarrassing mistakes, I guess," she said, laughing.

Addison looked at her intently. "I don't understand. Mistakes make you feel comfortable?"

Unconsciously, Molly stepped back a few steps, wanting a bit more breathing room between her and Wesley Addison. She slid the onion tart into the over to warm and made herself a kir.

A firm knock and Michel Faure came through the front door, opening his arms to Molly. "Salut at long last!" he said, and they kissed cheeks.

"I'm so glad to see you!" she said. "And where is Adèle?"

"She's coming, she just stopped off at her apartment for a moment on her way. We've missed you, Molls!"

"I think if I had been vacationing in the Seychelles, I wouldn't have missed anybody!" she said.

"I don't understand," said Mr. Addison. "Why would the location of one's trip have any bearing on one's feelings about who was not along?"

Molly took a deep breath. "Let me introduce my guest, Wesley Addison. This is Michel Faure, who has been traveling with his sister Adèle, who I hope will be coming any minute. And now if you'll both excuse me for a moment, I have some things to do in the kitchen."

For the first time, Molly wished she had the old-fashioned kind of kitchen, not open but safely behind a closed door, where she could escape and tend to her heavy apps and maybe drink half a kir in peace before facing Addison again.

She knew in her business you had to get along with everybody, and she tried to accept this first real challenge with grace, even if she didn't feel it.

BEFORE LONG, the big open downstairs of Molly's house was filled with friends laughing and telling stories. Ned and Leslie had come over, and Molly had seen Mme Sabourin in her yard and called out an impulsive invitation to her as well. The De Groots had begged off and were holed up in the pigeonnier. Adèle had arrived with a new handbag as a present for Molly.

Lawrence had contented himself with straight vodka and Molly's apologies over not having all the ingredients for a proper Negroni. "You do know you're an utter philistine," he said affectionately, sipping the vodka and reaching for an olive.

"Absolutely," grinned Molly. "I don't think of that drink with fondness," she added.

"I think there's a story there," said Michel, raising an eyebrow.

"Yes, but you can guess it. The only thing that makes it slightly interesting is that after two Negronis I got in a taxi with a killer."

"I don't think I can outdo that," said Michel. "And listen, my beauty—this *brandade* is perfection!" He dipped a toast in and chomped happily away.

"Michel has been eating everything that's not nailed down," laughed Adèle. "The boy has expensive tastes that were apparently neglected for far too long."

"You like handbags, I like caviar," he answered. "No need to judge."

"So does everybody have a 'thing'? Negronis, handbags, caviar...I'm not sure I fit in," said Leslie.

"I don't have a thing either," said Ned.

"You do too!" Leslie said. She shifted Oscar to her other hip and pointed at her husband. "This man has a shoe thing that you wouldn't believe. We had to bring a separate duffel bag on the trip just to hold them."

"Interesting," said Lawrence, giving Ned an up-and-down look. "You don't often find that in the straight world."

"I think of them as tools," said Ned. "Each one has its role. The slipper, the running shoe, the hiking boot—you want to wear a shoe that's made for the specific activity. Multipurpose shoes are sad little things: jacks of all trades, masters of none."

"I had no idea," said Molly, taking a look at Ned's feet. "But you're wearing moccasins now, not fancy loafers. If I told you those won't do, could you upgrade?"

"Of course he can upgrade," said Leslie, laughing. "He almost wore the loafers, just changed his mind at the last minute."

Mme Sabourin was smiling politely and sipping a kir. She only knew six English words and so the conversation was gibberish, but still she found it interesting that the younger people seemed to be inspecting each other's feet with so much good humor.

"And how about you, Wesley? What's your shoe collection like?

Wesley stared at Ned as though he couldn't quite make out what he meant. "I'm sorry," he said finally. "I am having some difficulty paying attention to what you are saying because I am listening to your accent instead of your words. I am a linguist," said Wesley, reaching out to shake Ned's hand. "Once wrote a paper on the Australian accent, discussing the degree of allophonic variation in the alveolar stops, to be precise."

Everyone paused.

"I haven't the slightest idea what you're talking about," said Ned. "So how about we get a plate of this incredible food and take our drinks out to the terrace and you can explain to me what the hell you just said."

"All right," said Wesley, making a half-bow.

"Hello little goose," Molly said, coming over to make faces at Oscar. Oscar shook his head and smiled at her. "I'm going to miss you guys so much," said Molly. "I feel like all three of you are part of the family now."

"We are sad to go," said Leslie.

A gust of humid air blew in as the front door opened and Frances swept in, followed by a glum-looking Nico. Frances was looking very dramatic, as usual, wearing a short shift-dress made of a filmy, barely-there fabric, and clunky platform shoes that made her legs look even longer.

"Well, hello, you nutter!" said Molly, giving her friend a kiss on both cheeks. "I hardly see you anymore! Oh my God, are you blushing?"

Frances flicked her black straight hair out of her face and lifted her chin. "I do not blush," she said. "And let me tell you," she whispered, "Nico is...he's such a man of mystery!"

"Uhm hm," said Molly, having heard this before from Frances concerning husbands one and two. "I'm happy for you. And so glad you came. You've got to try this brandade. It's my new fave, I think I'll be eating it three meals a day from now on."

Frances laughed and went off to say hello to Michel.

Molly went to the kitchen to get more *gougères* out of the oven. She tumbled them into a napkin-lined basket and then stood for a moment, looking out at the room filled with people she hadn't even known a year ago. Mme Sabourin was chuckling over something with Adèle. Frances was making Michel laugh, and Nico was glowering at them. Lawrence was standing by himself, petting the orange cat. Molly's eyes started to well up, she was so grateful for finding her way to La Baraque, to Castillac, and for having all these people in her life now who were so dear to her.

She was feeling so *verklempt* that even the stolid tone of Wesley Addison on the terrace as he lectured Ned about diphthongs made her smile with fondness.

Which is not to say that Molly had forgotten about Valerie. Once she was on a case, it was on her mind a hundred percent of the time, even if those thoughts were running quietly in the background. But that night, she felt as though the best thing any of them could be doing was to be together like this, laughing and talking about each other's shoes. It made facing the horror of what humans will do to one another more bearable.

It was the whole point of everything, really.

Chapter Seventeen

All week, Achille had been looking forward to Monday when the Salliac market took place. Yet here it was, Monday morning, late enough that he knew the vendors had set up and opened for business, and yet he kept finding reasons to delay.

It is possible, he was saying to himself, that Aimée would not do. She might be too young. She might want to talk about teenage things he knew nothing about. They might not be able to find enough in common. But then he thought of how lively she had been, talking to her friend on the phone, how she had tossed her head like a little filly, how her green eyes had lit up when he offered her a cannelé.

He wanted that liveliness near him. Wanted her to talk to him excitedly as he had overheard her doing with her friend. And yet, though it was true that Aimée's smiling and laughing attracted him, what made him feel connected to her was something very different. There was a shadow over the girl. A sense that she was wounded somehow, that something was wrong at home, maybe even terribly wrong.

Achille did not think about this directly. It was more of a vague feeling than anything else, though he had noted to himself her wrinkled clothes, the fact that she was at the market instead of school, and even that Aimée would accept a cannelé from a strange man. All of these impressions led him to believe that she needed him.

That there was something in her he understood.

Farm chores long since finished, Achille spent some moments in front of the mirror over the bathroom sink, trying to improve his appearance. Bourbon watched him closely, pacing back and forth behind him. He didn't have a toothbrush but he picked his teeth with some thin willow sticks he had cut by the stream. He combed his hair, making sure to work out all the knots. He grimaced at his reflection, wondering how he had turned into a man when he still felt so much like a boy inside.

The tractor was old but sturdy, and he maintained it well. So it felt like a betrayal when he climbed up and turned the key, and the engine caught and sputtered out. Nervously he turned the key again, careful with the pressure on the clutch in case he had let up too soon the first time. The engine did the same thing—seemed to come alive, but then gasped and died.

Achille jumped down, a knot in his stomach. The market in Salliac was that day, and only in the morning. He was not in control of when he might see Aimée: this was his chance, right now, and if he didn't get there in time, all could be lost.

Spittle collected in the corners of his mouth as he checked the hoses and the oil. He could find nothing out of order.

All right, he told himself, calm down. *Calm down.* The tractor is going to start this time. It *is*.

He climbed back up and turned the key. And it did start. Moving quickly from relief to overexcitement, he backed up and then gunned the accelerator, shot down the short driveway to the road, and turned left on the road towards Salliac.

He did not think about Valerie even once.

Now that the weather was sunny and warm again, many more people crowded the square in the center of the small village. He saw the woman who sold imported vegetables, a tall man selling organic spinach and lettuces, and another man selling pots and pans. On one side of the square a *crêperie* truck and a pizza truck were doing good business. Then, squeezed in between a fishmonger and two young women selling cheese, Achille spotted the old woman sitting at a table with her meager display of cannelés.

"Bonjour Madame," said Achille, his voice sounding a little quavery. "May I have six?"

She smiled at him. "Oui, Monsieur Labiche," and slowly put six of the dark golden treats into a bag. He startled at the sound of his name, but the woman did look familiar and he figured she had probably been a friend of his parents. Everyone knows everyone around here, he thought, with a shiver.

Achille had told himself he was not allowed to look for Aimée until he had the bag of cannelés ready. With devious insight, he understood perfectly that without the cannelés, the girl would have no interest in him. He couldn't just capture her like a baby frog—she had to be gentled first, and then lured.

Achille had practiced on a lot of girls over the years, even bringing them to point when he could have taken them, and decided not to at the last minute. He liked every part of it—looking for prospects, trying to see what they responded to, keeping an eye out so that he could disappear if anyone else appeared to notice him. Many weeks, even months, he had not been able to come to the Salliac market, or any market, because the presence of so many people was just too overwhelming. But once he had a prospect in mind, the other people did not really exist. He was focused on *her*.

And many of them liked the attention, even craved it. Valerie however—she was different, and had been since the first moment he saw her. She was the most animated person he had ever seen, positively bursting with energy, a happy imp that never stopped moving. Valerie had mesmerized him. And back then, he had not developed any of the methods he was trying to employ with the girl at the Salliac market; he suspected, looking back, that they wouldn't have worked on Valerie anyway.

Because she didn't need attention from anybody: she had no streak of sadness that Achille could spot a mile away, no vulnerability that he could exploit. He had stalked her, grabbing her one night as she came out of a friend's house on her way home. Not gentling and luring her, but taking her by brute force. It was a terrible risk, tying and gagging her right there on a street in Castillac, and bringing her home on the tractor, sitting between his legs—anyone could have seen, and he understood the trouble he'd have been in had he been caught. She almost made it impossible for him to drive with her thrashing, but he had gotten her back to the farm without a soul seeing what he had done.

He had worried that the necessity for force might make the kind of connection he was looking for impossible to have, that she would be angry and shout at him and continue on like that without ever stopping. But it hadn't happened exactly that way. She had been angry, but eventually the anger fizzled out. And Valerie had been his for seven whole years.

It was certainly regrettable that it was going stale. But not in his control.

He walked through the market with his back straight, fearful but able to hide it, looking for the girl. The thought of Aimée gave him strength and purpose.

Loved.

IT HAD NOT BEEN easy and several times Gilbert had thought she would never allow it, but at long last Maman had said he could forage by himself for nettles and other spring greens, and if he found enough, they could go to the Castillac market on Saturday to sell them. Gilbert had first had this idea back in the fall, during mushroom season, and had since been relentlessly trying to talk her into letting him, hoping that he could make enough money to buy a remote-controlled helicopter he had his eye on.

Maman said he was too young, that he would never be able to stick to the job long enough to make it worth it, that he was too lost in his own dreamworld to pay attention out in the fields. He would only disappoint himself. But Gilbert had finally worn her down.

Now the helicopter was forgotten, and instead he was desperate for a way to get back into the village so as to leave another note for the gendarmes, this time not forgetting the crucial information of Valerie's whereabouts.

After several days of chastising himself, he had gotten used to his mistake and no longer felt so guilty. Surely even the most famous detectives, Maigret and Poirot, made mistakes occasionally. Possibly even James Bond had made a mistake somewhere along the way, not that Maman had ever let him see a Bond movie. Looking ahead, he figured that by Saturday morning he would have managed to find the materials to make a second note; once in Castillac, he would tell Maman he had to go to the bathroom, and tape the note on the station door just like last time.

If only they don't think it's a dumb prank, he thought with a pang of prescience. *But there's nothing I can do about that.*

He and Maman had foraged for mushrooms and greens since he was a little boy, and he had no difficulty identifying the ones he wanted. He knew where the nettles grew and how to collect them without getting stung. He knew to pick young dandelion leaves, yarrow, and chickweed, and that older watercress leaves had more flavor.

It was true: he *was* daydreaming as he left the house and took off across the field behind the house. He was imagining nice rich ladies paying him handfuls of euros for his fresh spring greens. Maybe he could save Valerie Boutillier *and* get that helicopter!

It was no longer raining. The air was cool and the ground wet. He put on a pair of his mother's gardening gloves and harvested half a basket of nettles in just a few minutes. He wondered if Valerie was hungry. Did Labiche give her anything besides milk? He walked into the woods towards Labiche's farm, wanting just to check and see if she was outside.

As over-protective as Maman was, she had always allowed him to wander the farm and play in the woods alone as much as he liked, and he thought of the fields and woods as his territory, knowing the individual trees and the gentle slopes, the stream and the mossy banks, all the detail of the land with an easy intimacy. But now that he had seen Valerie, the long-lost girl, and realized that she had been stolen from the world and hidden away all this time—by his neighbor—now the woods no longer seemed as friendly as they had before.

Gilbert startled when a twig snapped behind him. He kept looking quickly around as if to catch someone spying on him. His fears were not centered on Labiche, although he dreaded seeing him; it was as though once the veil of safety and security was torn, everything turned scary, and suspect. The thick trunks of oaks were perfect for hiding behind and he imagined someone was there, getting ready to grab him.

At first all of his concentration had been on finding enough to justify the trip to the market the next day. But before long he was worrying about Labiche creeping through the woods and spying on him. And if his neighbor, who seemed so placid, a man more interested in cows than anything else—if he could turn out to be a sick criminal, who knows who else might be plotting something equally evil?

Gilbert turned around. The shadows of the wood made him jumpy. Maybe he should just forget this plan and go home, think of some other way.

Wait a minute.

He was not going to be like his mother, afraid of a million things that hadn't even happened. Labiche had been keeping Valerie prisoner for seven whole years, and not once had he made any move to add Gilbert to his prison. And also he had never seen Labiche in the woods, not ever. All Labiche ever did was walk in the fields with his dog and talk out loud to his cows.

The woods were Gilbert's home. He was safe there.

Wasn't he?

Chapter Eighteen

A chille had finished the evening milking, eaten his dinner, and washed up. The old television had broken months ago, and he was not fond of reading. There was nothing to do and he felt agitated.

He had been feeling ill-tempered since the Monday market in Salliac. He had gotten himself to the small village at long last, bought the cannelés, watched and waited...but the girl had not appeared. He was tormented with the thought that she had been there earlier and he had missed her. Maybe she had even looked for him, maybe she was hoping he would be there with his bag of fresh cannelés, and he had failed her. Disappointed her. And for what? He didn't even have a reason. He had come late to the Monday market because he had wasted time looking at a newspaper and then the tractor wouldn't start.

He had delayed because the market meant a crowd of people, even in a small village such as Salliac, and forcing himself to join them took time and effort.

Or maybe she hadn't come at all. Didn't even remember him.

To escape these agonizing thoughts he went to the root cellar.

He stood outside the door, listening. Valerie was quiet. The door was padlocked and he took out the only key, which was on a little chain attached to his belt. He hesitated.

It had gotten stale. Stale because Valerie was so different now, talking nonsense half the time, and not listening to him the way she used to do. She wasn't like she was when he took her, so lively and vital.

Put simply—he was tired of her.

But he opened the door, hoping maybe she had changed back like she used to be and they could have a night together like they used to have, talking about everything under the sun, and he would leave her and go back to his house and his bed feeling the warmth of companionship, of taking care of her, same as he did his girls and his dog.

That was all he was after. All he wanted was someone there to talk to, someone to take care of. Someone who wouldn't go anywhere. Wouldn't leave him.

He knew there were other men in his situation who took terrible advantage of the women they kept—he had read such an account in the newspaper years ago and that had given him the idea to build the bunker—but Achille was not like that and he despised the men who behaved that way.

"*Bonsoir*, Valerie," he said gently, coming in and closing the door behind him. He had brought a candle in a porcelain holder and he struck a match and lit the wick.

"Lala lali lo," said Valerie, not looking at him.

"It's going to be that again?" said Achille. "I'm not really one for music. We never had any music in the house when my parents were alive. I'm not used to it."

"Leeeeelaaaaaa—"

"Stop that!" Achille clapped his hands over his ears.

"I'm your Valerie," she said. She was huddled on her mattress, up in the corner of the root cellar. It was four paces long and three paces wide. In the early years of her confinement, she used to walk for hours, never able to take more than four steps in one direction.

"Yes," said Achille, feeling a momentary spark of tenderness for her. He reached out and stroked her hollow cheek. "It's just...I don't know what to do with you now."

"Do do do," said Valerie. She lay on her back and put her feet up on the ceiling. She was wearing a pair of jeans that Achille had bought at a store in Bergerac four years ago. It was always exciting, buying her clothes. He felt like he was practically telling the world that he had Valerie living with him, like he was giving a big hint to the world that he had a female, someone he was so close to that he bought her clothes. But no one ever seemed to pay any attention.

"I went to the market in Salliac today," he said, sitting on the corner of her bed.

Valerie said nothing.

"I'm just going to tell you outright. I went because I met a girl there last week. She has a brown ponytail. She reminds me a little of you, like a younger version of you."

Valerie said nothing. She pressed her feet on the ceiling and some bits of dirt fell down onto the mattress.

"Would you like some company?" Achille asked. "I mean, apart from me? Would you like it if I brought her here to live with you?"

Valerie lifted her head and stared at him. "I'm your Valerie," she said.

"Of course. Nothing can ever change that," he said, and meant it. "But I have so much work to do, I can't visit with you as often as we'd both like. So maybe you would like it if you had some company. I think the cellar is big enough for two, don't you?"

"La li la," said Valerie.

Achille felt a surge of anger. Why would she keep up that

meaningless nonsense when she knew how it irritated him? Why had she broken their connection that he had worked so hard for and risked so much to build?

Valerie pulled her knees into her chest and wrapped her arms around her legs, and rocked on the mattress, back and forth, back and forth.

Suddenly everything about the root cellar became intolerable to Achille: the smell, her singing, the blankness where she used to be, the darkness.

"All right, that's it then," he said, standing up. He took her dirty plate and bowl in one hand, and the slop bucket in the other, and said goodnight. Valerie did not answer but kept rocking.

Achille emptied the bucket into a deep hole he had dug, and tossed a handful of lime on top of it. He rinsed the bucket out carefully, unlocked the door again, and set the bucket back inside the bunker without a word.

This had been his nightly routine for seven years. Always when he returned the rinsed bucket he had said something affectionate, even just "goodnight, *chérie*," but that night he silently closed the door and locked it, and trudged back to the house, his heart heavy.

He was tired of her, and worse, in the moment he no longer even liked her. So now what was he supposed to do with her?

THE NEXT MORNING, Molly came out to the kitchen in her bathrobe and slippers to make coffee, but stopped in her tracks when she faced the destruction left from the night before. Lawrence had very kindly helped her load the dishwasher before he left, and Adèle had helped put away the food, but dirty glasses seemed to have sprouted up all over the place, crumbs carpeted the floor, and Bobo was standing in the corner looking very guilty about something.

"I'm sure you ate something you weren't supposed to," said Molly, scratching under her ears. "But hey, you should be able to live it up too once in a while. Just don't get sick, I beg you. I'm so not in the mood to deal with throw-up right now."

Bobo licked her chops and pushed her head against Molly's hand.

Just one cup of coffee, then I'll head to the market to get fresh croissants for everyone. I'll clean up when I get back.

She left Bobo and got out a mug, splashed in a generous dollop of cream, and got the French press ready while the water came to a boil.

Bobo growled.

Molly heard the heavy steps of Wesley Addison coming downstairs.

Dammit.

She tied her bathrobe firmly and put on her game face. "Good morning!" she chirped as he rounded the corner.

"Bonjour," he said, looking around the room with distaste.

Molly noticed his accent was quite good. "I'm just having some coffee before going into the village to get fresh bread. I know things are a mess but I'll tend to it when I get back," she explained. "Is there anything in particular you'd like me to get you? Any pastry you like above all others?"

"I don't eat pastry," said Wesley Addison.

"Gluten problem?" asked Molly sympathetically.

"No. I just don't like it."

Freak.

"Well, what else can I get for your breakfast then? I'm happy to make you some eggs. There's a farmer at the market who has amazing sausages, if you can wait until I get back."

"Raoul?"

"Yes," said Molly, "that's exactly who I mean. Just thinking about him makes my mouth water."

Addison looked alarmed.

"No!" said Molly. "I don't mean—I just meant that his sausages are very good, and I think I'll buy some for my lunch. So you know Raoul from when you were here before? Do you like to cook?"

"No."

Molly waited for him to elaborate. Eventually Addison said, "I don't cook. It was my wife who found Raoul, and cooked the sausages. Wouldn't stop talking about them either. Bought them every single Saturday and we usually ate them for dinner that night, every week for months."

Molly was nodding. Her mood was lifting just thinking about the cup of coffee that was almost ready. She tossed the filter and grounds into the compost bucket next to the sink and poured the magnificent dark brown liquid into her mug. "Oh!" she said, after swallowing the first ambrosial sip. "I'm sorry—would you like some coffee?"

"No," said Addison. "I don't drink coffee."

Crazy freak.

"My wife was an addict, however. I see you have the same fervor for the stuff that she had."

Molly smiled. "And where is your wife? Did she not want to make this trip this time? Hard to get away?"

"Oh, it's nothing like that," said Addison. "She's dead. She died near Castillac, actually."

"Oh! I'm...I'm very sorry," said Molly.

Bobo growled.

"Hush, Bobo-girl," said Molly, petting the top of her speckled head.

Molly wanted to know more of that story, but for the moment her wish for something to eat trumped her curiosity. She excused herself from Wesley Addison, washed her face, threw on some clothes, and headed down rue des Chênes towards Pâtisserie Bujold and the Saturday morning market. The sun was shining for the first time in days, her party had been a great success, and Molly wanted to enjoy it all—and just this once not think about anything ugly or sad.

Chapter Nineteen

Castillac was in a state of spring-induced euphoria. After the rains of the last week, the warm sun felt so good on everyone's skin, and Molly saw more than one person turn her face to the sun, eyes closed, drinking in the unfamiliar heat and brightness. The Saturday market was more crowded than usual. Every week it seemed as though more vendors crowded into the Place as they competed for warm-weather customers with fresh produce, cheese, and locally-raised meat. Molly could smell yeasty bread somewhere nearby, and coffee.

That scooter she had her eye on was rakishly parked on the sidewalk and she stopped for a moment to lust after it. The swooping chrome, polished and shining. The adorably cute dashboard with its well-designed dials and meters. Even just the small pads where the rider put his feet, and the elegantly shaped leather seat—it was all perfection.

She ran her hand over the handlebars, imagining herself cutting in and out of traffic like a slalom skier, a bag from Pâtisserie Bujold safely tucked onto the tiny luggage rack behind her.

"Pretty, isn't it?" said a familiar voice.

"Oh, bonjour Thomas," said Molly, her tone frosty, having not forgotten or forgiven when it came to Constance's ex-boyfriend's cheating ways.

"You're still mad."

"Of course I'm still mad!" said Molly. "Constance is my friend and you treated her abominably. Are you suggesting I should just get over it?"

"No, of course not. I'm...but I want you know..."

"Thomas!" said a young woman appearing from the crowd and tugging at his arm. "Let's go, we're going to be late!"

Thomas had the expression of a cow who is being harassed by a border collie.

"But still, nice to see you," said Molly, smiling to herself and moving on. She did love how the village was small enough that she would see plenty of people she knew at the Saturday market, but she could also see that in a place this size, if a relationship went south, it could get complicated.

Good thing I am dedicated to staying single, she thought, making her way towards Raoul's booth. She picked up a package of sausages, wondering briefly about exactly how Mrs. Addison had met her demise. She waved at her neighbor, Mme Sabourin, who was shoveling prunes into a paper bag.

"Manette!" she said, surprised to see her friend selling vegetables in a different spot than usual. "I'm totally discombobulated seeing you on this side of the Place. I thought everyone stuck to their usual spots."

"Usually we do," Manette said darkly. "It's that new fellow, the one selling whole-grain bread. And don't get him talking about the bread—he'll go on and on about how healthful it is until you want to club him over the head to shut him up. And if you're wondering about the taste, it's fine so long as you like bread with the flavor of wallpaper paste. And heavy as a concrete block."

Molly laughed. "I'm thinking I'll take peppers and eggplants to go with my sausages, please."

"Raoul's?"

"Of course. Now tell me how you're doing, Manette. Kids doing all right? How's your mother-in-law?"

"Still sick. Or acting sick, it's hard to tell which. But thanks for asking. The kids are good. Wild, wearing me down to my last nerve, but good." Manette winked at her and weighed the produce.

Something about Manette made Molly miss her own mother. She was so rosy-cheeked and good natured—things her own mother hadn't been, except rarely—and Molly couldn't help having a fleeting fantasy of going home with Manette and blending in, getting swept up in the happy mayhem of her big family.

But the market was crowded that Saturday and too many customers were clamoring for Manette's attention for Molly to keep chatting with her. She paid and arranged her vegetables in her basket and moved on with a wave goodbye.

A wizened man she'd never met was sitting at a small table, on which stood neatly arranged plastic containers of walnuts. The man looked something like a walnut himself, his aged skin in folds and deep creases, with lively dark eyes peeping out.

"Bonjour, Monsieur," said Molly, and then introduced herself. She had found almost all of the locals perked up considerably when they found out she lived in Castillac and was not just passing through.

But alas, though he was perfectly friendly, the Walnut Man had an accent that Molly could not get at all. It was so indeciperable that she couldn't even understand his name but stood with her eyes wide and a phony smile, just hoping the clouds would part and the meaning would suddenly become apparent. But it did not. Feeling a little embarrassed and also irritated with herself, she bought a box of the painstakingly shelled walnuts, gave Walnut Man a big smile along with some euros, and moved on.

❦

NEXT TO WALNUT MAN was a boy, also sitting at a small table. The boy looked troubled about something—his brow was furrowed and he was watching her intently— which made Molly's ears prick up just like Bobo's. On his table were heaps of wilted greens, and a few grungy-looking plastic bags.

"Bonjour, Madame," Gilbert said, so softly Molly could barely hear him.

"Bonjour," said Molly, wanting to touch his freckled cheek but restraining herself. "Did you find these yourself?"

"Yes," said Gilbert, his face flushing. This is the moment, he said to himself. Talk to her! Molly Sutton was the best detective in the whole village, maybe even the whole Dordogne! *Just tell her!*

But he could not make the words come out.

He could not make *any* words come out.

"They're wild? I've never actually foraged anything," she was saying. "I mean, I've foraged in the *supermarket*," she laughed at herself, "but not in the wild. Obviously not at all the same thing. I would be afraid to make a mistake. Not that I think *you* made a mistake—these look lovely and I'm sure you know what you're doing." Molly paused, and looked at him sideways. "You do know what you're doing, right?"

Gilbert froze. He nodded, now his face very pale. What is the matter with you! he yelled at himself, to no avail. He had not even come close to taping the note to the station door; every time he ran down the street to check, there was a crowd of people coming and going to the market. No way to do it without being seen.

Shy boys are so adorable, Molly was thinking. She almost had to physically hold her hand back with the other to keep from ruffling his hair, which was longer on top and a little curly.

"I am terribly fond of wild greens, especially nettles," she said. "How much are you charging? Can I afford to buy them all and have myself a real feast?"

"Oui, Madame," said Gilbert. "Five euros, that is all."

"You don't charge enough. For all this work? It must have taken you hours of foraging to find all these! Are you sure five euros is your price?"

Gilbert nodded, keeping back a smile.

"Molly! I was hoping to see you here!" Ben Dufort cut across the crowd and kissed her on both cheeks.

"Salut, Ben! Maybe we could go to a café once we're done marketing? I have an idea or two...."

"I'm sure you do," he said, smiling at her.

Gilbert watched them. If there was ever a moment to let loose with his information, this was it. Madame Sutton and Chief Dufort, together, right in front of him, and his mother out of the way talking to Manette.

Yet he said nothing. He watched the two of them together. Chief Dufort—well, Gilbert was going to keep calling him that even if he wasn't actually Chief anymore—he was so...so big, and strong, and good-looking. Gilbert was pretty sure Madame Sutton thought so too.

Surely it would be safe to tell them. They weren't yellers. They seemed nice.

Yes, they *were* nice. But that didn't mean for one second that they would believe what he told them. He was only nine years old. They would think he was daydreaming, just looking for attention. And he only had one chance. If they jumped to the wrong conclusion, he would have no way to convince them after.

He should just tell them anyway. Risk it.

Or maybe...maybe he could buy a camera with the money he saved from selling greens, and he could spy on Labiche and take photographs the next time he saw him outside with Valerie!

A dumb idea. That would take months.

"Hello? Are you daydreaming, my friend?" Molly was saying to him. "So five euros is your final price?"

Gilbert nodded, doubly mortified because now tears were

beginning to gather in the corners of his eyes out of frustration and not knowing the right thing to do. Sometimes he really hated being a kid.

He took her money and watched as the pair disappeared into the crowd, fully aware that his best chance to tell his secret had disappeared right along with them.

ॐ

MOLLY AND BEN made their way through the crowd to Café de la Place, where Pascal took their orders with his usual dazzling smile and disappeared into the kitchen.

"Is this too public?" Molly asked in a low voice.

"Not everyone is an inveterate eavesdropper like you," Ben said, with a grin. "But you're right, yes, we should be careful what we say. The success of our investigation may hinge on the abductor's taking it easy after all this time, no longer wary of being found out. We don't want half the village talking about what we're trying to do."

"I've been thinking the same thing," said Molly. "But I've been trying to think of some way to nose around a little without raising any suspicions, and I've got at least a piece of an idea."

Pascal returned with two café crèmes and plates of warm croissants, along with small dishes of sweet butter and raspberry jam. Molly dove in, starving. "Well, very simply—and of course, correct me where I'm wrong—I figure I need to get inside people's houses. I know there would be no way for me to really inspect anything, like if there are hidden compartments or something like that. Just getting invited in isn't likely to be enough. But it's a start, right?

"Anyway, my plan is to go door to door, with some sort of survey. I'll be armed with a clipboard and some forms, ask if I can come in and ask them some questions. Maybe say I'm doing historical research on the area, or geneological research. I wish I could say it was a government thing but they'll hardly believe an American would be doing that."

"And they'd be less likely to open the door."

"But so I was thinking...if you were keeping someone prisoner in your attic or whatever, wouldn't you be super nervous if a stranger came around at all? Do you think I'd be able to sense that nervousness?"

Ben swallowed a mouthful of croissant before answering. "Maybe," he said, but he didn't sound very confident. "Remember, we're looking for someone who has managed to keep this secret for seven long years. If he were the type to break a sweat the minute anyone comes near his house, he'd have been found out long ago. Some criminals are made of ice—they can lie and not have any of the physical manifestations of anxiety. That's why lie detector tests aren't perfect. Ironically, it's the biggest liars who don't get caught."

Molly nodded, feeling a little dejected. If Valerie was being held in a secret room somewhere, how in the world was Molly ever going to find out where? She could be right under their noses —upstairs at the Café de la Place, for all they knew. Days were ticking by and they were still at square one.

She looked into Ben's warm brown eyes and said, "You still think she was killed."

"I'm afraid so. The report from my end is that my friend in Toulouse is coming through for us—he's arriving sometime this week and bringing a trained dog. Supposed to be able to sniff out a cadaver in a large area."

"So what are you going to do, wander around the village with him on a leash?"

"I plan to make concentric circles, starting in the middle of the village and moving outward. My friend will likely give me direction on how to use the dog most efficiently. I want to get out into the countryside rather quickly. Unless Valerie Boutillier is in someone's freezer somewhere," he added, his voice low, "I expect that's where I'll find her. Out in the woods—the forest of La Double has many secrets. And possibly this dog will uncover at least one of them."

Chapter Twenty

After the talk with Dufort, Molly was determined to make headway on her part of the investigation. So that afternoon while cleaning up the wreckage from the party the night before, she composed a persona for herself of a bumbling genealogical researcher, interested in the old names and families of the area. She figured that would be unthreatening as well as not require any special knowledge on her part. In her old life in America, Molly had been a fundraiser, quite used to approaching strangers, putting them at ease, and getting them to write checks before they knew what was happening.

Well, she hadn't been very good at that last part. Or at least, she hadn't enjoyed it very much. But this job, this investigation, was fundamentally different: a woman's life was potentially at stake. Which was a whole different thing from some school's being able to build a fancy new building they didn't really need.

In bed that night Molly read her questions aloud to Bobo, who was allowed on the bed just that once. She made a form online and found a notebook to fill with copies of the form along with some pages of fake notes, dug up some decent pens, and considered herself all set.

The next morning she left some not-quite-fresh croissants on the counter along with a note for Wesley Addison, and took off for the village, wishing she could take Bobo with her for protection. For a practice run, she stopped at the house next door where Mme Sabourin lived.

"Bonjour, Mme Sabourin!" she said, enthusiastically.

"Bonjour Molly," the old lady answered. They kissed cheeks. "I had a lovely time the other night. You have some colorful friends," she said with a small smile.

Molly ran through her questions, and Mme Sabourin answered gamely, though Molly thought she could see her wondering what in the world this was all about. And then, just to be methodical about it, she went to the next house on rue des Chênes and introduced herself and went through her list of questions, and then the house after that and on and on, marking down on a map when no one was home.

The houses in Castillac varied from the very old—some as old as fifteenth century in parts—to so new the stucco had barely dried. Molly was grateful that many people (mostly older women) invited her in and offered her a cup of coffee or tea, and were more than happy to go into the details of their family histories as well as the history of the Dordogne. She heard about the torture of aristocrat Alain de Monéys in 1870, and about the disruption caused by the religious wars of the sixteenth century. About groups of Huguenots leaving France for England and Sweden. About the heroes of the Resistance, who showed such courage in standing up to the Nazis. About the foreigners who came, over the decades, mixing their blood and their names with those of Castillac.

Over the course of a very long day, she learned a considerable amount about these families, their interrelations and connections to other parts of the country and beyond. But not once did she get so much as the tiniest inkling that anyone was up to anything remotely untoward, nor did she spy a single shred of evidence that Valerie Boutillier was living anywhere nearby.

THE NEXT MORNING Achille woke up and instantly leapt out of bed. It was Monday, the day of the Salliac market, and he was not going to waste half the day doing nothing this time. He was going straight there, right after the morning milking.

He was not going to miss her again.

The morning chores seemed to take forever: get the girls in from the far field, hook them up to the machine, turn them out in the west field; take Valerie her breakfast and empty her bucket; take a bucket of slops to the hog; feed the dog.

All the animals seemed to move in slow motion, and it was frustrating to Achille that there was nothing he could say or do to move them along any more quickly. When he urged Bourbon on, she turned and looked askance at him, and he kept quiet after that.

At long last, he was ready to go. He considered showering and combing his hair but did not want to take the time, so he climbed on the tractor smelling of manure and sweat, his hair sticking up in back, in a terrific hurry.

The tractor coughed and sputtered but the engine caught, and slowly moved down the short driveway to the main road, and off to Salliac.

Achille sold his milk to a cooperative, and had just received a payment. He was feeling wealthy and full of optimism, envisioning the moment when the girl climbed on his tractor to go home with him, and how it was going to give him more pleasure than anything ever had in his entire life. He kept picturing it, running the image in his head over and over, changing small details and running it through again.

He knew perfectly well that even if he could convince her to come home with him willingly, she would never want to stay there with him. He was under no illusions on that score. But holding her, being in charge of her completely, responsible for everything having to do with her—being her whole world—that was part of the point. The best part, he admitted to himself sometimes.

At first, the new girl would have to stay in the attic. It would be warmer there at night anyway, although he would likely have to endure some shrieking and crying.

He didn't like crying.

That was why he had been forced to build the root cellar where Valerie lived. It had been a massive undertaking and he still felt proud of himself for having managed it. After a few months with Valerie in the attic, he had had enough of her crying and screaming, all night long. He had a milking schedule to adhere to and nothing was allowed to affect that. It had taken him months to build the cellar, even using the digger attachment on the tractor for the bulk of the digging. He had to research, to gather materials—imagine building an underground dwelling all by yourself, and making sure the roof wasn't going to cave in!

It hadn't been easy, no. Not on top of all the daily responsibilities he already had. It's not like Valerie was going to pitch in. She had spent those months screaming herself hoarse. He had been very lucky none of the neighbors had heard anything.

As he drew close to Salliac, he pushed any thought of Valerie and the farm out of his mind, and focused all of his attention to finding the girl.

He knew she was there, he could feel it.

It was a beautiful day, warm with a light breeze, with more people walking around than the last time. A man bumped into him from behind and Achille startled violently, then shuddered at the thought of the stranger touching him like that without any warning.

The market felt dangerous. Any second, someone might start talking to him, and he would have no idea what to say back.

And then he saw her. It felt like a moment out of a movie, he could actually hear music playing as though someone had turned on a radio or an orchestra had risen up out of nowhere. He lifted his gaze and across the Place the girl stood with the sun illuminating her as she leaned back, one knee bent and her foot against a wall, talking with two friends.

She is the one.

Achille wanted to run to her, to take her hands in his and look into her pretty face. He wanted to start their conversation now, the conversation he expected to go on for years and years. But he held himself back.

He knew rushing was a mistake. And there were her friends to contend with. He would have to be patient.

At least that was one useful thing his father had taught him during those agonizing hunting trips. They would have to sit in the woods, not moving for hours on end, waiting for game to appear. Checking the wind direction, their clothes brown and green for camouflage, waiting and hoping. Time had felt endless.

That part wasn't the agony—it was the killing Achille didn't like. The hunting trips would have been wonderful if he had been allowed to bring the animals home, to keep them and care for them. His mother wouldn't have objected, because she was gone much of the time. In a special hospital, was all his father ever said. All Achille knew was that she was there, and then she was not, and she left over and over until she finally never returned.

Always leaving. Always leaving him behind.

Achille never took his eyes off the girl. Finally one of the friends wandered off, and he saw the girl kiss the other friend, a tall girl with legs so long they reminded him of spider legs.

He had forgotten the cannelés!

Quickly he scanned the tables ringing the Place, looking for the old woman who sold cannelés. He couldn't see her anywhere. But she was necessary; he couldn't approach the girl empty-handed—she was depending on him to provide for her.

He felt his throat start to close up from over-excitement. His hands trembled and suddenly all the other people at the market felt threatening again. They were too close and moving too erratically. Someone might bump into him again, someone might ask him a question.

It was overwhelming.

Achille turned and walked quickly back to his tractor. The day wasn't right. There were too many difficulties. He need to get home and calm down and think everything through.

But as he put his hands on the seat of the tractor and was about to hoist himself up, the image of the girl standing in the sunshine flashed into his head, and he paused. He dropped his hands and turned back around.

I can do it.

He looked again for the cannelé-seller and still did not see her. So instead he went into a shop that sold candies and bought a handful of caramels. He smiled at the proprietor and put the caramels in his pocket, and went to find his soulmate.

Chapter Twenty-One

On Monday morning, Molly wandered around outside drinking her first cup of coffee and looking at the daffodils. "Bobo! Don't trample the flowers!" she shouted, as Bobo flew straight into the border and began digging furiously.

Molly stepped in and dragged her back out, then bent down and inhaled the sweet scent of the flowers, closing her eyes so that all her attention was on the complicated, exhilarating smell.

"Okay, I'm doing it," she said, standing back up with a sudden clarity of purpose. She could not have explained why sniffing the daffodil had made her decide to buy the scooter that day—maybe something about carpe diem and living for the moment—but whatever the reason, she went inside to grab her handbag and set off for Castillac and the little shop on the far edge of town that had an array of scooters outside in a rainbow of gleaming colors.

"Stay, Bobo!" she said, and Bobo ran back and curled up on the front step as though she'd intended to do that before Molly said a word.

It was around a half hour walk to the scooter dealer's shop. Long enough for Molly to try to come up with a better plan than canvassing houses, and fail. Long enough to think about how kind Ben was, and how remarkable that he treated her as though she made meaningful contributions to their investigation, when he had years of training and experience and she had zero.

Long enough, of course, to swing by Pâtisserie Bujold and buy a croissant aux amandes. She was in such a good mood that she greeted Monsieur Nugent with more friendliness than usual, and sailed out of the shop almost giddy with anticipation about her new scooter.

But then she stopped in the street. "Lapin!" she said out loud, and then checked behind her to make sure no one heard. I need to talk to Lapin, she thought. His career is all about poking around in people's houses, and right after someone dies—a moment of great vulnerability for anyone, but maybe especially for someone with a terrible secret. Wouldn't Lapin, more than anyone, have some ideas about who might be unbalanced enough to take a hostage for seven years?

Regretfully she turned in the opposite direction from the scooter dealer and went straight to Chez Papa, where there was a decent chance she could find him.

"Sorry, you just missed him," said Nico, who was sweeping. "He came in for a quick coffee and a croissant and then hurried off. I have to say, I'm a little curious? I thought you and Lapin weren't exactly friends."

"Eh," said Molly, waving her hand. "We get along just fine." And indeed they did get along, but that didn't mean she was looking forward to calling him up and arranging to meet. It would have been much better just to have a few words at Chez Papa, having run into each other by chance. Or at least it would seem like chance to Lapin, which was the main thing.

"Want coffee or anything?"

"Nope!" said Molly. "I'm off to buy a scooter!" And the door shut behind her with a bang as she headed across the village once again.

❧

THE GLOSSY EMERALD green scooter of her imagination was not what Molly ended up with. As often happens, her dream collided with her pocketbook, and she ended up with a ten-year-old model, battered and dented but which the dealer swore ran like a dream. It was the color of mud.

Molly loved it.

The dealer had given her a quick lesson in the parking lot and Molly had taken to it like a duck to water. She felt powerful riding around the village on it—she could get places so quickly! Take sharp corners! Feel the wind in her face!

No buyer's remorse, not even a little, despite knowing she had spent money that should probably have been spent on a new water heater. She would probably need a car as well, eventually; it was something of a miracle she made it through the winter without one. But next winter was a long ways away, Castillac had a new taxi driver now for her guests to use, and so all was right in the world of transportation, at least for now.

Molly checked the map in her fake genealogist's notebook. She had made considerable progress going door-to-door, covering nearly a third of the village. Now that she was mobile, she figured why not check out some of the places on the fringes of Castillac —after all, Mme Gervais had suggested she look at the farms, and now she could do so without wasting the whole day walking to get to them.

First she made sure she had plenty of gas, then chose a street at random and took off. Like so many French villages, Castillac was set in the middle of the countryside with no suburb to speak of, so she was riding by farmland within a few minutes. No one home at the first farmhouse. At the second, a nice older woman asked her inside and talked her ear off about cheesemaking. She sampled the woman's cheese and smiled a lot and moved on.

The third farm belonged to Achille Labiche, according to the map from the *mairie*.

Molly came down the driveway and lovingly parked the scooter next to a tree. It was such lovely countryside, in May everything was so green it almost glowed, and she admired the herd of black and white cows out in the field. A border collie crept out from behind a tractor and watched her intently, as border collies do.

"Hey there," said Molly, speaking French because it was, after all, a French dog. The dog did not move, did not acknowledge her greeting, but kept watching.

Molly walked up to the door and gave it a hard rap. She had been to so many houses that the routine had numbed her somewhat. She no longer felt much worry about approaching strange houses, even though she was looking for someone with a dangerous secret. Much as she tried to remain observant and stay on her toes, it was difficult for her to maintain a high level of focus when she was having the same conversation over and over, never seeing a single thing that seemed remotely suspicious.

Was anyone home? She considered looking in the kitchen window but instead called out, "Bonjour? Monsieur Labiche?"

She heard slow steps inside the house and waited.

The door opened a crack.

"Monsieur Labiche? Salut! My name is Molly Sutton. I moved to Castillac last summer, and I'm doing some genealogical research on people in the area. I was wondering if you would mind giving me five minutes of your time? Please understand— I'm not selling anything! Just want to know a little about your family names, if you don't mind talking to me for just a few minutes."

Achille wanted to slam the door and go back inside. His hands were trembling. But the last thing he wanted to do was attract attention by seeming rude. He didn't want this foreigner blabbing all over town about unfriendly Labiche who had refused to talk to her.

He took a deep breath and held it for a moment.

"All right," he said, coming out into the sunshine and closing the door behind him. "I don't know anything about my family history. My last name is Labiche. My mother's last name was Maillard. That's all I really know."

Molly smiled. "What I usually find is that people know more than they think," she said. "Are your parents still alive?"

Achille nodded. "They're out in the back pasture, taking care of some fencing," he said, and the instant the words left his mouth, a voice inside his head shouted: *Fool! She will find you out with your stupid lies!*

He put his trembling hands in his pockets. He saw the scooter and wondered if Valerie had heard it come down the driveway. Would she start yelling?

"All right. Maybe it would make sense for me to come back later, when I can speak to them?"

"They're very busy," said Achille, over the loud voice and roiling darkness in his brain. "I can probably tell you anything they can."

"Excellent," said Molly, tucking a handful of curls behind one ear. "Are they both from Castillac?"

"Yes."

Not a talker, she thought. *Oh, I enjoy a tough nut every so often.* Reaching down to her shoe as though to adjust it, she stepped back a step or two to give the man some space. She did not make eye contact but looked across the green fields with a smile—but not too big a smile. She was trying not to overwhelm the skittish man, thinking how oddly fitting it was that his name was *la biche*, which meant deer.

"Your pasture looks like it's in great shape," she said, pointing. "Have you always raised Holsteins?"

"Yes," said Achille. *Couldn't she take a hint? Just go away. Please. I'm begging you.* But he could not find any words to make her go, so he just stood there with his hands in his pockets, feeling trapped.

"Is it just you and your parents here?"

"Yes."

"Any other relatives nearby? Did your parents have any brothers or sisters?"

"I don't know."

"Really? That's unusual," Molly said, in a friendly sort of way, not in a your-family-is-a-bunch-of-weirdos kind of way. "I got dragged to so many family things when I was a kid. My aunt Bethany? Oh my Lord, she could talk the bark off a tree. Not what a kid wants to do on a Saturday afternoon, you know?"

Labiche took a step backwards, bumping up against the door.

Molly opened her notebook and pretended to glance over her notes. Then she looked around the farm, trying to find something that would get Labiche talking. She saw the milking barn and the hog pen. She saw a door set into a little hill, probably a place to overwinter potatoes or something like that. She saw the border collie working, circling around the tractor, watching them.

"Your dog looks very intense," Molly said lightly. "Does she herd the cows?"

"Oh yes," said Achille, smiling in spite of himself. "I never trained her. She just knows what's to be done. Drives the girls crazy the way she harasses them."

Molly laughed. "I've got a dog, I think she's got some shepherd in her, maybe some kind of hunting dog too? She's a little crazy but she's good company. I live alone," she added with a shrug, hoping that a bit of sharing might help him loosen up.

But the momentary smile when he talked about Bourbon flickered and disappeared, and Achille said nothing else. Molly figured she was never going to get invited inside the farmhouse, so she shrugged and thanked him for his time.

As she started up the scooter for the ride back to La Baraque, there was no nagging feeling about Labiche, no alarm bells, no intuition. Instead, the most famous detective in all of Castillac—according to nine year old Gilbert—was only thinking about how glorious it was to ride fast on a narrow road, and about what to have for lunch.

Chapter Twenty-Two

Achille went back inside the house and paced around the kitchen. He made a fist and put it to his mouth, chewing on a knuckle.

This is bad, he kept thinking, over and over. *Bad.*

That redheaded woman was a chatterbox, anyone could see that. She was going to go into the village and say things about him. She probably hadn't wasted a minute, was talking about him right now! Sitting at a bar in a crowd of people, going on and on about his farm and everything she had seen and heard.

She would tell people something was wrong with him. He knew how it went. He saw how she looked, how she stared.

Achille paced and paced. He thought about her standing there, looking at him, holding that notebook. That was where she wrote everything down. All of her judgments, her diagnoses, everything that was going to get him into trouble. And if they took him away, what would happen to his girls?

What would happen to Valerie?

Well, it wouldn't do. He couldn't allow it. She might already be headed to the gendarmerie! And then a horde of people would descend on his farm, poking their noses where they didn't belong.

He knew all along those people had been looking for an excuse to take him away—and she was going to give it to them. They'd put him in that same hospital where they had put his mother, and they didn't let her out even though she'd begged to come home.

He chewed on his knuckle, breaking the skin and sucking on the trickle of blood.

They would find her.

And he would go to jail. He was not at all confused about that. He knew they would never understand, would never be able to grasp what he and Valerie had meant to each other all these years.

He would have to take care of it, and he had better act quickly.

Achille went out, banging the door behind him, squinting into the sun. He trotted to the tool shed and picked up a hatchet. Bourbon moved beside him, watching.

He unlocked the door to the bunker. Valerie was lying on her back, with her feet up against the ceiling.

"Hello," she said.

That gave him pause. She had not greeted him like that in months; she'd had been silent or else singing that nonsense that grated on his nerves so. But Achille was not changing his mind now. It was better for her this way.

She had lost her grip on sanity, anyone could see that. And if an animal went crazy, what was the humane thing to do?

Put it down.

Put *her* down.

But the blood: he would have to do it outside, where the rain would wash away the evidence.

He left the house, whistling for Bourbon. His body felt tense. Muscles were twitching in his calves and along the sides of his neck.

To calm himself, Achille started to go to his cows, to walk in among the herd and feel their animal warmth, but in the driveway he stopped. He stood remembering one of the times they'd taken his mother away. How he'd stood in that same spot, watching, not saying anything, afraid they would take him too. She was humming, his mother, and the memory of that tuneless sound was enough to make Achille want to scream just to block it out.

But he did not scream. He had years of practice being quiet, as the neighbor no one could object to. He had taught Valerie to be quiet too, though it had taken quite a while for her to understand.

This was *bad*.

"Come on, Bourbon!" he called, climbing over the gate to the west pasture. The dog sped towards him and sailed through the boards of the fence, looking like a thoroughbred in a steeplechase. Achille laughed.

He didn't want to kill her. He was no murderer. But on that Tuesday afternoon in May, he was not seeing any other way. Once it was done, all the gendarmes in the département could come to search his farm, and there would nothing to find.

It would be unpleasant, but many things in life are unpleasant. And once it was over, he could concentrate on the girl in Salliac. He would be patient with her, go very slowly, and maybe all the talk in Castillac would die down. They would let him alone.

If only that foreign woman had stayed away. She shouldn't go poking around in other people's business, she just shouldn't.

🙰

THE DAY MOLLY had been dreading had come: the Australians were leaving, going all the way back to Sydney, and it was time to say goodbye to little Oscar. She knew that if she were going to make a real go at this gîte business, she couldn't be getting so attached to every child who came to stay at La Baraque. Clearly she would need to develop a way to keep them, if not at arm's length, then not quite so close to her heart.

"Mum!" shouted Oscar, raising his chubby arms when he spotted her walking towards him. Ned and Leslie were packing up their car, and all three watched Oscar crawl over the grass and then pull himself up on Molly's leg.

"You know you're going to be walking very soon," she said, scooping him up. "You'll be running all over the place, getting into all kinds of wicked trouble!" Stifling a sob, she leaned her forehead on his head, smelling his baby smell one last time. "I will miss you very much," she said, her voice a little shaky.

She managed to pull herself together to have a last chat with Ned and Leslie about their trip home, then hugs all around, and the family was in the car and moving away down rue des Chênes. Molly ran straight in the house to her bedroom, threw herself on the bed, and sobbed.

She cried about probably never seeing Oscar again. She cried about how hard it was to say goodbye to anyone she cared about. She cried about the babies she wanted but did not have, about how lonely it was living alone, about every other thing that had given her a moment's sorrow over the last few years. She cried about her artichoke seedlings dying because she forgot to water them. She cried over not making the tiniest bit of progress in finding poor Valerie Boutillier. She let the sound and emotion pour out, wailing without holding anything back.

And then she was done. She cocked an ear, listening for Wesley Addison, having completely forgotten she was sharing her house. Her face looked as though a grenade had gone off nearby, but the tears did make her feel better. Until her thoughts drifted back to Valerie.

She considered throwing herself back down on the bed and crying some more, but that felt too much like giving up. She pulled out the thin file Ben had given her, and settled in to read it through once more.

Chapter Twenty-Three

I t was regrettable, certainly. But Achille had thought and thought and could see no other way.

He had plans for next Monday market day in Salliac. He hoped to make a giant step of progress with the girl. He didn't know her name, but he had firmly decided that she was the one, she would be his. Not next week—no, it was going to take patience. This time, he didn't want to force her, he wanted the girl to climb up on the tractor of her own free choice. He was ready to invest some time getting to know her and smoothing the way. As much time as it took, he wasn't afraid of running out of patience.

But he couldn't manage it with this new fear blossoming in his chest. Thanks to that meddling woman, that Molly Sutton, the gendarmes from Castillac were about to descend on his farm and start searching. They could show up any minute!

Valerie had to go.

The way he saw it, he owed her that much.

Achille knew very well that if he merely unlocked the padlock and opened the door, did not tie Valerie but walked away so that she could get away—he would soon hear the blare of the gendarme's siren and find himself shackled and in custody. He knew he would never be able to make them understand. He had no illusions about that.

In a way, the whole thing was very simple. That's what Achille kept telling himself as he went about the morning milking in the pouring rain. As he made his breakfast and then took Valerie a jug of fresh milk and three eggs scrambled in butter.

It's very simple.

He had lived in the country his whole life; he knew how to kill animals. He never liked it, it wasn't a part of farming he enjoyed, but he had killed countless cows and hogs over the years, and chickens too when he was a teenager and his mother had kept poultry for awhile during one of her lucid phases. His father used to take him hunting and they shot wild boars and doves, although he did what he could to get out of those days with his father—because what Achille wanted was not to shoot the animals, but to trap and and keep them, which his father did not understand.

Valerie would pose no difficulty, technically speaking. He could probably do it when she was asleep and she would barely even know what was happening.

But *he* would know. And thinking about how he would feel afterward gave him a sick feeling in his belly that wouldn't go away. Confusingly, the idea of Valerie gone filled him with both overwhelming relief and unendurable sorrow.

So, not so simple after all.

The rain was really coming down, so hard he could barely see the trees bordering the field towards the Renaud's farm. He sat in the kitchen looking out of the smudgy window thinking about how to do it. It felt wrong to use a method of killing he used for farm animals on a woman he had loved, even still loved. But on the other hand, he was comfortable with those methods, felt confident with them.

A razor blade had a lot of advantages...but so messy. He

wanted it to be quick, as quick as possible, so quick she didn't have time to register what he was about to do.

He didn't want to do it. He was not a murderer.

But sometimes you had to do things you didn't want to do, isn't that what his teachers and his father had told him over and over?

And thanks to that snooping foreigner, he had better hurry.

ON WEDNESDAY MOLLY picked up her notebook and climbed on her scooter, planning to spend some hours continuing the survey because she didn't know what else to do. Trying to be methodical about it, she rode through the village and turned in the driveway to the farm next to Labiche's.

The farmhouse was small and tidy. Molly heard roosters crowing. As she parked and looked towards the house, she saw two heads looking at her out the window.

On Wednesday afternoons school let out early, which explained why the boy, running out of the house with a wide grin on his face, was home.

"Well, hello, mighty warrior of the forest!" she said, recognizing Gilbert from the market.

"How did you learn to speak French?" he asked.

"Oh, you can tell I'm not a native?" she said, smiling.

Gilbert's mother came outside, wiping her hands on her apron. "Bonjour, Madame," she said to Molly, her expression not nearly as welcoming as her son's.

"Bonjour, Madame," answered Molly. "I met your son at the market last week. The wild greens made a delicious salad!" Madame Renaud said nothing, so Molly quickly delivered her genealogy spiel as she opened her notebook and got out her pen.

"Ah," the woman said, looking a fraction less suspicious. "My husband's family name was Renaud. My family were the Tisons.

NELL GODDIN

Almost no one left on my side of the family now. Well, I've got that cousin who went to America. Barely ever hear from him now." She glared at Molly as though it was her fault. "You are American, I take it?" she said.

"I am. Although I don't plan to move back. I'm quite happy here in Castillac."

"What about your family? They don't mind?"

"I don't have much family left," said Molly. "No, it's all right— my parents died some time ago, and my brother and I aren't especially close. That's life, right?"

The boy had walked around behind his mother, and was looking at Molly intently.

"Hey!" he said suddenly. "Want to see the hens? Maman and I raise chickens. Mostly for the eggs but of course we eat them when they get too old to lay." Gilbert looked hopeful. "I'll show her, Maman, you can go back inside."

But Mme Renaud turned to her son and put her arm around his shoulders, giving him a brittle smile.

Gilbert looked crestfallen.

Molly was trying to decipher the obvious tension but she had no clue what it was about.

Mme Renaud talked for another moment about some relatives that had moved farther south, but Molly had trouble paying attention. Gilbert had ducked out from under his mother's arm and then had circled back behind her again. He was staring at Molly, his eyes wide and communicating something. But what?

"Oh, I see you have such a nice *potager*," exclaimed Molly. "Would you mind showing it to me? I'm just getting started on mine, and honestly, I'm way behind schedule. I see your spinach has been producing for quite some time, is that right?"

In Molly's experience, gardeners liked to talk about their gardens. She did, anyway. Mme Renaud was reluctant, but walked over to the fenced *potager* and pointed out the greens, naming each variety in turn, though she seemed to take no pleasure in talking about it.

The potager was lovely. Orderly rows of lettuce looked like jewels in the sunshine, bright green alternating with crimson and purple and dark green, all sparkling from a shower that had come and gone just before lunch.

Maybe the boy is just bored? Hi mother isn't much fun to be around, that's for sure. On the dour side.

Impulsively, Molly said, "Hey Gilbert, there's a meadow behind my house that's absolutely brimming with all kinds of plants I can't identify. Maybe you'd like to come over for lunch one day and you could give me a lesson?" Molly looked at Mme Renaud, asking her permission with her expression.

"I don't believe so, no," snapped Mme Renaud. "Madame Sutton, I don't know how things are over in America. I've never been there and, frankly, I have no desire to go. I see on television that people are killed just going to the cinema. Here, we do things differently. I'm sure you're very nice but I am not going to allow my child to visit your house by himself. You're a stranger to us, and a foreigner on top of that…No.

"Come along, Gilbert, go into the house. I have several chores remaining for you before it's time to play." And with that, Mme Renaud put the death-grip on Gilbert's shoulder and marched him inside without another word to Molly.

Gilbert turned his head just before going through the door, and Molly thought his face looked positively anguished.

Shaking her head, she climbed back on the scooter and rode to the next farm on the road, feeling less optimistic about her search the farther she went.

Meanwhile, Gilbert sat down on a kitchen stool as his mother informed him that he was no longer going to be able to sell greens at the market, if she couldn't trust him to stay away from people they did not know and did not want to know.

"But I *do* want to know her!" he protested. "She's like the only person in the whole village who solves any crimes!" With a flash of perception, he wondered if that's why Molly had been here, working a case, and the genealogy business had just been a cover.

"Well, solving crimes is not your job, Gilbert," his mother said firmly. "Your job is to make sure the crimes don't happen to you. And that means sticking with people you know and trust, do you hear me?"

"Oui, Maman," said Gilbert dejectedly.

"We will skip the market entirely for the foreseeable future. It's spring, the garden is producing nicely and we have everything we need right here. Just attend to your studies and play outside when you have extra time."

Yesterday, in his worry and discouragement about what to do about Valerie, he would have said that he didn't think his situation could have gotten any worse, but it just had. For a brief exciting moment, he thought he would be able to take Molly to the henhouse and tell her everything. He could practically taste the relief that telling her would have brought.

And now...now what?

Chapter Twenty-Four

"Hup, ho!" Achille said. He shoved the handle of the hatchet under his belt and picked up the thick rope. "It's a beautiful day," he said. "Let's go for a little walk in the woods." His voice sounded normal even though he felt like everything inside— his brain, his stomach, his heart—was shaking and on the point of breaking down.

Valerie got up and allowed him to tie the rope around her waist. "A walk in the woods," she repeated.

"A walk in the woods, yes."

She stood with her hands dangling down at her sides, watching him tie the ropes. She used to watch everything he did with such interest, her eyes so intelligent and curious. But no longer. She barely seemed to register that she saw anything at all. He led her out of the bunker and through the farmyard, heading for the pasture and then the woods.

And her gait had gotten strange. She no longer walked beside him in a regular way but jerked one way and another, not trying to get free but as though she could no longer understand the logistics of the rope and being tied to him.

He felt impatient and angry at her for making him have to do this.

All he wanted on this lovely May day was to take care of his cows, and daydream about the girl at the Salliac market. All he wanted was a simple day, uncomplicated, to plan and daydream while he went through the calming routine of his chores.

He did not want to walk in the woods, he did not want to take a hatchet to her neck, he didn't want to, he didn't want to.

They climbed a low hill, Valerie getting tangled in bushes several times along the way. Achille pulled her roughly along.

I'm not a murderer, he said to himself, as he looked keenly at her neck, planning where to aim the chop.

Valerie stood still. She closed her eyes and lifted her chin, looking as though she were preparing herself, resigned to whatever was going to happen.

Achille slid the hatchet out of his belt. He took good care of his tools and he knew the edge was sharp, but he flicked it with his thumb anyway, nearly cutting himself.

"I'm sorry," he mumbled, raising the hatchet over his head.

Valerie did not move or open her eyes. It was perfect, really—if he aimed just right, she would be gone quickly. But Achille let the hatchet fall from his hands. It bounced once and lay on a pile of damp leaves, glistening in a shaft of sunlight.

She was his *Valerie*.

He wasn't ready. He couldn't simply butcher her like she was an October hog.

Dejectedly, he led her out of the woods and back down to the root cellar. She began to sing her nonsense again which made the muscles in Achille's neck spasm. He thought of Molly Sutton and the poison she was spreading about him in the village, and he knew he was going to have to find a way to finish the job.

He just wasn't ready.

Not yet.

§

"I KNOW THAT LOOK," Frances was saying as she carried their lunch plates out to the terrace at La Baraque. "You're working on something. I can tell. It's that Boutillier person you were talking about at the dinner party, isn't it? Spill it, girlfriend. You know you want to."

Molly looked sheepish. She did want to. But she guessed Ben would not be in favor of her talking about the case to anyone else; she had already blabbed to Madame Gervais.

"Come on, Molls. Don't tell me you found another dead body!"

"No, no, nothing like that," said Molly gratefully. "In fact— what I'm hoping—is that this time, it might be just the opposite. Finding someone alive who everyone assumes is dead." She paused, her conscience making one last effort to keep her from telling. "You're right, I'm looking for Valerie Boutillier," she said.

"She's...who is she again?"

"We talked a little about her at the dinner party awhile back. Remember my telling you about how there were two missing women in Castillac that I hadn't known about before I moved here?"

"Well, how would you know, anyway? It's not like the real estate people give out crime reports, do they?"

"Right. Well, Valerie's been missing for seven years. A young woman about to go off to university, just disappeared out of nowhere."

"And so—not to be rude, of course I respect your powers. But why in the world do you think she's still alive? Or anywhere you could find her?"

Molly told Frances about the note and her collaboration with Ben.

"I knew he would never make it as a farmer," laughed Frances.

"I mean really, he's no more suited to that life than I am! Okay, so what have you got?"

Molly looked down. She lifted her fork and put it down, staring off into the meadow. "Nothing."

Frances dug into her salad and waited for Molly to elaborate. Bobo streaked around the side of the house and disappeared.

"I've started going door to door, asking questions about genealogy, pretending to be working on a project. But I don't think it's getting me anywhere. If someone is hiding her, standing in the foyer for ten minutes isn't going to clue me in, you know? And if I get invited to sit down and have a cup of coffee, that doesn't mean the person has nothing to hide, right? I don't know what I was thinking—that she would be upstairs and pound on the floor? Yell for help?

"If somehow somebody has managed to keep her hidden this long, it's going to take more than five minutes to discover where she is. She's not going to be where the mailman or any stray visitor would be in earshot, you know?"

"Hmm. Yes, agreed. You need...another plan."

"I know. But I can't think of anything, Franny. You got any ideas?"

"Pour me a glass of that rosé. Let me think about it."

"I'm so frustrated, even though it's been fun, actually, meeting so many people from the village. And they're so nice—most of them invite me in, listen to my prattle, do their best to be helpful. I swear, I love this place, I really do."

"Obviously it's grown on me as well," said Frances with a sly smile.

"Nico treating you right?"

"Almost too right," Frances said with a slightly befuddled expression. "But so...listen, back to Valerie. Did she have a boyfriend or anything?"

"Apparently not. She was an ambitious girl, about to leave

town to start her new life at a prestigious school. Her family is close, she has a little brother and both parents are alive."

"Have you talked to any of them?"

"I want to. But it seems insensitive at this point. I mean, we've literally got nothing except a note that looks like a parody of a ransom note that may or may not be talking about their daughter. If I thought it would really make a difference, maybe I'd call them up. But right now it seems like it would just be stirring them up over nothing.

"Ben's getting a dog trained to find cadavers, actually I think he's going to be starting that search this afternoon. I guess the family would be relieved just to know one way or the other, and have her remains to give her a proper burial."

"Did he not look for her body seven years ago?"

"I'm sure he did. But maybe she was killed after the search, or maybe he just didn't look in the right place. There are so many possibilities, and no leads to steer us one way or another. Nothing except for the note."

"I wouldn't feel that way," said Frances. "I mean about the burial. The whole idea of bodies being buried totally skeeves me out."

"Yeah. Well, I'd agree that the whole idea of 'closure' is way overrated. No matter what happens, when someone you love dies, there isn't anything about it that's ever finished."

The women ate for a few moments in silence. "You doing okay with that little kid gone?" asked Frances, knowing how attached Molly had gotten to Oscar.

Molly shrugged. "I know it's ridiculous. It's not like he's my family, or that I even spent that much time with him. Just a day here and there over the course of two short weeks. But...."

"It's killing you."

"Yes. Honestly, sometimes I think love just really sucks."

Frances nodded. "I hear you, sister. So does that mean you're not chasing after a certain organic farmer who's quite hopeless at his job?"

"Shut up, Frances," said Molly, grinning, as she hopped up to go get another baguette.

᪥

ACHILLE WAS DRINKING a cup of coffee in his his kitchen when he heard a knock on his door. He froze.

He thought of Sutton standing outside and his throat closed up and his mouth started watering as though he were going to vomit.

Must calm down. Hide your fear. They aren't coming to take you away—they don't know anything.

He got up from the kitchen table and went to the door. He was so grateful to see Madame Renaud instead that he beamed at his neighbor with far more friendliness than usual.

"Bonjour, Achille," she said, her voice high and tight. "Have you seen Gilbert?"

"No, Florence, I have not. But I just got up from taking a rest and have not been out and about for a few hours."

"The bus dropped him off after school, as always. He did his chores in the henhouse. But since then I haven't seen him anywhere. I've called and called and he doesn't answer!"

"I'm sure it is nothing. He is just a boy, he likes to roam around in the woods!"

"I'm sure I sound over-protective. It's that American woman, she's got me feeling on edge."

Achille looked at her sharply. "American woman?"

"Yes—her name is Molly Sutton. Apparently she's moved to Castillac now. She came sniffing around the other day, asking a lot of questions. Do you know she actually invited Gilbert over to her house? A perfect stranger? I tried to tell her that we don't do things like that here...we don't let our children wander off with people we've never even met and have no idea who they are...but I don't think she understood me. It makes me very nervous, Achille, strangers like that. We have no idea what they might be capable of."

"She...she had no business trying to take your son away from you like that," said Achille, feeling outrage on Madame Renaud's behalf. "You are a good mother. You stay home, you look after your boy. You worry about him, like a mother should." Achille's hands started to tremble and he stuffed them into his pockets. "Molly Sutton," he said with a sneer. "You don't think he's gone to her house?"

Madame Renaud gasped. "I didn't even consider that! Well, I don't really think Gilbert would disobey me that way. And she lives on the other side of Castillac from us, at that old place, La Baraque—you know it? I don't think he would get it in his head to walk that far, and his bicycle is still in the garage.

"But then where on earth *is* he? It's nearly dinnertime. We always eat at the same time and he knows he's supposed to have finished his homework and chores by then. It's very hard for me, you understand, Achille—it's very hard, a mother alone like I am, with no one to share the worry...."

"I will keep an eye out, I can tell you that," he answered. "He may even have come home by now, you'll see."

Florence nodded, although her forehead was still wrinkled with anxiety. "Thank you, I will go check and see. Keep your eye out, please."

Achille opened the door for her and watched her go, cutting through his farmyard on her way back to her place. If Valerie called out, Madame Renaud would surely hear her.

But Valerie did not call out.

Calm down. No one knows.

And Achille was going to make certain it stayed that way.

Chapter Twenty-Five

He had only been messing around in the forest, daydreaming, and building tiny houses for make-believe creatures out of bark and bits of moss. Maybe Gilbert had heard his mother calling but transformed the sounds into the howling of a beast in his fantastical daydream, but in any case he had not stopped what he was doing to go home. He was angry about not being allowed to go to Madame Sutton's house and so he took his time, getting home just before the sun went down even though he knew his mother would shriek at him and likely punish him for not coming when she called.

The next day he was back to worrying about Valerie. Gilbert wasn't sure what his new plan was going to be, but wisely he decided to do what he could to get in good with Maman while he figured it out. It was Wednesday, when he only had a half day of school, so as soon as he got home he went to the garden to do some weeding, a job Maman usually had to nag him to get started on.

The garden was so hot, out in the baking spring sun. He kneeled down and yanked out some celandine, making a pile to one side. If only he'd been allowed to talk to Madame Sutton alone. It was agony to think of how close he had come to being able to tell her the secret that was like a poisonous weight in his pocket he couldn't get rid of.

Of course, Gilbert could have just blurted it out. He could have said, "Hey listen, the neighbor is keeping Valerie Boutillier captive! She's been right next door *all the time!*"

He stopped weeding for a moment and imagined what would have happened if he had opened his mouth and let the whole thing come out. Maman would have probably gotten hysterical and sent him to his room. Or she would have given Mme Sutton one of those looks grown-ups gave each other, a look that said, *Don't mind him, he's off his gourd. Always telling tales.*

And Mme Sutton would have chuckled and they'd have gone on talking about where Maman's cousins lived, pretty much the most boring conversation ever in the history of the universe.

Or maybe that's not what would have happened. Maybe he wasn't giving Mme Sutton enough credit. You don't solve two serious crimes by dismissing the truth when it's spoken right at you, he thought. Maybe Mme Sutton would have listened. Maybe she would have taken out her cell phone and called Dufort right away—they were friends, he'd seen them talking at the market—and the gendarmes would be speeding with sirens going straight to Labiche's farm by now.

I probably blew it again, he thought, as his lower lip—to his horror—began to tremble.

Gilbert yanked out some more celandine, breaking off some of the root.

But if the gendarmes went to Labiche's, they would need to know where Valerie was. Gilbert had only seen her outside, tied to the neighbor's waist. He had no idea where she was being kept.

He jumped up, leaving the pile of wilted weeds in the potager, and raced through the field, trying to get over the hill before Maman saw him and called him back. He didn't feel the hot sun now that he was moving and had something important to do.

Gilbert reached the cover of the woods, panting. He wished he wasn't wearing a stupid bright yellow shirt. To keep from being seen, he crouched down low and went from bush to bush, moving to the edge of the property line, eyes scanning for any sign of Labiche.

The farm was quiet except for the occasional moo; the cows were all in the near field. Because of the heat, most of them were lying down, clumped up in the shade of a few trees. Gilbert could see the large barn, and the farmhouse beyond. He snuggled down in the leaves to hide his shirt completely, and waited, watching.

Waiting is not all that easy at any age, but at nine years old especially not. He fidgeted. His fingers picked apart leaves while he forced himself to keep his eyes on the buildings so that he would see if anyone came outside.

The image of Dufort at the market drifted into his mind. The former chief seemed so capable, so strong. Gilbert remembered how he had looked at Mme Sutton with such an interested expression. Like he would listen to you without making fun or pooh-poohing no matter what you had to say.

And then suddenly, the thought coming with such force it was like a slap to the side of his head, Gilbert thought—*maybe Chief Dufort is my father.* Maybe the reason Maman wants to keep me home all the time is that she thinks I'll find out if I'm hanging around the village. Someone will tell me. People in the village, even Dufort himself, might even realize the truth because we sort of look alike.

He lifted his arm from the leaves and inspected it, as though he would be able to discern some connection to Dufort in the way his arm looked.

Then Gilbert lay his head down for a moment, his eyes shut, knowing that what he was thinking was not reality, but sucking every last little bit of pleasure out of it anyway: his father coming for him, and scooping him up in his strong, tanned arms, hoisting him up on his shoulders and giving him a bumpy ride, and then, when they were done playing, listening carefully to whatever Gilbert had to tell him.

And then he would solve this business with Valerie. He would be able to fix it all. Everything.

He would know the right thing to do.

&

"WELL, Mr. Addison, I'm not saying you have to move to the cottage. I'm only saying that now that Ned and Leslie and dear little Oscar are gone, it's free if you would like to have it. Of course, if you'd prefer to stay where you are, you're more than welcome to do so."

Molly wished almost desperately that Wesley Addison would move to the cottage. Financially it was better for him to stay where he was, because she sometimes got last minute bookings, and it made sense to keep the cottage available since it slept more people than the haunted room where Addison was staying upstairs. But still...she would much rather have her house to herself.

It was turning out to be a pleasure, running a gîte business. She liked meeting new people, the people were mostly interesting and pleasant, and it was fantastic not to have to get all dressed up to go work in an office, cooped up all day, and on the phone. This work suited her far better than her former job of fundraising.

But at the same time, boundaries were always good, and she had found out, thanks to Wesley Addison, that she would rather the guests be confined to the cottage and the pigeonnier, and not walking around her house late at night, almost giving her a heart attack since by now she was so unused to living with anyone else.

Yet Wesley Addison did not want to move to the cottage.

"Well then, it's settled," he said. "I'm thinking of extending my stay another week," he said, and Molly's heart leapt up at the unexpected income only to come crashing down at the prospect of yet more Wesley Addison. "You see, when my wife and I were here seven years ago, she died suddenly. It's...I felt it was important for me to come back. Perhaps that is hard for someone else to understand."

"No," said Molly, feeling some sympathy. "It's not hard to understand. But it does seem as though it would be difficult. Painful. Do you mind my asking what happened?"

Wesley Addison bowed his big head. Then he lifted it abruptly and steepled his fingers together. "She fell. We were sightseeing at the Château at Beynac. You know it, of course?"

Molly nodded, her eyes wide.

"Then you know it stands at a great height, overlooking the Dordogne."

Molly nodded again, not really wanting to hear the rest of the story but at the same time badly wanting to know what happened.

"She slipped," said Addison, and shrugged. "Smashed to bits on the rocks. As I said, the place is at a very great height."

Molly's hand flew to cover her mouth as she gasped, imagining how horrible that must have been. "I'm so terribly sorry," she said, impulsively reaching out to touch his arm.

Addison jerked away. Molly felt for the big man; what could be worse than having your spouse die in an accident while on vacation?

And then *seven years* set off a little alarm in her head. "Seven years ago, Mr. Addison? Do you happen to remember a girl going missing when you were here? It would have been in all the newspapers and on television. Her name was Valerie Boutillier."

"I remember nothing about a girl. As you might imagine, my attention was taken up by the necessity for making some rather complex arrangements in order to have my wife's body sent back overseas. I was not hobnobbing at the local bars, listening for the latest local news."

"Of course not. I meant...well, again, I'm so sorry for what happened."

"'Hobnobbing'. Interesting word. Old English, as I'm sure you won't be surprised to hear. Comes from hob and nob, meaning to toast each other, buying alternate rounds of drinks. So you see, I used exactly the right word just there."

"Yes, I see," said Molly faintly. "Well then, I have some gardening chores that just won't wait. Have a good evening, Mr. Addison." And she went straight out to the garden and called Bobo, who ran around the side of the house and slammed into her legs. Molly squatted down and let the dog lick her face.

"Just keep me company for a bit," she said to Bobo, and began pulling up weeds with fervor, feeling lonely and a little upset. Sometimes it felt as though too many terrible things happened in the world, and there was no escaping them.

She sighed, and then sighed again, and the rhythm of weeding and the nearness of Bobo soothed her spirits.

"Life is messy, that's all there is to it," she said to Bobo as she stood and headed back inside for a kir.

Chapter Twenty-Six

Molly had taken a shower and put on clean, if not very fashionable, clothes. She was pouring herself that kir when she heard a creaking sound coming from the front yard that she guessed was Constance's bicycle.

"Salut, Constance!" she called as the front door opened, and got out another glass.

"Molls! How are you? I hear you're working on a new case."

"What?" said Molly, putting down the bottle of crème de cassis. "How do you know about that?"

"Couldn't get any details though. What's going on? Don't tell you me discovered another body!" Constance hooted as though Molly's propensity for stumbling across dead bodies was hilarious.

"First of all, not funny, and second of all, is there any privacy in this village at all? Does everyone have spy-cams running 24/7 or what? I don't know whether to be delighted or disgusted."

Well, it's not like you don't enjoy a little gossip, Molls. *Castillaçois* are the same way. While the rest of the world obsesses over Prince William and Kate Middleton or whichever celebrity is in rehab for the tenth time—we in Castillac are more interested in what's going on with the people we know. Or if not know, then at least see on the street from time to time."

"I just...well, to be honest? I want to know what everyone else is doing too, but that doesn't mean I want anyone else knowing what *I'm* doing."

"*Absolument!* " said Constance with a laugh. "That is the way of the world, and I'm sort of shocked that for once it's me schooling you instead of the other way around."

Molly laughed. "All right, here's a kir, sit and tell me the news."

The two friends plopped down on the sofa and sipped their drinks. Constance let out a long, theatrical sigh.

Molly cocked her head. "Thomas?"

Constance nodded slowly. "I don't even want to talk about him. I don't want anything to do with him. But at the same time, all I can think about is him showing up at my door begging me to take him back."

Molly thought this over. "Do you think that might happen?" she asked.

"When hell freezes over," said Constance glumly. "I haven't even seen Thomas in weeks and weeks. I guess he's spending every minute with that wretched, hateful Simone Guyanet."

"I guess it wouldn't help to tell you I had a relationship like that once? A guy I couldn't let go of, even though we didn't even really have any fun together and he was right to break it off. Do you think it's mostly hurt pride that keeps you spinning around?"

"If he did come back, I wouldn't mind shoving it in Simone's face," said Constance, her eyes lighting up at the idea.

Bobo came racing in through the terrace door and flung her paws up on Constance. "Well, hello!" she said, scratching the speckled ears. "My mother always said no one will love you like a dog. I think she was right."

Molly considered. "I think she was right too. At least...dog love is so uncomplicated. They see you, they're happy, you're happy, that's all."

"Yeah."

They sat in silence for a long while, sipping their drinks and thinking about love and dogs. Finally Molly decided to go ahead and talk to Constance about the case; it was on her mind all the time, and since Constance and Valerie were reasonably close in age, she might have some little nugget of information no one had managed to unearth.

"So, Constance...."

Constance stopped petting Bobo and Bobo put her head on Constance's knee, looking up at her hopefully. "What?"

"Valerie Bou—"

"Boutillier! I *knew* it! I'm actually a little hurt you didn't call me up and ask to interview me. I did know her, after all."

"I wondered about that."

"Yeah, she was a couple years ahead of me, but I knew her all right."

"So tell me about her. What was she like?"

"She was like a...kind of like a...I can't think of anything to compare her to, a whirlwind or tornado or something. You never knew what was going to happen next when Valerie was around. She was super smart and full of herself—the kind of girl you sorta want to hate, but in her case? She deserved to be full of herself because she was pretty awesome. Really funny, for one thing. Always coming up with these crazy pranks that the teachers wanted to get mad about but they'd end up laughing along with everyone else."

"Can you remember any of them?"

Constance looked up at the corner of the room, thinking. "Well, she would fill random rooms at school with balloons, so you'd go to class and open the door and balloons would be spilling out into the hallway and you couldn't even get inside there were so many. One time she got into the computer room and put some kind of seed down in the keyboards, where you couldn't even see them, and later on plants started sprouting up between the keys!

She almost got in trouble for that one. Schools get a little protective of their computers. But it turned out not to cause any problems.

"So like, she was a prankster, but not a mean one, you know? That's what people liked so much about her. She made everything more fun but not at anyone's expense."

Molly nodded. "I wonder...this quality she had that you're describing...do you think a stranger would be able to see it? You're talking about her as though she practically glowed just walking down the street."

"Well, yeah, I mean—she'd be the girl in the center of a group of people, all laughing. She'd be the energy, you know?"

Molly nodded again. She was thinking that if Constance was right, a stranger could easily have been attracted to Valerie's energy and obvious popularity. Someone local, or just someone who was in Castillac long enough to see her around the village.

"Was she beautiful?" asked Molly.

Constance screwed up her face. "Well, no, not really. Not beautiful, I wouldn't say. But totally, totally appealing. Everyone wanted to be her friend."

"And...I know this was a long time ago, but do you remember having any ideas at the time about what happened to her?"

"All the mothers thought she'd been snatched up by a molester. We couldn't go anywhere alone for months. I don't remember feeling afraid or anything myself—my friends and I were all trying to get our mothers to calm down. I wondered if something had happened to make her run away. I didn't know her that well, didn't know her family or anything, so I don't think I had any guesses about why she might have run.

"And heck, maybe I just liked that scenario better than some of the other ones people were talking about, you know? Valerie running free, instead of Valerie dead, or being held captive somewhere, some freak's prisoner."

They finished their drinks and sat in silence for some minutes.

"You know a lot of villagers, right?" asked Molly.

"Sure. I mean, not everybody! But you know, I like being out and about, I like chatting..."

"So if you think over all the local people you've met over the years, do any of them strike you as being...is off-balance the right word? Utterly nuts? Sadistic?"

Constance scratched her head. She picked at a loose thread on her pants. She scraped her teeth over her lips a couple of times. "I don't know, Molly," she said finally. "People are weird, you know? A lot of people are weird, and probably Castillac is the same as anywhere else in that department. But what kind of weirdo do you have to be to do something like that? And would anyone be able to tell just by looking at you or having a conversation? Or, say, waiting on you in a café or something?"

"That's it, that's pretty much the question, right there."

They both nodded. They had the question, but answers were turning out to be extremely scarce on the ground.

§⋅

LÉON, Dufort's friend who worked at the Toulouse gendarmerie, had come and gone, leaving him with a burly Belgian Malinois. The big dog was named, perhaps too obviously, Boney. There hadn't been time to give Dufort much of a training session but Léon seemed confident that the dog would know what to do.

Boney sat next to the door, watching Ben with his intelligent black eyes.

"You want to get to it, don't you," Ben said. He petted him between his ears that stood up, admiring his black muzzle. He was a serious dog, no little ball of fluff, and it was clear he wanted to work. Ben had never been allowed to have a dog; both of his parents had worked long hours out of the house and had thought a dog would get too lonely by itself all day. He felt a little awkward with Boney now that they were alone together. He imagined the dog thought he talked too much, or could see he was not used to handling dogs.

And he was right. But Boney didn't particularly care either way, as long as he got to work. He stood by the door, looking over his muscled shoulder at Ben as he cleaned up the breakfast dishes and got ready to go out on their first search.

Boney was trained to search for dead bodies, and only dead bodies. Only *human* dead bodies. His training had been extensive and Léon had told Ben that Boney would not be put off course by dead rabbits or deer. He could air-scent; that is, he could pick up the smell of death as it wafted by, and follow it until he found its source, even over hills, up streams, anywhere the scent led.

Ben had dressed in long sleeves and canvas pants plus heavy shoes, expecting to have a rough day in the forest. "I'm just putting this on you for now," he said to Boney as he attached the leash. "Don't be insulted. But if something happened and you dashed into the street and got hit by a car, I think Léon would dismember me."

He led the big dog to his car and the dog hopped in back as though it were a familiar place.

"Make yourself at home," said Ben, looking at him in the rear view mirror. He wished now he'd invited Molly to come along. In fact, he wished it so much he turned around and drove out rue des Chênes to ask her if she'd like to join them, and Molly jumped at the chance since she was feeling a little crowded by Wesley Addison, who had shown no sign of leaving La Baraque that day.

"It's not exactly a light-hearted way to spend the morning, is it," said Molly, apprehensive as she climbed in the Renault. "I mean…I don't *want* to find her body, you know?"

"Look at it this way," said Ben. "If we search all around Castillac, and all through the forest of La Double, and Boney doesn't find her? Then she's not there. I admit, it's hardly proof she's still alive, but it's at least something in that direction, right?"

Molly wasn't so sure about that. "If you want to get rid of a body, there are a million ways to do it besides burying it in nearby woods. If it were me, I'd probably chop it up and drive to the ocean, rent a boat, and go way way out...."

"Really," said Ben. "You seem to have given it quite a lot of thought."

"I'm just saying," said Molly. She turned in her seat so she could reach back to Boney. "He doesn't really like petting," said Molly. "He's just tolerating me."

"He wants to get started," said Ben. "And so do I. As soon as I get a little farther up this road, I'm going to pull over and we can watch him do his thing. You ready to walk?"

"I'm ready."

Ben stopped and backed his car into the woods far enough that another car could get by. Then he opened the door to the backseat and Boney leapt out.

Then the dog froze. He lifted his nose in the air and sniffed, and took off into the underbrush.

"If I lose that dog...." said Dufort.

"Don't worry," said Molly with a laugh. "But come on!" She ran through the woods trying to keep Boney in view. The dog was zigzagging, up and back, up and back, covering fifty, a hundred times the ground the humans were.

And that was how the rest of the morning went. Boney ran in patterns, often stopping to lift his noble black muzzle in the air and sniff, and then he would duck his head down and run as though being pulled along by his nose. Ben and Molly walked and often ran to keep up with him.

After three hours, Boney had found exactly nothing. Ben and Molly stopped by a stream and the dog waded in and lapped up water, then lay down and let the water come up over his back.

For a moment the humans were too tired to talk. They stood in the quiet woods, by the stream, and Ben hooked his finger in the belt loop of Molly's jeans and gave it a playful tug.

"Now what?" she said, her face red from exertion.

"We're almost done with this loop. How about afterwards we go to your house and you make me lunch?"

"All I've got is some salami and stale bread."

"Sounds excellent." Ben looked at Boney. "You ready, boy? Go have a rest and come back later?"

Boney stood up and trotted out of the stream. He shook, giving Molly and Ben a more or less welcome cool spray, and the three of them headed back to the car.

No bodies. No Valerie. It was hard to feel pleased, spending all day looking for something and not finding it, but not finding Valerie in the woods was exactly what they were hoping for.

Chapter Twenty-Seven

The next morning was Saturday. Molly lay in bed, which was unusual for her since normally the instant she awoke she zoomed straight to the kitchen to make coffee. But instead she rolled over under a light quilt thinking about yesterday in the woods with Ben, and the cozy lunch they had after. About Valerie and Oscar, about Constance and her broken heart, about the little boy whose mother was so protective...all the threads that wove together to make her recent days in Castillac.

Upstairs she could hear Wesley Addison moving around, and she knew she'd better get up if she wanted to dodge a lengthy exegesis of her Boston accent. The cottage was still empty, and the De Groots staying in the pigeonnier had rarely been seen. As far as Molly could tell, they ventured out for wine and pastries and then scurried back inside. Ah, newlyweds....

Bobo had been very interested when Molly came back after the day in the woods with Ben and Boney. And just who is the Other Dog you spent your day with? her speckled face seemed to be asking. Here it was the next day and Bobo was still a little bit stand-offish.

"I know, Bobo, I did sort of cheat on you. But it was work, not play! I was expressly told that you were not allowed to come. Boney needed to work without you distracting him. But I promise, I swear on a heap of liver treats, that I will take you to La Double for a long hike one day soon. You will adore it."

Bobo allowed Molly to rub her chest but she did not make eye contact.

"You're a tough nut, Bobo," murmured Molly. "Now you stay and I'll go to the market and get some bones for you from Raoul. How's that?"

She heard the heavy step of Addison on the stairs, and slipped out the terrace door and walked quickly to her scooter and zoomed into the village.

The Saturday market never failed to put Molly in a good mood. Every month, she knew more people and felt more at home there. She remembered how hesitant she had been at first, how uncomfortable it made her that people knew who she was before she even met them. And oh, the state of her French! But now she could communicate, even if the subjunctive was still sometimes out of reach. Molly was part of Castillac, no longer a stranger.

Which was partly why Madame Renaud's reaction the other day had surprised her. On her rounds doing her phony survey, almost everyone had recognized her, either as the owner of La Baraque or the person who had solved a crime or two. Had she said something to offend her? Her little boy was adorable, and Molly kept going back to him in her mind, wondering why he had been looking at her so intently.

Was his mother mistreating him in some way, and he needed Molly's help?

She would keep an eye out for him at the market, and maybe she could have a private word with him and find out if something was wrong.

Molly and Manette had a laugh when a dignified old lady dropped her basket and muttered *merde* under her breath. She chatted briefly with Rémy, and they joked about Ben being the hardest-working and least talented farmer ever. She got some lardons and bones from Raoul, as promised to Bobo. And she continually scanned the crowd—a big one, now that the weather was so nice—looking both for Gilbert and anyone who seemed, well, like a crazy teenage-girl-stealer.

"La bombe!" boomed a voice not three inches from her ear.

"Bonjour, Lapin," said Molly, turning to see the big man standing with his arms open, a big grin on his face.

"I hardly see you anymore," he said kissing her on both cheeks. "How did the furniture for the pigeonnier work out?"

"It's lovely, thank you," said Molly. "Got the place rented out as we speak, I'm happy to say. Thanks to you and Pierre."

"I'm very glad to hear it. I don't know if you've heard, but I have a commercial enterprise of my own, just getting off the ground. I'd appreciate your support."

"Sure," said Molly, crossing her arms over her chest as Lapin's eyes drifted in that direction. "What kind of thing is it?"

"I'm opening a shop," he said proudly. "Something I've been meaning to do for years. My garage was full to bursting with things I'd put aside over the years, with just this plan in mind. So please, do me the honor of dropping by. It's down at the far end of rue Baudelaire. I know it's a little bit out of the way but you know how rents are in the center of the village."

Molly nodded. "What are your hours?"

"Mornings, 10 to noon. Closed Wednesdays. You give me a call anytime, I'll run over and open up for you. Don't hesitate to call, my dear!"

"I'll definitely drop by," she said, causing Lapin to widen his eyes in surprise. He was used to Molly keeping him at arm's length whenever possible.

"Actually," she said in a low voice. "Do you have a minute? I've been wanting to have a word with you."

"By all means," said Lapin, beaming. "Step into my office," he said, with a grand gesture towards the empty alley.

Molly snickered and then looked serious. "Listen, Lapin, this is private, what I'm about to say. But I've been thinking maybe you could help with something. It's important."

"I'm all ears."

"We—I—there's been an indication, and I don't want to say how or why, that Valerie Boutillier might still be alive."

Lapin took a step back. "What? Where did you get that idea?"

"I told you, I'm not going into details. But what if she *were* alive, Lapin? What if, instead of being murdered, like everyone assumes, even her family—what if instead, she's been held prisoner all this time, right here in Castillac?" She watched his face closely.

Lapin thought it over. "Well, I have read in the papers about cases like that. Is it unusual? I don't know. Could it possibly be the case with Valerie? I wouldn't want to bet on it."

"No one's asking you to bet. It may be wildly unlikely, I know. But...if it's possible, even a small percentage possible, we should check it out, right?"

"Of course. When you put it that way."

"Right. So what I was thinking is that you of all people might be helpful in this situation. You've poked around in more attics than anyone. You see people when their defenses are down."

Lapin shrugged.

Molly leaned in, next to Lapin's ear. "Can you think of anyone in or near the village who might be capable of something like that? Of holding someone prisoner for seven years?"

Lapin took a deep breath and the inhalation seemed to go on and on. "Not off the top of my head. Molly, I'll give it some thought. But my gut reaction to what you're suggesting...is that if Valerie was being held at a house where I went to work, I never suspected a thing. Like you say, when I show up, people are in a state of upset. Someone important to them has just died, there's confusing paperwork to attend to, and all the change and adjustment that happens after a death.

"So if people act a little odd, I give 'em a pass, you understand?"

Molly looked crestfallen.

"Listen, I'll give it some thought. Can't do much more than that, right?"

"All right, Lapin. I figured it was worth a shot. Keep thinking about it though—sometimes stuff doesn't occur to us right off...it takes a little percolating to get there, you know?"

Lapin nodded and they said their goodbyes.

Molly had to drop by Pâtisserie Bujold to get breakfast for her guests, and then take it back to them before it got too late. She hurried through the rest of her marketing, filling her basket with fresh vegetables and goat cheese made by a farmer about a mile away from La Baraque.

She was so taken up with inspecting the produce and chatting with the vendors that she did not notice a man following her, at a distance, as she went from one stall to the next. Achille Labiche was wearing overalls and he had his hands tucked under the bib. He did not appear to pay attention to anything at the market but Molly, his eyes pinned to her as he moved his hands nervously under the bib of his overalls, stroking his fingers and cracking the knuckles.

It's her fault, he thought over and over.

I'm not going to let her ruin everything.

Lapin had let Molly go reluctantly. He found her tremendously attractive, though it must be said that he found most women so. He bought a croissant from a vendor next to Manette, and then walked the many blocks to his new shop on rue Baudelaire.

Lapin was a junk dealer or purveyor of fine antiquities, depending on whom you talked to. And as he had told Molly and the interior of his shop proved, he was not lacking in inventory. In the front he had tables and counters heaped with jewelry and small bibelots, then farther back small furniture such as a child's desk and several footstools jammed the aisle, and all the way back he had arranged large pieces: armoires mostly, along with some big mirrors and a grand-looking settee with gilt flourishes. The walls were covered with art ranging from Impressionist imitations to ancient portraits to a few modern pieces that people would either love or hate.

When someone died anywhere around Castillac, Lapin was there in a flash, offering to help organize, assess, and also sell, if the heirs wished him to. He was not on the whole an unscrupulous businessman, although he did believe that by rights the owners should have some idea of the worth of their property, and if they didn't ask specifically and Lapin really didn't like someone, he might not be inclined to let them know that the scratched-up old chair in the attic was actually a *fauteuil à la Reine*, made and stamped by one of the grand eighteenth-century *ébénistes*—Jacob, for example—and worth a decent year's salary. Though he had only stooped to that sort of lie by omission a few times in his career, when the heir in question had been particularly odious.

He was good with people who were grieving, and his service gave them comfort. It helped to have someone who knew his way around during those early days after a death in the family, when there seemed to be so many unfamiliar legal and administrative tasks, all clamoring to be performed right when the family was simply trying to deal with the massive upset of losing someone they loved.

Of course, all families weren't so loving, and some people were missed more than others. Lapin had gotten into his line of work because he had always liked nice things, especially old ones; he had not expected to be a sort of therapist to the families, or to see the seamy underside of the proper public personae that most families managed to put forth.

Lapin was hoping to get his first customers that day. He wasn't in the most convenient location, but surely some would see the notices he had pasted up all over the village and in Salliac too, and be curious enough to drop by. He fussed with the counter by the front door, knowing that it would be the first thing anyone would see when they came in. There was an old ceramic bowl holding numerous rings. A platter with earrings arranged on it. A stand with five or six necklaces hanging from it, catching the sunlight quite nicely.

Then his cell phone rang and he got distracted. He failed to continue hanging the necklaces for display and simply left the cardboard box containing them sitting on the counter beside the earrings.

Nestled in the box, on top, was a silver chain with a star charm attached to it. The metal was tarnished and there was no identifying tag. A silver necklace with a star charm...to Lapin it meant nothing. The chain was real silver, but it was not valuable beyond that. It was just another trinket to toss in a box and hope someone would buy someday.

To Valerie's family and friends, however, the necklace would mean everything. It might mean, finally, a piece of evidence, a lead, something to hang onto after seven long years.

Chapter Twenty-Eight

La li la, la li lo.

She could tell it was spring. She could *smell* it. She spent so much time in the dark that her senses other than sight had sharpened, and as she lay on the filthy mattress Valerie imagined she could smell the leaves of the trees unfurling, could smell the frogs hatching out in the pond, the bulbs cracking open underground and sending up fat green shoots—the flowers, of course: she could smell them opening as June approached and even the nights were no longer chilly.

La li la.

She had counted so carefully at first, as though knowing how many days she had been held captive would help her, keep her connected to her old life in some way. But about three years in, she had become despondent and stopped walking back and forth in the bunker, stopped counting the days, and just lay face down on the mattress, not eating. She had no idea how long that phase had lasted because she wasn't counting anything anymore.

She wasn't feeling anything anymore.

Valerie was waiting to die, and the prospect of death, of

delivery from the endless incarceration in the bunker—death was the only thing she had to look forward to.

But Labiche had gotten upset. He couldn't bear it when she wouldn't eat. And so he made some unusual effort in the kitchen, even finding a cookbook in a secondhand bookshop and making her recipes from it. He had no talent as a chef but he did have fresh milk and butter, pork and beef from his own farm, and fresh vegetables from the market in Castillac, when he managed to gather up enough courage to go to it.

And even though Valerie felt angry and hopeless enough to want to die, that spirit deep inside—or maybe just her nose and her taste buds—wouldn't release her that easily. Labiche would come with a bowl of cream of sorrel soup, or beef stew redolent of rosemary and thyme and Burgundy, and she would sit up and eat ravenously, wiping the bowl with crusty bread. Sometimes he brought her little egg custards with a dusting of nutmeg. And he seemed so pleased to see her eating that at first she had allowed a little spark of hope to ignite.

Maybe he does care about me, and wants me to be happy. Maybe eventually he will finally let me go.

The sparks of hope were really the worst thing. Because whenever one lit up, and then extinguished, it was so much worse after. It was like waking up with a giant's foot firmly on your chest, a weight there was no squirming out from under, caught, held, so squashed you could barely breathe.

ACHILLE HAD NOT BEEN to the Saturday market in Castillac for many months, perhaps even a year. Lately of course he had other interests over at the Salliac market, interests that had to be put on the back burner for now, until he could take care of the immediate—and possibly dire—problem here in Castillac.

He was uncomfortable in the village. The market was far too

crowded, and he couldn't shake the feeling that people there were laughing at him behind his back because of what had happened to his mother.

She *had* been odd, he knew that. There had been times when the oddness went too far and his father had called for help and his mother had been taken to the hospital. Seven or eight times that happened. That's what the hospital was for, wasn't it? Achille didn't understand why people had to gossip so. He could sense them staring and then looking away if he turned to look at them. He could hear them whispering.

It was a hateful village full of hateful people, and he wouldn't have come at all except he had a pretty good idea that Molly Sutton would be there.

And he was not mistaken.

He had parked his tractor way down at the far edge of the village because the streets were too narrow and crowded to get much closer. He passed Lapin Broussard on the street, giving him an awkward wave and then looking away. Lapin had come to the farm after his parents died, and taken away some of the old clutter lying around that Labiche hadn't wanted. Gave him a good price on it too.

But he didn't like seeing Lapin because he reminded Achille of those unfortunate days after his parents' deaths. His father had taken good care of him—so good, in fact, that Achille had not been entirely sure he would be able to manage on his own. He knew how to take care of his herd, and his hog, but himself? That he had to learn, and it took some time.

Lapin was like the grim reaper, thought Achille, putting as much distance between them as possible. Always coming around the minute the funeral is over. And maybe that's kind of a sign, thinking about the grim reaper. A sign that he should do to that woman what he had already considered.

He was not a murderer. He would never be able to see himself that way no matter what.

But the thing was...Molly Sutton was nosing around where she didn't belong. He had been in a state of high anxiety ever since her visit, expecting to hear the shriek of sirens any second—and who can live like that?

In some moments, he was certain she knew. Certain she had seen the bunker and realized what was inside. Certain she was going to tell on him, and he would spend the rest of his life in prison.

He knew he would never, ever be able to make them understand.

It was easy to find her. In the central part of the market where the stalls were jammed up together and the crowd was thickest, there was the American woman, putting her hands in her tangled red hair as she laughed with the man selling leeks. Achille stood frozen, watching her.

If he could get her on a side street with no one around, he could come up behind her and snap her neck right quick. Then walk back to his tractor and go home. No more worry about the sirens. Free to get on with his various plans.

Achille moved around behind her, giving her plenty of room because *Mon Dieu* he certainly did not want her to spot him and talk to him. That would be completely unacceptable. He stood behind a stone pillar that held up the porch of an old building, and he waited.

The woman sure was a talker, thought Achille. He watched her joking and smiling with each vendor in turn, filling her basket with lettuce, potatoes, mushrooms. He watched her spend a long time with Raoul, the pig farmer, talking with her hands in the air until a line had formed behind her. Maybe someone pointed that out because she whirled around to look behind her, and her hand flew to her mouth and she stepped aside. Achille could hear her apologizing. Her accent grated on his ears.

He moved around the pillar so she would not see him.

She walked on to the next stall and then the next, taking an eternity to finish.

Achille was not a man with an appetite for food. His mother had been a terrible cook and his father had done all the work in the kitchen as well as run the farm. The food had been healthy but very plain, barely more than a sprinkle of salt for flavoring, and as a result Achille had never cared much about what he ate. The temptations of the market—the piles of croissants, the bundles of just-picked asparagus, the truffles and cookies and duck—made no impression on him.

He loved to feed Valerie, but for himself, he stuck to boiled meat and boiled vegetables, maybe with a bit of butter but never any sauce, or herbs, or even pepper.

She was getting to the end of the row of stalls now. Achille's fingers worked under the bib of his overalls; he clasped his hands together and then pulled them apart, stroking his fingers one by one. He was excited. He thought that snapping her pale neck might bring a certain satisfaction.

With a wave Molly said goodbye to the last vendor. She kept scanning the crowd as though looking for someone in particular. She began to walk and then turned around abruptly, searching—and saw Achille. Their eyes met. Achille could not hold her gaze and he looked down at his feet and then moved behind a large group of people who were speaking English too loudly.

He waited just a few seconds, mastering his fear. Then he stepped around the crowd and Sutton came back into view. She was taking a side street away from the Place, a narrow little street that would be perfect for what Achille had in mind.

Quickly he trotted to catch up with her, taking his hands out from under the bib of his overalls, and feeling a tingle in the back of his neck.

Chapter Twenty-Nine

Molly had hoped to see Gilbert selling his wild greens. The more she thought about him, the more she worried that something was really wrong and he had needed her help the other day. But she didn't see how she could go back to the Renaud farm —his mother had been quite clear that she wasn't welcome, and Molly feared showing up again might make whatever was going on worse.

She walked briskly down the narrow street and then onto the wider rue Saterne. Stragglers were still headed to the market and she was glad she'd gotten there relatively early. All that was left on her morning list of chores was a visit to Patisserie Bujold, and then back to the scooter and home again.

Achille watched her enter the pastry shop, and waited.

There was a line at Patisserie Bujold and they were out of réligieuses, which was probably a blessing, thought Molly, because if she didn't start to curb her pastry consumption she was going to have to buy a new wardrobe. She got croissants for the De Groots and Wesley Addison, hoping they didn't mind how late she would be getting back, and left the shop with a wave to Monsieur

Nugent who was too taken up with customers to pay her his usual unwelcome attention. On the street she found herself in a crowd of tourists, something you didn't see every day in Castillac.

"Excuse me," said a woman in strangely accented French, "can you tell us where the market is?"

"I'm headed back in that direction right now," said Molly, smiling. "Follow me!" And she led the group of six or seven middle-aged women back down rue Saterne and then along the narrow street to the Place, chattering the entire way about her favorite places to visit nearby.

Achille watched her go. There was no way to get her alone now and he felt frustration boiling up inside.

I should have acted. I had the chance, and I let it slip away. What is wrong with me? Why am I always so paralyzed?

Achille took off for his tractor, glowering at anyone he passed on the street. Out of habit he looked all around as he walked, never wanting the unpleasant situation of being sneaked up on. He glanced in all the alleys and side streets as he went by.

Down one such alley he saw an old man kneeling on the cobblestones. Erwan Caradec was known to the villagers of Castillac—he was homeless and an alcoholic, and the villagers fed him and looked out for him, sometimes giving him a place to sleep in a garage or hayloft. That morning Erwan had had the great good fortune to find a bottle of brandy in a brown paper bag, just sitting on the sidewalk, and he had indulged in so many gulps that he was now more or less lost to the world.

In several strides Achille was upon him. Erwan smelled ripe and the smell twisted into Achille's mind—the smell of filth, of illness, of madness. It enraged him and he reached his strong hands down and took the man's face in his palms and wrenched it so hard he thought the head might come right off.

Erwan gasped, and fell back on the street. He was still, and his skin drained of color so completely there was no doubt he was dead. Achille looked down at the crumpled body, and then he put his hands under the bib of his overalls and walked back to the tractor. He did not look back and he did not, even a little, regret what he had done.

Chapter Thirty

Molly stayed up late Sunday night, reading through the Boutillier file for the fourth or fifth time, and when Bobo began barking on Monday morning she was still fast asleep, and it took some minutes for her to claw her way to consciousness and remember who and where she was.

Someone was knocking on the door, and she threw on some clothes and went to answer it.

"Bonjour, Pierre! Come on in. You don't mind if I make some coffee?"

"Not at all, Molly. I just dropped by on my way to another job to see if the roof repair has held up?"

"Well," said Molly, thinking. "The pigeonnier is rented at the moment so I haven't been inside in nearly a week. But I've heard no complaints from the guests, so that's good."

"Indeed," said Pierre. "I'm happy to hear it."

"Although it hasn't rained, has it? I can't really remember. But it may be that the roof hasn't been tested with any wet weather."

"We've had a few light showers, but you're right, it's been lovely out recently, hasn't it? My wife is a devoted gardener like you and she was out dawn to dusk all weekend."

Molly smiled. She'd never met Madame Gault but knew she worked at the *cantine* at the *primaire* in the village, cooking excellent food for the young students. One night at Chez Papa, Lawrence had told her about how French children are served four course meals at lunchtime and taught table manners as well.

Impatiently she stared at her French press, willing the life-giving liquid to drip through faster.

"Hey," she said, suddenly struck by a thought. "You do all sorts of stone-work, right Pierre?"

"Yes. As you know, the buildings in this area tend to be made from stone, at least the older ones are. I have no lack of work repairing these old buildings, along with stone walls."

"Do you ever do other sorts of building? Do you ever make anything from scratch or is it all repair?"

"Oh yes, I've made new buildings when a customer wants it. There's another gîte business on the far side of Salliac, have you met Madame Picard? She hired me to build a series of bungalows around a small lake on her property. They turned out rather well, I believe. Are you looking for something like that?"

"Possibly," said Molly, thinking hard. "Okay, this is going to sound like an odd question, but I've been doing a lot of reading about the Resistance, and talking to Madame Gervais about the war. And I'm wondering if there are any...any buildings, structures, anything you can think of...where either Jews or Resistance fighters might have been hidden. I'd like to have a look, if anything like that remains."

Pierre stroked his chin. "I'm not sure I know of anything like that," he said. "As far as I know, from the stories I've heard—people were hidden in barns and attics for the most part. During the war, people most likely didn't have the resources for building something new—it was a very difficult time, economically, as you know. And on top of that, a new building would attract attention, which of course was the opposite of what they would want."

"Right," said Molly. "Okay, let's say just for the sake of argument that you were hiding someone and for whatever reason your attic wasn't suitable. Maybe you had no attic or barn. And you decide to build something to keep this person in, safe from prying eyes. You have to build the hiding-place with materials that weren't that hard to come by. What would you do? What would it look like?"

"May I have a coffee?"

"Oh, of course! Sorry, I'm just barely awake." Molly got out a cup and poured Pierre come coffee.

"Just black," he said, and then took a long sip. "Well, what I'm thinking—your imaginary person lives in the country, I take it?—I'm thinking I would build a sort of half-underground room, make it look like a root cellar. Dig out enough space from a hillside, bolster the ceiling with some good sturdy beams. The advantage of that is you've got evenness of temperature. Because it's dug into the earth, it won't get too cold or hot in there. Here in the Dordogne, it would stay above freezing all the time. And of course you don't need materials for walls, because the walls are dirt.

"You planning to hide away one of your guests?" he added with a chuckle.

"Ha," she said, thinking of Wesley Addison. "Not exactly. Though I did have the sweetest little boy here for awhile. Oscar. He's back in Australia now and I'm afraid he took part of my heart with him."

"I suppose that's the downside of your business, eh? Though sometimes I too meet a young child and feel a pang that my wife and I never had any children."

"Oh!" said Molly. "I hope I haven't—"

"No, no, you haven't said anything wrong. Iris and I tried when we were young, but it didn't happen. All feels like a long time ago now. And of course she is with children every day at work, at the *cantine*. She loves that about her job."

"I bet," said Molly, understanding perfectly, and also knowing that most likely her love for the job was bittersweet.

"So, back to my purpose in coming—are the guests at home now? Could I take a quick look at the roof just to make sure all is well?"

"They barely leave the pigeonnier," laughed Molly. "Newly-weds, you know. Why don't you drop by after the next hard rain, and we'll give it a look?"

Pierre finished his coffee and took off.

Molly called Bobo and wandered around outside, happily finding some tulips blooming around the side of a falling-down outbuilding she hadn't been able to figure out a use for. But maybe Pierre could give her some ideas, she thought. He had certainly given her plenty to think about this morning: a root cellar would be the perfect place for Valerie.

But oh, thought Molly, how dark it would be in there. Dark and damp. She shivered, her imagination making the dank hole in the earth feel all too real.

❧

ON MONDAY MORNING Thérèse Perrault took the call and ran straight from the gendarmerie to the location in an alley off rue Saterne. It was early morning and a group of people stood in the street, peering into the alley at the body of Erwan Caradec.

She kneeled beside him, putting two fingers on his carotid artery just for form's sake—no one seeing his gray face (or whose nose was working) had any doubt that he was dead.

"All right, who found him?" she asked as she stood up.

"I did, Officer Perrault," said a boy of about nine, stepping forward. "I live here," he said, jerking his head at the house next door. "I was taking out the trash, that's my job every morning before school. And so that's when I saw him." The boy's eyes went to Erwan again, widening as though surprised to see him still lying there.

Perrault called Maron and then Florian Nagrand, the coroner. She asked the onlookers to step back, reminding them that until she determined otherwise, the area was considered a crime scene. Though she spoke with little force, since she expected, as did the others, that Erwan had died of some alcohol-related problem.

"Poor man," said Madame Tessier, the village's most dedicated busybody who happened to live on rue Saterne. Her eyes were bright and she gestured down the block. "I saw him over there, by the bench in front of the Villar's house, just day before yesterday. In a state of advanced inebriation, of course. But we did exchange pleasantries about the weather before his chin sank to his chest and he slid off the bench onto the sidewalk."

"How did his health seem otherwise?" asked Perrault. "Did he complain of feeling unwell, anything like that?"

Mme Tessier shook her head. "He did not. Monsieur Caradec never complained about anything, actually, unless he had nothing to drink. Then he would complain about *everything*."

The group tittered.

"Come on now, François, you'll be late for school!" shouted a man out the back door of a house.

The boy who had found the body looked at Perrault. "Can I go? Will I need to come to court or anything?" he asked hopefully.

"Sorry, you're out of luck on that score," said Perrault, though she had great sympathy for his desire to get out of school on any pretext, and especially one as exciting as discovering a dead body in the alley behind your house. "I'll be in touch if I need you."

"It's sort of amazing Erwan lasted as long as he did," said a woman with her hair in a kerchief.

"He loved roast duck," said an older man, shaking his head.

And that was the extent of the eulogy given to Erwan Caradec on that Monday morning in May, in the village of Castillac in southwest France.

Chapter Thirty-One

While Perrault waited for the coroner to arrive on rue Saterne, Achille Labiche, newly-minted murderer, was riding his tractor to the Salliac market, intent on seeing Aimée and making some further progress with her. It was another beautiful day, sparkling and green, and he was pretty sure anyone who could be outside on such a day would be, so he was not anxious she would not be there. Anyone would be tempted to skip school on a day this nice.

As always he timed his arrival for just before lunch. He parked his tractor at the edge of the village as he always did. He was wearing the same pair of bib overalls he had worn the day before, and he tucked his hands up under the bib as he had then, pleased to have discovered this new place to put them. All his life, Achille's hands had felt awkward when he was around other people, making him self-conscious. His hands were large and dangled off his arms and fluttered sometimes and attracted attention. Safely under the bib was much better, and it was comforting to lace and unlace his fingers.

He reached the Place and looked around for the girl, making sure not to be obvious about it. He felt some pressure, from deep inside, the dead center of his body, to hurry everything along. It had been forever since he had someone to talk to, and his loneliness had reached such a painful point that he began to fear for his sanity. At least now that he had proven to himself he could kill not only livestock but a human, he believed his next try with Valerie would succeed.

With no Valerie to confuse things, no Valerie with her tuneless singing and lying on the bed refusing to speak any sense—with Valerie gone, the way was clear. As soon as the girl was ready, she could move to his farm with him. Maybe she would even live in the house with him, and he could bring her meals on a tray. He wondered if she would like to eat the same things that Valerie did, or whether he would need to expand his repertoire. He looked forward to getting to know all of the girl's quirks and preferences, to doing his best to keep her happy.

The cannelé-seller was in her usual place, and Achille did not have to work up his courage to speak to her as he usually did, but walked confidently over to her table and bought half a dozen, then changed his mind and asked for a full dozen. He felt so expansive, so optimistic after yesterday's "bit of work," as he was calling it to himself.

Biting into the fresh cannelé and smiling at the flood of memories it brought back, he turned and scanned the crowd again. And as though she were waiting for him, there stood the girl stood beside a bicycle, right in front of him, her hair in a ponytail, once again talking on her cell phone.

With a smile he started towards her, one hand under the bib and the other holding the bag of cannelés. When he was a mere twenty yards away, to his horror, he saw Molly Sutton coming from the other direction, heading straight for him.

Achille quickly turned and walked away. Thankfully she had been rummaging in her handbag and he was fairly sure she hadn't seen him. But the Salliac market was so small there was no crowd to get lost in. He ducked around behind a truck, his heart racing, clenching his teeth so hard his jaw began to ache.

What was that woman doing here? She was going to ruin everything!

He peered around the side of the truck. Sutton was talking to the vegetable seller, laughing as usual. Did she think the whole world was a joke, Achille wondered bitterly. He decided to walk away from the Place to try to calm himself. If Sutton was there looking for him, and he thought the likelihood of that was high, wouldn't she check behind the trucks right off? He had better find someplace else to hide.

Salliac was a small village with only four streets: two wide streets ran from north to south, and two narrow streets, barely wider than alleys, connected the other two. The houses ranged from stately to ramshackle, all made of stone, all built in other centuries. The green neon cross of a pharmacy blinked farther down the street. He passed a shoe store with dusty shoes in the window, a *boulangerie* with stacks of rolls on the counter along with baskets of baguettes, and a tiny café with two tables on the sidewalk and a bored waiter in an apron leaning against the doorway.

No one else was on the street and that was good. He could breathe.

But if he stayed away too long, what would happen to the girl? She might already have jumped on that bicycle and ridden away, and he had to see her that day, had to talk to her.

Had to give her the cannelé she was waiting for.

Abruptly Achille turned and trotted back to the Place. He wasn't going to let that Sutton woman wreck what he had planned and dreamed about for so long. He would find a way to deal with her, all right. Hadn't he had proved that he could do difficult things?

The girl was what mattered. Maybe he could get close to her, out of Sutton's sight, and call to her. She would look up and grin and come to him, right under that woman's nose, and wouldn't that be thrilling?

He slowed as he reached the Place, easing his head around to see where the girl was, and Sutton as well. They were both exactly where he had left them, the girl standing next to her bicycle, and the redhead chattering to the vegetable seller.

Sutton's not looking for me, he thought. Or if she is, she's being awfully crafty about it. And I think she *is* crafty. My mother used to—well, never mind about her. I'm not thinking about her right now.

He took a deep breath, settling his eyes on the girl. She moved around while she talked on the phone, putting her hand in her back pocket and taking it out again, brushing hair back from her face, hopping on one foot.

He thought the hopping on one foot was so sweet. She was young—he wasn't going to make the same mistake twice, and had spent untold hours criticizing himself for choosing Valerie when she was already a young adult. A young teenager will be so much more adaptable, thought Achille. She'll get used to her new circumstances. She'll be happy at the farm, happy with me.

Nervously he looked over at Sutton. Her back was to them; he could stroll right over to Aimée and Sutton wouldn't see a thing. But she could always turn around. She might be just waiting for him to make a move and then she'd pounce.

A small van was parked not far from Aimée, and Achille edged up alongside it, using it for cover. It wasn't ideal. He couldn't get as close as he wanted to. But at least he was out of sight of Sutton for the moment.

"Bonjour, Aimée," he said, his voice light and friendly. It amazed him, the tones that came out of him when he had the courage to reach out to someone like this. He sounded normal. Like anybody. Not like who he really was—and he was grateful for it.

"Hey," said the girl, flashing a smile. Then she stepped back a step, then two.

Achille was crestfallen. But he knew not to follow. "You know I can't miss a Salliac market," he said, not looking directly at her. "Can't get cannelés like this in Castillac, oh no." He drew one out of the bag and the sun caught it, making it look like a golden trinket a royal might carry.

The girl's eye was on the cannelé. Achille extended it just a few inches, a few inches of invitation.

Aimée made another quick smile and took the cannelé from his hand.

Mon Dieu, I thank you.

Achille had a sudden fear run through him and he needed to know where Sutton was—but the van was in the way. He moved up to the front of the vehicle and tried to look through the windows but couldn't see Sutton or the vegetable seller. His hands slipped under his bib and he stroked his fingers quickly, biting his lip.

"Okay then, thanks again," Aimée said as she flung a leg over the bike.

"Wait," said Achille, his voice calm and paternal. She stopped and cocked her head, waiting to hear what he had to say.

PART III

Chapter Thirty-Two

He had to go quickly. This was his chance.

After he came home from school, Maman had driven to a sick friend's house with a jug of soup. She was so rarely away from the farm that Gilbert knew he had better go now even though if she ever found out he had ridden his bike into the village by himself, the punishment would be unforgettably severe. His plan was to ride into Castillac, tape a new note to the door of the station—this time telling where Valerie was—and be back home long before Maman. She would doubtless talk for a long time with the sick friend, and he should have plenty of time; he wasn't even going to allow himself to go the épicerie for candy.

Straight there and back, that was all. And then—if the gendarmes did their jobs—Valerie would finally be saved. It wouldn't take them more than a half hour to check out Labiche's farm, and if they knew she was there, they would find her. Wouldn't they?

Gilbert watched as Maman's car disappeared around the curve in the road and then ran to his room. Carefully he pulled the note from his desk drawer where he had hidden it under some school papers. Once again he had used letters cut from a newspaper, so again it looked like a ransom note from a movie:

VaLerie B at LABiche faRm
HURry

HE OPENED his math book and slid the note in and closed it, then put the book and a roll of tape into his backpack, and ran outside. It was cloudy and a little chillier than it had been, but Gilbert did not notice the weather or the the roosters crowing or the sound of birds twittering as they made their spring nests. All his focus was on getting to Castillac as fast as possible, and taping the new note to the door.

He felt a little like Superman as he rode his bike—never had he pedaled so quickly and felt the wind in his face as forcefully. It was a slow Monday and there was no traffic. The road wasn't hilly and it was only six kilometers into town. In no time at all Gilbert was in Castillac and almost at the station—

"Salut, Gilbert!" yelled another boy.

It was his schoolmate, François Bardon. Gilbert hadn't thought in advance about running into any friends. "Can't stop right now!" he called back, and sped up.

The street in front of the station was empty. Perfect. He let his bike clatter to the sidewalk and slipped off his backpack. His hands were shaking as he unzipped it and took out the math book. Laying it on the sidewalk, he got out the tape and tore off a piece, then another. He pulled the note from the book and taped it to the door. Looking around and seeing no one on the street, he used another piece of tape, and then another.

The feeling as he rode back through the village was indescribable. The guilt of having failed to tell the gendarmes where

Valerie was had been so oppressive that he had barely felt a moment of joy since. But now he flew through the narrow streets with a huge grin on his face, taking his hands off the handlebars which would horrify Maman, his arms up over his head as though crossing the finish line at the Tour de France.

"Gilbert!"

He had forgotten about François. His intention had been not to stop for anything no matter what, but now that the note was safely taped to the door, he changed his mind. Maman would probably take forever at that friend's, talking about knitting and the weather and all that other boring stuff. He wheeled over to the sidewalk.

"I thought you weren't allowed to ride your bike to the village," said François, who was desperately excited to tell Gilbert the news of how he found the dead body of Erwan Caradec right in back of his house, but delaying the pleasure as long as he could.

"I'm not allowed, so what," said Gilbert, shrugging. François was so annoying.

"Guess what I found this morning before school."

Gilbert shrugged again.

"A dead body. Right in back of our house, over there." He pointed in the alley. "My father called the gendarmes and everything."

Gilbert's eyes widened in spite of himself. "A real dead body? Who was it?"

"Monsieur Caradec," answered François, wishing it were someone more unexpected.

"Wow," said Gilbert. "What did he look like?"

"He was all slumped down and his skin was gray. It was weird. I mean, I've seen Monsieur Caradec passed out a million times, but I could tell the second I saw him that this wasn't like the other times."

"Probably choked on his own puke," said Gilbert.

François nodded, sorry that he couldn't claim it had been murder.

The two boys stood without speaking, looking at the spot where Erwan had breathed his last. "Well," Gilbert said finally, "I've got to get home. See ya later." François nodded and went inside.

As Gilbert left the village, pedaling fast and swerving around cars, he forgot about François and Erwan and was suffused with the pleasure of having corrected a painful failure. The worry that his mother would find out he had been gone nagged at him, but manageably so.

It was only when he was almost home, when the skies opened up and rain came pouring down in buckets, that he gave any thought at all to the weather. Would the tape hold through a rainstorm like this? he wondered. And how could he possibly know, one way or the other?

This is horrible, Gilbert thought as he turned into the driveway of the farm, soaked to the skin, seeing the car already parked in front of the house.

Horrible.

෫෪

"BUT WHO IN the world would want to kill Erwan?" Perrault asked Maron as they sat in his office talking about their newest case.

Maron shrugged. "I don't think Nagrand could be mistaken about a broken neck."

"But couldn't he have fallen and broken it that way?"

Maron sighed. "Not according to Nagrand. He says the neck was wrenched around with great force. Not at all what you would see in a fall. Plus the only falling Erwan could have done was from standing to lying down. He wasn't near any steps, nothing like that. Nagrand was unequivocal."

Perrault was wrestling with her usual conflicted feelings about the situation. Things had been awfully slow around Castillac for months, and she was privately thrilled to have a murder investigation to sink her teeth into. On the other hand, of course she would never have wished Erwan ill—he had enough problems without getting murdered to top them all off.

"All right then, Chief, now what?"

"Let's start with the usual. We'll canvass the neighborhood, see if anyone saw or heard anything."

"I already talked to Madame Tessier. She'd spoken to Erwan on Saturday on her way back from the market, around eleven. Said he'd got a bottle of brandy and had put a pretty good dent in it. But he was alive, if not sober, when she left him."

Maron furrowed his brow. "I was hoping Tessier might come through for us again. *Bon*, let's get to it."

Perrault jumped up and put on her slicker. The big rainstorm had passed but it was still sprinkling outside. "I'll take west of rue Saterne?" she asked Maron.

Maron nodded. He thought Perrault a decent-enough officer, and got along with her better now that they weren't both vying for Dufort's attention. She would likely be reposted in the next few months, and he would miss her—which for Maron was high praise.

They left the station. Perrault was deep in thought, trying to come up with any reason why a person might want to kill a pathetic soul like Erwan Caradec. She reached down and picked up a soaking piece of paper on the street. She did not look at the side with the carefully arranged cut-out letters. The tape hadn't held and the whole thing was a soggy mess, and thinking it was litter, she dropped it into a trashcan on her way to find someone to interview.

Chapter Thirty-Three

Molly rode her scooter up on the sidewalk outside Chez Papa, leaned it on its kickstand, and hurried inside.

"I laugh every time I see you on that thing, " said Nico, drying a glass with a dishtowel.

"You're just jealous," said Molly. "And who wouldn't be, she's so gorgeous."

"So are you, my dear," said Lawrence, looking at home on his usual stool with a Negroni parked on the bar in front of him.

"Why, thank you," said Molly, genuinely happy for a compliment. She had not been feeling tip-top of late, she and Ben having made zero progress on the Boutillier case. "Now what is this latest bit of gossip you have for me? It's not like you to be so coy when you text me."

"It's not gossip, actually—it's news. And since it happened a few days ago, you've probably already heard." Toying with her, he paused for a long sip of Negroni.

"Kir?" asked Nico, already with crème de cassis in hand. Molly nodded.

"There's been another murder in the village," said Lawrence.

Molly gripped Lawrence's arm. "*What?* Really? Who?"

"Erwan Caradec. You've seen him around the village, no doubt...most of the time drunk off his wrinkled old bottom?"

"You mean the guy who hangs out down by the Desrosiers mansion?"

"That's the one. He was a fixture of the neighborhood. No place to live, and alcoholic, obviously. The neighbors looked out for him—gave him food, shelter when it got really cold, that sort of thing."

"That's kind of them," said Molly distractedly. "Was he a bad drunk? Yelling, violent, anything like that?"

"No, I don't believe so. Sometimes he would get worked up about politics and go up and down the block ranting about how the right wing was a bunch of proto-Nazis and should be run out of the country. But I don't think he ever directed any of his ire at anyone here in the village, not that I ever heard about."

"Are you sure he was murdered? How did you find this out?" asked Molly, always wondering about Lawrence's sources.

"Definitely murder. Perrault and Maron spent yesterday afternoon going door-to-door, to see if anyone knows anything."

"Nico, can we have two plates of frites?"

Nico nodded and went around the corner into the kitchen. No one else was at Chez Papa that Tuesday, early in the evening. Molly got off her stool and paced back and forth.

"I do notice you come alive when someone dies," said Lawrence drily.

"I'm just thinking," said Molly. "It just seems so random, doesn't it? A homeless guy—harmless—that everyone knows—is killed out of the blue? It doesn't sound right."

"Well no one would say there was anything right about it. I haven't heard if Perrault and Maron have any leads."

"But who would do something like that? What could the motive possibly have been?"

"Maybe there was no motive," said Lawrence. "Maybe the murderer did it simply because he could."

Molly shook her head. "Maybe in some places in the world, that would make some sense. But that kind of cold-blooded depravity, here in Castillac?"

"I do love the way you hold on to your fantasies. It's a charming thing about you. But Molly, why would you imagine anyplace—including Castillac—to be magically free of sociopaths?"

"I didn't say that," she answered grouchily. "Or, I didn't mean that, exactly. You know, supposedly the percentage of people who are sociopaths is higher than you might think, something like four per cent. It's just that while most of them are incredibly difficult, they aren't violent."

"Duly noted," said Lawrence, smiling as Nico returned with the frites. "You've utterly spoiled me, you know. I used to eat at proper mealtimes the way the French do, and now I'm stuffing in frites any time of the day or night, thanks to you."

"Glad to be of service," said Molly, plucking a scorching hot frite off the top of the glistening pile. "So Nico, how's Frances? I barely see her anymore."

"She's got a screw loose," said Nico, glowering.

"Uh oh," laughed Molly.

The door opened behind them and the sweet smell of spring livened up the room. "Salut, Dufort," said Lawrence.

"Salut Lawrence, Nico, Molly," said Ben, then kissed Molly on both cheeks.

"So who could have killed Erwan Caradec?" Molly asked.

Ben stepped back and raised his palms in the air. "Whoa, Molly, you jump right to it, don't you?"

"Lawrence just told me. What the hell? I mean, murder for a reason is one thing. But now random people are getting killed, here in Castillac? The place I thought was going to be all calm and serenity?"

Nico and Lawrence laughed. "Has it occurred to you yet that you don't actually like those things all that much?" said Lawrence.

Molly shot him a look. "Seriously, guys. Just give me one halfway believable motive and I'll shut up about it."

No one said anything.

"How was he killed?" she asked.

"Neck broken," said Ben.

No one said anything. Lawrence bowed his head.

Ben asked Nico for a glass of whiskey. When he leaned over to the bar to pick it up, he got close to Molly and she smelled the forest on him. It smelled good, until she remembered why he had probably been out there.

"In the woods today?" she asked.

He looked into her eyes and nodded. And then pressed his lips together and shook his head.

Molly wanted to ask for details but knew the arrangement with Boney had to remain private—and so with Nico and Lawrence looking on, she changed the subject to which vegetables needed to be started inside before planting in the garden, which none of them, including the full-time organic farmer sitting next to her, knew the slightest thing about.

THE NEXT DAY Molly worked in the front flower bed in the morning, trimming and weeding and daydreaming. And then, feeling restless, she hopped on the scooter and went into the village, thinking she would walk around the Desrosiers neighborhood again and check out where Caradec had been killed. She wasn't really trying to solve the case, just feeling curious about Castillac's latest murder, which as far as she could tell, was entirely without motive.

I guess it couldn't possibly be connected to Valerie, she thought, having parked the scooter and wandered down rue Saterne. It's funny how our minds always want to make patterns and connections even where there aren't any.

"Bonjour, Madame Tessier," she said to the old woman sitting in a chair outside her front door. They had not been introduced but each knew who the other was, and had a certain semi-professional respect for the other, busybody to busybody.

"Bonjour, Madame Sutton," the old woman answered. "I was just about to go inside and start dinner, but the weather is so spectacular, isn't it? No sign of another big rainstorm this afternoon."

Molly smiled in agreement. She wanted to ask exactly where Caradec had been found but thought it would be rude to leap right in with it, so she talked instead about the salad she had made the night before with frisée, lardons, and a mustard dressing. Mme Tessier nodded her approval and then, appearing a bit impatient, told how she was the last person to talk to Erwan Caradec. Molly was relieved at the change in subject.

"Unless, of course, the murderer talked to him," added Mme Tessier. "Can't speak to that, of course. Officer Perrault didn't seem to know when he was killed. That alley isn't frequented much. I won't say he could have been lying there for days because as I said, I spoke to him the day before he was discovered. Did you know it was a little boy who found him? François Bardon, lives in that house right over there, backs up on the alley, you know. Was taking out the trash like a good boy, and stumbled on poor Erwan." Mme Tessier shook her head sadly.

"Death is part of life," she said, waggling her finger at Molly. "But I think we can agree it is not the most pleasant part, even if it does give one a brief spurt of happiness when one realizes it was someone else's turn and not one's own."

"How true that is," said Molly gravely. The two women said their goodbyes and Molly kept walking to the end of rue Saterne, glad to be out in the sunshine getting a little exercise. She turned onto rue Baudelaire and admired the lamps in the window of the lamp shop (which always seemed to be closed) and passed Mme Gervais's house. And then, without having intended to go there at all, she found herself looking in the window of Lapin's newly-opened shop. Laurent Broussard, the sign said, his formal name outlined in gold, and looking very serious.

She pushed open the door to the tinkle of a bell. He wasn't kidding about having plenty of inventory, she thought, looking at chairs stacked up against one wall and several boxes of antique toys at her feet, the whole place nearly filled to the rafters with other people's junk and treasure.

"Lapin?" she called.

She heard some rustling in the back, then cursing. But no one appeared.

"Lapin?" she called, louder.

More rustling, more cursing.

Then she saw Lapin's big head appear over a stack of boxes. "La bombe!" he said. "I thought I heard the bell a minute ago. You do me great honor, paying my humble shop a visit," he said, moving through the furniture and boxes to where she stood by the front door, and kissing her firmly on both cheeks.

"Now, I know a thing or two about customers," said Lapin, his eyes bright. "I've worked enough flea markets to learn some things: some people like to be shown around. They like having the good bits highlighted, they like the personal touch. You?" he laughed. "You, Madame Sutton, are the type who likes to browse without any guidance, am I correct? So that if, say, I suggested you might like some of the jewelry I have right here—these necklaces for example—you'll bristle and want to be left alone."

Molly laughed. "Nailed it, Lapin," she said. "Although not left alone, exactly. Just no hard sell. Let me look and decide what I think before you try to tell me what I should think, you see?"

"Oh yes," he said with a grin, "I see."

Reflexively Molly crossed her arms and walked down a crowded aisle. "So all this stuff is from people's estates?"

"Almost everything. This and that I picked up at attic sales and the like. But mostly, when someone dies, a pile of objects remains that the family doesn't want, and that's where I come in. Or the family wants to make a little extra money, so they have me in to appraise what they're willing to part with."

"So. much. stuff," said Molly, coming back up the other aisle. "It's weird thinking that at some point people were really attached to everything here, you know? Someone's child sat in that little chair and learned to read, or some woman looked in that mirror every afternoon to fix her hair before her husband came home."

"I always knew you were a romantic, Sutton."

"Don't get any ideas," said Molly. "All right, it's time I went home." She stopped at the front counter and looked at the rings piled on a gold-rimmed platter, and slipped one on her hand. "Pretty," she said, holding out her hand and looking at the delicate silver ring with a small blue stone.

"Since we're old friends," he said, "I can make you an unbelievably low offer on that. It's extremely rare, that sort of ring. A real original."

"We're not old friends and you're so full of it, Lapin," laughed Molly. She slipped the ring off and put it back on the platter. Then she let the hanging necklaces lie across her fingers, gold and silver, someone's former treasures.

She started to peek into the box where, unbeknownst to her or Lapin, Valerie's necklace lay, but just then the bell tinkled and another customer came in, and Molly turned around, waved goodbye to Lapin, and went home.

Chapter Thirty-Four

Molly was lying in bed listening to Wesley Addison clomp around over her head, delaying getting up in the fruitless hope that he would leave La Baraque for the day and give her some peace. Her window was open and the racket of birds was astonishingly loud. A fresh breeze stirred the curtains. Bobo was outside performing her post-dawn patrol of the grounds, the De Groots had not been spotted in three days, and she had finally gotten a booking for the cottage—another family for two weeks —and would be able to pay off Pierre Gault and stop worrying about the electric bill.

Everything at La Baraque was as it should be...except, of course, for the continually nagging problem of Valerie Boutillier.

She was expecting Ben to come by for a planning session and so she gave up on avoiding Addison and put on a pair of shorts and a T-shirt, thinking that after Ben left she would spend some hours in the garden.

Coffee, a hunk of yesterday's bread smeared with some sweet butter, and she was ready to go.

Bobo barked her "hello, friend" bark (which sounded much different from her "who is this stranger?" bark) and Molly went to open the front door before Ben had time to knock. They said their bonjours, kissed cheeks, and then looked at each other with expressions of disappointment.

"The thing is," started Ben, "I don't know whether the note was just a hoax and we've been on a wild goose chase, or whether we've—or rather I—have failed her again."

Molly nodded. "I know." She gave him a cup of black coffee. "Want to walk around outside while we talk? It's such a beautiful morning."

They strolled through the meadow, Ben throwing sticks for a delighted Bobo, the orange cat shadowing them at a distance.

"So you got nowhere with Boney?"

"Well..." said Ben, "as far as Valerie is concerned, that's right. I would make a pretty large bet that her body is nowhere near Castillac. Boney and I covered a lot of ground. I only had him for a week, but I asked Rémy for some time off so I could do as much as possible before Léon came to pick him up. That dog is amazing, he really is. I swear I think he understood exactly what I wanted him to do and why.

"He did however find something else of interest, unrelated to the Boutillier case. A body buried deep in the forest of La Double. No telling how long it's been there—Florian is investigating and I hope to have some information by early next week."

"Jeez—*another* body!"

"It could be quite old, might be nearly impossible to get anywhere with it. Or of course a natural death with no crime involved at all. But there is a list of missing persons, both for the département and all of France—hell, we might have to look on the international list—so hopefully we'll get some useable DNA and Florian can give me some idea of how long the body has been there."

"Will he still report to you since you're no longer at the gendarmerie?"

"Well, not 'report'. But I think he will make time to have a conversation," said Ben with a small smile. "Florian and I annoy each other. But that's a matter of style more than anything else. Respect is mixed in there as well."

"Do you miss the gendarmerie?"

"No. Yes. Well," he said, laughing, "I don't miss the stress. I really enjoyed this week with Boney, being able to focus on one thing without worrying about neglecting other duties or having to justify the time spent. I really, really like being my own man instead of part of a military unit."

"So you're not going back?"

"I don't think so. That means I'll have to find something else... it turns out organic farming is not where my talents lie, according to Rémy."

"He told me you buried the spinach seedlings under a foot of mulch," said Molly, laughing.

"Oh, that was an early mistake. I've done much worse since then. He gave me the day off today even though it's peak season and there's a ton of work to do. The poor man would have fired me long ago if he weren't such a good friend."

They passed the pigeonnier where all was quiet, and reached the end of the meadow.

"Have you explored these woods much?" asked Ben.

Molly shook her head. "Want to keep walking?"

"Let's do," he said. "I did come through here with Boney, so at least I can assure you that you won't be surprised by any bodies."

"Glad to hear it. So...Valerie."

"Valerie."

"I was just so sure that the note was real," said Molly. "Of course I had no basis for believing that, and I understand that detective work is about tracking leads and finding evidence and using your brain, not just having feelings. But I couldn't see who would bother making a note like that, you know? I wasn't seeing —and still don't see—what the payoff would be. Wasting the gendarmes' time? Why would that be at all satisfying?"

"Remember that you found the place on the door where the note had been taped, and it was low? Probably a kid. And kids do things that make no sense all the time. Might've been a dare, something like that."

"I guess," said Molly. "I wish there were a way to measure the height of the note and then approximate how tall the kid is likely to be, and then canvass all the kids at school within that range of height."

"Very scientific of you," said Ben, reaching his hand out but then letting it drop.

"I just can't believe we spent all this time and effort and we've gotten absolutely no new evidence at all, not one teeny tiny shred."

"Welcome to my world," said Dufort. "No doubt Perrault and Maron are struggling now with Caradec's murder—when I spoke to them, they had absolutely nothing to work with."

"That's another thing I do not understand. Who would have anything to gain from killing that poor man?"

"You're making the mistake of assuming the murderer acts logically," said Ben. "And while there is always a certain underlying logic in a murderer's thinking, there is often a wild streak of insanity, of chaos. And it is that streak that a good detective tunes into."

Molly kicked the leaves and thought this over. "It was never this frustrating for Nancy Drew," she said, and this time Ben reached for her hand and took it, and they walked for a long time taking in the beauty of the woods in spring and not saying anything at all.

IT'S a simple matter of tying up loose ends—that's how Achille thought of it as he rode his tractor around Castillac to the north, turning onto rue des Chênes on the other side of the village. The street didn't have a shoulder for him to park on, so he drove past the cemetery and kept going until he got to a field, and tucked the tractor in next to a tree where it did not look at all out of place. Achille didn't know anyone on that side of town so had no idea whose field it was, but he wasn't worried that anyone would look twice at a tractor beside a field. It would blend in and attract no attention at all, just as he himself had managed to do all these years.

He set off on foot going south, back towards La Baraque, where Florence had told him Sutton lived.

Molly Sutton, he thought darkly. With her snooping and laughing and incessant talking: coming right up to his house, and knocking on his door! Interfering with Madame Renaud and her son! It was unconscionable, meddling in a family like that.

Intermittently he remembered Erwan Caradec and how easy killing him had turned out to be after all, much easier than killing a farm animal when you got right down to it; that realization gave him a bright new sort of confidence in his ability to do whatever a particular situation warranted. Even if it seemed too hard when he first thought about it.

Achille couldn't help thinking about how stunned his father would be if he found out Achille had killed a man—Achille, who had never been able to pull the trigger while hunting without closing his eyes, who always tried to talk his father into trapping the animals and turning them into pets.

He was a man now. It was shame his father was long dead and not there to see him, but Achille puffed his chest up a little as he walked along the road. His father would probably abhor the killing, since he had hunted to put food on the table and not from any pleasure in killing for its own sake. But Achille was sure that deep down his father would have been proud, too. He had done what needed to be done and wasn't that the whole problem with his mother—that she could not? That she would be mumbling in a corner of the kitchen, talking to people who weren't there, not doing what needed to be done?

Why oh why had he told Sutton they were still alive? If he had only kept his mouth shut!

A car was coming from the direction of the village and he jumped into the woods and stood still until it had gone past. Where was that house? He was impatient, looking forward to the moment when he first fixed his gaze on Sutton, and could watch her without her knowing he was there.

He knew he could kill her, he had proven that to himself. But he wasn't so tunnel-visioned that he couldn't see the potential in that for making his circumstances worse. If someone killed Sutton, maybe the Americans would send over the FBI and who knows how many detectives and police, the whole village would be crawling with them. It's not like he could run, not with Bourbon and his herd to take care of.

It's not like he could run with Valerie, either. Not to mention Aimée.

When he was about fifty meters away from La Baraque he slipped back into the woods. Now that it was late May, the leaves hid him from view almost immediately. He had no particular attachment to woods, always preferring to be in the fields where his girls grazed, but he appreciated the cover once he caught sight of the house.

He stayed still, well-hidden, and watched.

It was dusk. He saw a light come on, and then another. A shape went quickly past a window but he couldn't tell if it was Sutton or not. He needed to get closer but he worried that she might have a dog that might bark at him or even try to bite him.

And of course, Molly did have a dog. But at the moment when Achille Labiche was spying on Molly's house, turning over the idea of snapping her neck and shutting her up for good, Bobo was deep in the forest chasing after a red squirrel. She might have protested, if given a chance to defend herself, that she wasn't really a guard dog...though if anything happened to Molly she would never get over it.

When it was not quite dark but dark enough, Achille crept out from the trees and walked towards the house. It was a hodge-podge sort of place, he thought, lacking the pleasing symmetry of his farmhouse. It was hard to figure out where anything was from the outside—was the kitchen over that way? Was her bedroom in this addition, or the one sticking out in the other direction?

He kept one ear cocked, listening for anything that might give him away. He thought his father would be happy to know he had taught his son to move quietly, to listen, to anticipate problems as he stalked his prey.

There she is.

Achille could clearly see Molly making dinner in the kitchen. As far as he could tell, she was alone, standing at the counter, piling lettuce into a big bowl. Then she chopped something and threw that in. Poured herself a glass of rosé. Broke the end off a baguette, smeared it with butter, and ate it standing up, next to the refrigerator, as though she were so starving she couldn't wait another second.

Achille thought her almost grotesque, with her unkempt hair and her blue jeans. His mother had been demure, her hair in a neat bun and always dressed in a skirt, even while she did farm chores.

Molly Sutton was no one's mother. No one would even miss her.

Chapter Thirty-Five

Wesley Addison was in his room, sitting in an uncomfortable chair, looking out of the one small window. He had taken a long rest that afternoon, having fallen asleep while reading a monograph on dialects of southwest France.

He did not like to nap. Naps made him feel groggy afterwards which made him uneasy.

So it was groggily that he sat in the uncomfortable chair, looking out at the meadow and thinking about his wife. Seven years is a long time, but he had had moments, in the Dordogne, of feeling as though she had only stepped into the next room. Moments when the sound of her voice and the feel of her soft skin was so vivid he nearly spoke out loud to her.

She had understood him, his wife. She had been able to laugh at him in a way that helped him to laugh at himself, and she had somehow been able to hear all the things that he meant but was not able to find ways to say.

Wesley watched the speckled dog fly through the meadow and into the woods, and he would have smiled at the dog's energy except he considered himself a cat person and so smiling at a dog would be a sort of betrayal.

The window had been cleaned recently, but the glass was old and had a foggy patch in one corner, and spots in the glass itself; his view was not crystal clear. So perhaps this imperfect view would account for why he thought he saw something in the woods, right on the border of the lawn. Not something —someone.

He leaned closer, nearly pressing his nose against the glass. Dusk was falling fast and he squinted, losing the person's shape and then finding it again. Wesley stood up with a sigh. His wife had liked a cocktail at dusk, and making it for her had been one of the daily traditions of their life together, and so every day for seven years he had drooped at the cocktail hour.

He thought, since I am on vacation after all, I will have a cocktail myself for once. I'll ask Miss Sutton to toast Catherine with me. And then I will see to packing, and be ready to leave in the morning.

He clomped downstairs. He passed a window in the hallway.

"Miss Sutton!" he called out when he saw her standing at the kitchen counter.

Molly startled violently. "Mr. Addison! Good evening," she said, trying to recover. "Sorry, I'm feeling a little on edge. Have you seen Bobo?"

"Oh yes, she was after a rabbit, off like a rocket," he said, as he thought: though I am a cat person.

"Ah, she does love to chase rabbits. Can I get you a drink?"

"That is precisely what I came to ask for," said Wesley.

Just outside the window, hidden in a viburnum, Achille saw the big man come into the kitchen. He couldn't quite hear what they were saying but he could see the size of the fellow—his gigantic feet, his hands as big as toasters. Achille crept along the side of the house, away from the window. And then he hurried across the lawn and back into the woods, and ran all the way back to his tractor, which took four tries to start.

He knew where she lived, and that was a start. But he was not going to try anything with that bear of a man hanging around.

He wasn't crazy.

🙠

GILBERT HAD MANAGED to keep Maman from finding out he had ridden his bike to Castillac. Thinking quickly when he saw that she had gotten home before he did, he put his bike in the garage and wiped it down with a rag, and then went in the back door with a convoluted story about a fort he was building up in the woods and how he had hoped the roof he built was waterproof but sadly it turned out to leak.

He got Maman talking about the different ways you might be able to make a watertight roof out of sticks as she heated him up a cup of broth to warm him, and got him some dry clothes.

It was a miracle her suspicions had not been aroused, especially since her sick friend had told her all about Erwan Caradec and how he had been murdered. A story like that would normally have made his mother even more fearful and apt to overreact to any little thing, even getting wet in a rainstorm, but thankfully for once she told him about it without adding a long list of things he would no longer be able to do because of it.

Caradec would have been a major excitement at any other time, but Gilbert was single-mindedly focused on Valerie. Not to mention that the elevation of Caradec's death to murder was going to make François completely impossible to be around.

In any case, neither the illegal bike ride nor Caradec's murder had led to more tightening of restrictions for Gilbert, and so he was able to get away that Thursday after getting home from school and doing his chores, and sneak over to the Labiche farm to check on Valerie.

Once he was out of sight of the house, he slowed down. Gilbert was a boy who noticed things, and he touched the rough bark of the oak, saw the dappled shade made by the bright green leaves, listened to the birds. All his senses came alive in the woods and he felt happy and free, and full of purpose.

When he got to the edge of the woods bordering Labiche's farm, he settled down in the leaves as he had before. This time he had worn a brown shirt so he wasn't as worried about being spotted.

All was quiet. The cows were out of sight, probably in the west field. Gilbert could hear the odd moo in the distance, along with crowing from his mother's roosters coming from behind him.

Okay, where could she be? he asked himself. In the house, maybe in the attic. Or a secret room Labiche made just for her. The barn is gigantic, there's got to be room enough in there. Or what about that root cellar, dug into the hill just past the barn.

Seven years in a root cellar? Just thinking about it made Gilbert gasp for air, imagining the endless darkness.

He watched, his chin on his hands, looking for any sign of life, and listening hard for any cry for help. He wondered whether Valerie had yelled at first but no one had heard her, which to Gilbert seemed like pretty much the worst thing he could think of.

The sun beat down on his head, comforting and warm. It had been a long day at school and he had played hard at soccer during recess.

His eyes closed, and he fought against it for a moment, then fell asleep.

It was such a peaceful sleep, lying there in the soft bed of leaves with the gentle sun on his face, that it was all the more jarring when the dog started to bark nearby. Gilbert's eyes flew open and he saw a border collie racing up the hill straight for him, and Labiche standing about thirty meters away, watching the dog.

Uh oh.

He knew it was hopeless, but all he could do was jump up and run as fast as he could. He darted through the woods, his heart in his throat, the dog nipping at his heels. He was fast, for nine years old, and having been sound asleep only seconds earlier.

But not fast enough. Labiche caught up to him and grabbed the neck of his shirt and then quickly held Gilbert's wrists behind his back.

"What do you think you're doing?" Achille asked him, leaning down near the boy's face. "Spying on me? Taking notes?"

"No, Monsieur," stuttered Gilbert. "I was just out looking for greens, you know, to sell at the market. And I must have fallen asleep..."

"Greens? What greens were you finding hidden down in the leaves on my property? You think I don't know what you're doing? You think I don't know who sent you?"

His large hands squeezed Gilbert's wrists painfully as he pulled the boy back to his farm.

"What? Nobody sent me!" protested Gilbert, but he could see his neighbor did not hear what he was saying, and in fact didn't plan on listening to him at all.

Chapter Thirty-Six

Maron spun his chair away from his computer screen and rubbed his hands over his face. He had been working long hours since the discovery of Erwan Caradec's body but had little to show for it. Florian Nagrand placed Caradec's death sometime Saturday, though he hadn't been discovered until Monday morning. His body had not been moved so he had been killed in the alley where he was found. There was no weapon and hence no opportunity for fingerprints. A forensics team had come from Périgueux and they had found a few clothing fibers that were not from the clothes Erwan had on, but that meant little— they could have been acquired in casual contact such as brushing against someone on the street or a hug. Though who would want to hug Erwan Caradec, Maron could not say.

He and Perrault had found no eyewitness, nor anyone who heard anything. They had no ideas for a motive, no suspects, no evidence, no leads.

Here it was the end of Thursday. Time to go home to his apartment, cook a little skirt steak he had gotten at the butcher's that morning, sautée some mushrooms, pour himself a glass of his favorite Pecharmant to go with it...but there would be no satisfaction in it, not with this wretched case hanging over his head.

Oh, how he missed the days when Dufort had all the responsibility. And to think how he had grumbled, not liking being bossed around. Being bossed around turned out to be infinitely more preferable to this...this inability to let a case go because the success or failure lay completely on his head. This feeling that if the case did not come to some kind of resolution, he would feel such shame it would be a struggle to walk down the street without wanting to hide.

Impulsively Maron grabbed his cell and called Nathalie, the manager of La Métairie, and asked her if he could take her to dinner that Saturday night. She sounded surprised but agreed to go, and Maron patted himself on the back for salvaging his mood by taking action. He stood up, trying to think of some kind of direction he could give Perrault before leaving for the day when the station phone rang.

It kept ringing.

"Perrault!" he called out, but got no answer.

She is entirely too independent, he thought. She could at least let me know where's she's gone off to. He picked up the phone himself. "Chief Maron," he said, even though technically he was only the officer in charge and did not have the title of Chief.

Howling on the other end of the line.

"Hello? Slow down, Madame, I can't understand a word you're saying...what?...Your son is missing? Can you tell me your name please?"

Maron's body became more and more rigid as he stood at Perrault's desk, listening to Madame Renaud's sobs. His back got ramrod-straight, his thighs tense, the muscles in his face hard.

"Madame," he broke in finally. "Yours is the poultry farm just out of the village, on route de Canard? I will come immediately."

They hung up and Maron called Perrault's cell. "Thérèse! Where have you been? I need you to meet me at the Renaud farm...Yes, that's the one...Her son Gilbert is missing...No, it hasn't been long at all, he was at school today. I've heard from her before, she sees abductors hiding in every bush. He hasn't been gone more than a few hours and she's hysterical. I expect the boy is just off playing and lost track of time, but we can go have a look around and maybe that will calm the mother down...yes...on my way now."

Maron strode to the door and wrenched it open as though the doorknob was the source of his difficulties. He decided not to take the police vehicle but chose the scooter instead, and drove quickly through the village.

As a child Maron had heard the story of the boy who cried wolf, but he didn't think of it as he made his way to the Renaud farm. He tended to shut down when anyone got very emotional. And he did not pause long enough to consider that even a person who overreacted time and again, getting dramatically upset when nothing was actually the matter—that even a person like that might not be overreacting this particular time.

IT WAS DARK. The kind of dark you get in the country, without any glow from nearby cities to brighten the sky. There was cloud cover and no moon, and so the blackness was complete.

Gilbert sat on the concrete floor of Achille Labiche's barn, crying off and on. An iron ring was set into the floor and he was chained to it, a tight leather belt around his small waist, with the chain linked right to a metal loop on the belt. He could see no way to pry off the loop with his fingers and the buckle was locked with a padlock.

The barn floor was cold and he shivered, even though the night wasn't chilly.

He could see the door to the root cellar, where he guessed Valerie was. But he was afraid to call to her, afraid that Monsieur

NELL GODDIN

Labiche might come back. And he did not want to imagine what Labiche might do to him if he made him madder than he already was.

Labiche had dragged Gilbert out of the woods and straight to the barn. Gilbert hadn't screamed because he was too afraid, and he knew he was too far away for anyone to hear anyway. It was possible his mother might, if the breeze was blowing the right way and she was standing outside in the exact right spot...but the last thing Gilbert wanted to to was alarm his mother, though he knew that when he didn't come home, she would be...he didn't want to think about it.

Monsieur Labiche had muttered about Gilbert being a spy, sent by Madame Sutton. Gilbert would have thought that hilarious, or even felt pleased to be thought so dangerous, if he were not so scared. Chained to Labiche's barn floor, it was terrifying to understand that the man thought him such a threat. He had thought Labiche was going to kill him right then and there, once they reached the barnyard. At least he guessed Labiche was thinking about it, judging from the fiery look in his eye.

But then Labiche had done the evening milking and brought Gilbert a mug of milk, still warm.

Maybe at least he isn't going to kill me right away, otherwise why waste the milk?

The chain between his belt and the iron ring was fairly long, so Gilbert could stand up and even walk around a little bit. If he leaned against the chain, he could see out of the room he was in, out to the long milking stand with troughs, the drains, everything very modern and not what he was used to.

He tried to figure out how to communicate with Valerie. He wanted her to know about the note he had left on the station door, not having given up hope that someone had seen it, that someone would finally come to save her.

And now him.

All he had wanted to do was free Valerie Boutillier, and now he was as trapped as she was.

He cried a little, letting waves of self-pity wash over him, his shoulders shaking. But when the waves stopped, he sat up straight and wiped his eyes on the back of his hand. Valerie had survived like this for seven years. He could do it too. He wasn't going to die—he'd fight back if Labiche tried anything. And eventually—somehow—he would find a way to get free, and run straight to the root cellar and let Valerie out. Then he would sneak her into the woods and away from Labiche forever, and the two of them would run home and use Maman's cell phone to call the gendarmes.

He should have gone to the station and just told them, he thought. He should have told Madame Sutton at the market.

I'm never keeping a secret again. No matter what.

Chapter Thirty-Seven

Achille sat at the kitchen table eating canned lentils and sausage he had heated up in a saucepan. Usually he scraped his meal onto a plate but that night he ate straight from the saucepan with a big spoon, his hands trembling.

During the evening milking the herd had been restless and skittish, as though a wolf were lurking in the woods with his eye on them. But Achille knew there was no wolf. There was only Molly Sutton and the gendarmes, and he was afraid.

He did not want the boy. The boy was the last thing he needed now. His plan for weeks had been to get rid of Valerie—quickly, painlessly—and then Aimée could come to the farm. He had spent countless hours on the plan and believed it was solid. He wondered if Aimee might be able to learn how to make cannelés herself and they could eat them together at dawn before he did the milking.

The plan was simple: Valerie out, Aimee in. No room for any boy.

Plus, Achille knew Mme Renaud would be hysterical, and he did not want to be the cause of it.

He tucked his quaking hands into the bib of his overalls and went out into the field. Bourbon trotted at his heels. He found the herd and walked in among the cows, patting their flanks and smelling the sweet, earthy fragrance of manure. But nothing he did would stop the trembling of his hands, or the insistent voice that said *do it do it do it* so that the words were the rhythm track under every step he took.

MARON ARRIVED at the Renaud farm at about seven o'clock, a few hours from sunset. He wanted to wait for Perrault but squared his shoulders and knocked on the farmhouse door.

"Officer Maron!" Madame Renaud shouted as she opened the door. "You see? You see what time it is now and Gilbert still not home?" She tapped the face of her watch. "I tell you, I knew something like this was going to happen. I felt it coming for years! People—"

"Madame Renaud," said Maron, trying to make his rough voice sound gentle. "Madame Renaud, please, I need to ask you some questions."

She glared at him and started to say more but then closed her mouth and nodded.

"How old is Gilbert?"

"He's only nine," said Mme Renaud, bursting into tears.

Inwardly Maron cursed Perrault for not being there already. "Hey now," he said awkwardly, "it's only been a few hours. The likelihood is that he'll turn up, probably out in the woods with his mates, something like that—"

"No! People told me I was over-protective, but now here's the proof that I was not. It's a dangerous world, Officer Maron, a dangerous world. We should be out looking for him right now! Have you organized search parties? Why are we standing here doing nothing when my little boy has been *abducted?*"

Maron took a deep breath. He felt like slapping Mme Renaud

but was not close to giving in to the impulse. "What was Gilbert wearing when you last saw him?"

Mme Renaud tore at her hair and looked up at the ceiling. "I can't tell you that!" she wailed. "I'll say one thing—that American woman, Molly Sutton, she might know something about this! She was over here just a few days ago, sticking her nose where it didn't belong. She actually invited Gilbert over to her house, if you can believe that!"

Maron cocked his head. "Do you know Madame Sutton?"

"No, I don't know her. Never been introduced. That's why I'm saying it was strange. It was suspect behavior! Who goes over to someone's house they've never met and invites their child over? Something's not right about that, Officer Maron, you know I'm speaking the truth!"

A knock on the door and Maron let in Perrault.

"Bonsoir, Mme Renaud," said Perrault, reaching out to touch the woman's arm.

Mme Renaud was swept away by another gust of tears.

"Her son, Gilbert, nine years old. Missing since…what time did you last see him, Madame?" asked Maron.

"It was around four-thirty, I believe. I wasn't hanging around glued to my watch! But he came home from school as usual and did his chores. I haven't seen him since." She dropped into a kitchen chair and looked mournfully at Perrault.

"We're talking about a few hours?" said Perrault, shooting Maron a look.

"Oh, sure, minimize it!" accused Mme Renaud. "What does she know, an old chicken-farmer! I'm telling you right now, some-thing is wrong, my child is missing, and you need to get going, get searching right away! I don't care what your rules are, do you want to serve the citizenry or stand around twiddling your thumbs? You know as well as I do that the first hours after someone is missing is the best time to find them!"

"Any places he likes to go?" asked Perrault, chastened at having been caught out. "Was he upset about anything, a fight with one of his friends, struggling in school, anything like that?"

"No, no, no," said Mme Renaud. "Gilbert's a good boy. Does his work and stays out of trouble. I keep him right here on the farm and he does his chores and his homework and doesn't get into any trouble."

Another fountain of tears. "And she was asking about my relatives for some reason. *Nosy,*" she said emphatically to Maron.

Perrault looked at him questioningly.

"Molly Sutton," he said. "Came here a few days ago for some reason."

Perrault looked back to Mme Renaud. She wanted to comfort her, to put her arms around her and tell her it was all going to be okay. But first, Mme Renaud was the kind of woman who did not accept comfort from another woman—she wanted to lean on Maron, she wanted Maron to fix the problem, Maron to listen to her wailing.

And second, even though two hours wasn't a worrisome amount of time to be missing, Perrault had no idea whether it was all going to be okay or not.

Chapter Thirty-Eight

The following day was no easier for Achille. When he took the boy some breakfast, he noticed his tear-stained cheeks, and the sight made him feel sick to his stomach. He never wanted the boy! And his thoughts were so fractured and jumping around that he could not think of a single plan for what to do with him.

He kept having ideas—fantasies, really, and he well knew it—such as giving the boy some medicine that would make him forget he was ever in Achille's barn. Forget that he was a spy, trying to ruin everything for his neighbor who had never done anything to him.

Achille kept to himself, he had never made any sort of trouble for the boy. Why had the youngster turned against him like this?

Well, first things first. With great effort, Achille pushed the problem of the boy out of his mind. It was time to deal with Valerie.

Time to cross at least one problem off his list.

Achille's hands weren't trembling now. He went to the barn, to the back room where he kept his tools, and found a crowbar. It was heavy and lightly oiled, without a speck of rust. Achille's father had taught him how to take care of things. He always said a man's got to do what needs to be done.

Achille went back outside and strode towards the root cellar, Bourbon trotting beside him. It was the middle of the morning, a drowsy time at the farm, sunny and warm. The air full of bees. Smells of rot and earth and animals.

Right as he put his hand on the door-handle of the root cellar, it struck him: If Valerie is gone, there was nothing to stop him from simply letting the boy go. He hadn't realized it before, but now he saw that this was a classic "kill two birds with one stone" situation. Because if there was no Valerie, there was nothing for anyone to see. Gilbert could run back over the hill, meet up with Sutton, the gendarmes, or anyone at all. He could tell them any old story about what he had seen—and if they came to look, what would Achille care?

There would be nothing for anyone to find, and they would think the boy was making it all up. Achille would fill the root cellar with potatoes and empty crates. It would mean waiting until things calmed down to bring Aimée home, which would stretch his patience. But surely if they came looking and found nothing, any suspicion would blow over quickly. If only he hadn't lied to Sutton, he thought, for the ten thousandth time, his mind running in circles trying to come up with an excuse he could make.

But it's not time to worry about that now, he thought. This is Valerie's time.

"Hello," said Valerie, when Achille stepped into the root cellar, holding the crowbar behind his back.

Her eyes were boring into him. She seemed more alert than usual.

"Good morning!" said Achille. "I was wondering if you would like a short walk. It's warm and the sun is out."

It would be so much easier to just do it here, he thought. But I need for it to happen outside, where it will rain.

Valerie did not answer but lay down on the mattress and rolled over, her back to Achille. He got out the rope and tied one end to his belt. "Valerie? My girl?" he said, his voice breaking imperceptibly.

Somewhere way down deep, he hoped she would roll back over and grin at him, the way she used to. The hope was such a tiny flicker that it almost went by without his noticing it.

"Valerie?" he said softly, tightening his grip on the crowbar, his eyes darkening.

"Oh, all right," she said, swinging herself up and standing next to him so that he could tie her to him.

He lay the crowbar on the mattress. Valerie looked at it, then into Achille's face, searching.

"You're not singing today," he said.

"No," said Valerie.

Achille picked the crowbar up and led her, stumbling, out of the root cellar. She blinked and raised her hand up against the sun. The warmth felt terrifically good against her skin after the dank dampness of the root cellar; she could practically feel the nourishment of the rays spreading through her whole body.

"I am tired of the dark," she said quietly. "If I am very good and quiet, could I come back to the house?"

"We've been over this," said Achille. "How many times have I agreed to that, and then you come and start shrieking?"

"That was before."

"I know it was before. It was before I told you that the root cellar was where you were going to stay for the rest of your life because you wouldn't stop singing and shrieking."

The root cellar for the rest of her life? *No.* Valerie felt something like a cozy blanket fall over her body—a comforting, warm feeling, if a little suffocating—because she knew very well why Achille was carrying the crowbar, and she understood that he was going to deliver her from the agony of seven years that she saw no other way to end.

Perhaps having her head bashed in wouldn't be pleasant, but at least it would be quick, and she would never have to go in the root cellar again. She could at least die outside, with a breeze on her face and the sun shining on her.

Achille led her through the back field. He felt as though he wanted this awful thing to occur as far from his house as possible while still remaining on his land. Valerie was doing her usual thing of veering away from him, pulling on the rope and stumbling, and he felt irritated with her. With a thudding feeling in his belly he understood that his plan had a gaping hole in it—

—he had not even considered what he would do with her body, once it was over. He had too many things to think about, and with Sutton breathing down his neck it was impossible to think clearly!

He would just have to do it now and figure that part out later. He could always bury her in the woods—the woods went on and on and there was no way to search it all. Whatever needed doing, he would find a way to do it. He was a man now.

Do it do it do it

They passed the graves of his mother and father, under an oak in the middle of the field, a small pair of headstones side by side in the shade. If only they really were still alive, like he'd told Sutton. If only his father was still here to make things right.

If only he were in the house eating cannelés that Aimée made for him, and all this fuss and bother were behind him.

His grip tightened on the crowbar. Should I do it in the woods or in the field? he wondered. Does it make any difference?

Valerie walked along behind him, eyeing Achille's hand on the crowbar. Her body was flooded with adrenaline and it made her thinking sharp. Was there any way she could wrestle that crowbar away from him and bash *his* head in? I would have to be very very lucky, she thought.

"La li la," she sang, with a dreamy expression on her face. She tried to make her limbs look floppy and relaxed even as she watched for any chance to grab the crowbar.

Bourbon ran along behind them, watching them both. A dormouse rustled at the edge of the field but she paid no attention.

Thinking of Molly Sutton, Achille stopped suddenly. He turned and raised his arm, waving the crowbar above his head. "I am sorry!" he said, pausing an instant before bringing it down towards Valerie's head.

But Bourbon was faster than Achille. She sprang between them, clamping her jaws around Achille's wrist so that he yelled and dropped the crowbar. Valerie screamed and ran but the rope yanked her back as it pulled Achille towards her.

Achille was in shock, rubbing his wrist, unable to comprehend what had happened.

Bourbon was running around behind them, circling, yipping, urging them back towards the farmhouse, and before long Achille moved in the direction Bourbon wanted him to, and Valerie stumbled along behind, the crowbar left behind in the field to rust.

Chapter Thirty-Nine

Now that the rental season was underway (though bookings were still a little spotty for some weeks) Fridays were the calm before the whirlwind at La Baraque. On Saturdays Molly said goodbye to one set of guests, then she and Constance got everything cleaned up just in time to welcome the next set of guests. So there was no way to do any of Saturday's jobs ahead of time. Nothing to do but enjoy the easy Friday by puttering in the garden and thinking about how lovely it had been to hold Ben's hand when they walked in the woods the other day.

Not that Molly was interested in romance anymore. No, that chapter was closed, and all to the good. *I have Bobo to keep me company,* she thought just as Bobo came flying around the house with something smelly in her mouth, then leapt in the air and streaked back in the other direction and out of sight.

She had almost gotten the nasty vines out of the front border. It had taken months, but the border no longer looked like a jungle and it was time to take a trip to a gardening center to see what was available for planting. A lot of the flowers she loved—peonies and poppies, for starters—wouldn't bloom until next year. Molly wasn't that great at delaying reward, but she was trying to learn.

Or rather, La Baraque was teaching her whether she liked it or not.

"Molly?" said a hesitant voice.

She leapt to her feet, startled and on her guard. But it was only Thomas, on his bike, looking sheepish.

"Good heavens, Thomas, you scared me." She took off her gardening gloves and tossed them on top of the trowel, then brushed her hands together.

Thomas smiled awkwardly and came over to kiss cheeks, Molly stiffening at his touch. "Sorry, Molls, I know what you mean, though. Things are unsettled in the village again. I swear, until those women started disappearing, back whenever that was? Before that, Castillac was just your typical sleepy little town. Not murders and abductors left and right like it is now."

Molly nodded. "Yeah, it does feel a little like I dropped into the Bermuda Triangle of the Dordogne. So, um, what can I do for you?" She felt a little uncomfortable chatting away with Thomas after the hurt he had caused Constance. Of course, it was none of Molly's business. But at the same time she didn't want to act as though nothing was any different, either.

"Listen, Molly. I...I value your...your wisdom...."

Molly waited. Thomas squeezed the handbrakes on his bike over and over, and looked everywhere but at Molly.

"Oh, for crying out loud, Thomas, just come out with it!"

"I want Constance back!"

"Oh, really?"

"Yes, really! Molly, it was a stupid thing I did. I let Simone...I mean, I can't put the blame on her, I know it was me...but oh man, I don't want to be with Simone. We're not suited to each other, we're really not—"

"So you've broken up with her?"

"Well, not yet, I mean, I'm about to—"

After pointedly rolling her eyes, Molly turned away and put her gardening gloves back on. "Well, what's stopping you? You want to find out if Constance will take you back before you break it off with Simone? You realize that makes you a—" She stopped herself, realizing that her mastery of profanity was incomplete because she didn't know the French word for what she wanted to say. "And anyway, this is a conversation you should have with Constance, not me."

Thomas was hanging his head. "I know, I know," he mumbled. "It's just that I think I might have one more chance—maybe—and I'm afraid I'll blow it."

Molly shrugged. She squatted down and yanked out a vine with more force than usual.

"Say," said Thomas, "didn't you know that kid who disappeared? I thought I saw you talking to him at the market a few weeks ago."

Molly was about to give the root a hard wrench but she paused. "What little kid?" she asked, slowly.

"Name's Gilbert Renaud. Everyone in the village is talking about it. Why aren't you coming to Chez Papa as much as you used to? I was there last night—Frances and Lawrence were hoping you'd show up."

"You're saying Gilbert Renaud is missing?"

"That's what I heard. Was at school yesterday, got home, hasn't been seen since."

"Thanks, Thomas, for telling me that. I've got to go." And she turned and ran inside the house, looking for her cell to call Ben. A young boy—that was a whole different thing. It didn't fit with their theories at all, it must be a different perpetrator than the one who took Valerie. She needed to find out what Ben thought, what the gendarmes were likely to do.

Oh, that sweet little boy. A mischievous glint in his eye, if she had understood him right. It was impossible that anything bad should happen to him. His mother seemed slightly unhinged but Molly had decided she was just over-protective, as any single mother might be. And now…either the mother had been correct to worry, or the mother...but no, Molly couldn't believe she had anything to do with it.

*

EARLY FRIDAY MORNING Perrault and Maron met at the station. They now had both a murder and a missing child to investigate, and sorely felt the absence of Benjamin Dufort.

"Just call him up," urged Perrault. "I bet anything he'd be happy to help. From what I hear he's not exactly cut out for farm work."

"He resigned his post," said Maron, glumly. "I can't—"

"Well, I can," said Perrault. "Tell me what you want me to do this morning and when I'm on my way I'll call and ask if there's any way he would at least be willing to consult with us. Informally, of course." As far as Perrault was concerned, once a detective, always a detective, and she couldn't believe Dufort wouldn't want to get in on these interesting cases. And also restore order in Castillac as soon as possible.

Maron pressed his lips together and looked out the window. They had done everything they could for Erwan Caradec, but so far it was turning out to be a perfect murder: no evidence, no suspects, and no further ideas for where to look for either one.

He turned back to Perrault with a sigh. She was asking for direction but he had none to give her. "The Caradec investigation is a brick wall, as far as I can tell. Are you seeing something I'm not? Because all I see is a murder with no apparent motive. Like someone in the village or visiting the village just walked down the street one day and decided to snap the man's neck for fun. What are we missing?"

Perrault stopped herself from answering too quickly. She sat down and closed her eyes, imagining Erwan's last moments. Imagined that she was Erwan, standing in the sunshine by the alley on rue Saterne, pleasantly drunk, happy that spring had come. She waited, hoping that her imagination would guide someone into view, but got nothing.

"I don't know," she said finally. "Obviously whoever killed him did it for some reason, we just haven't been able to figure out what it was. What about little Gilbert? I'm not sure there's anything else to be gotten from his mother. I guess all that's left is for us to start searching? I could round up some friends to help, and we could at least cover the Renaud farm and anyplace else you can think of where he might be."

"Not yet. First go over to the school and talk to his teachers, the principal, and his friends. Let's see if they can give us some guidance on where we might look more efficiently."

"You're thinking he's just run away?"

Maron shrugged. "Could be." He narrowed his eyes at Perrault. "I know you're thinking about Valerie Boutillier, now that we might have another abduction on our hands. But one thing I think I could bet my career on is that the same person did not snatch Valerie and Gilbert. Entirely different profiles, if that's in fact what has happened to Gilbert."

"How lovely it would be if it turned out to be one person doing it all—Valerie, Gilbert, and Erwan." said Perrault.

"In your dreams," said Maron. "Now get going. See if Gilbert had any reason to run away. Don't be afraid to lean on his friends if you think they know anything. We'll start organizing the search as soon as you get back."

Chapter Forty

A part of Valerie had wanted that crowbar to hit her skull, had even prayed for it to come down hard and finish her in an instant. But it is not so easy to wish for death, even when your circumstances are horrendous and have been so for an eternity. Even as she prayed for deliverance, another part of her rose up to fight against the assault. Bourbon had saved her, but making the effort—struggling to live—had woken her up and brought her back to herself.

No longer lost, not drifting, but once again fiercely clinging to the faith that she would—somehow, some way—get out of the root cellar and away from the disturbed man who had held her prisoner for so long.

Achille came in the next morning after the milking, as he always did, bringing her breakfast of fresh milk and toast with strawberry jam, her favorite. He did not look her in the eye and when she reached out for the jug of milk he startled violently.

"Achille," she said softly, trying to soothe him, thinking correctly that a nervous Achille was more dangerous than a calm one. "It's all right. Nothing has changed between us. I'm still your Valerie." She worked to arrange her face in an affectionate expression and he flicked his eyes in her direction but then looked away again.

"It's just..." he started to say, and then stopped, because the memory of raising the crowbar over her head burned in his memory and in the moment he could think of nothing else. "I do love you," he said softly, and the words seemed to cause his insides to sag, almost to collapse, and now instead of the crowbar what he saw was his mother's drooping shoulders as she was led to the car for the last time, being taken to the hospital where he wasn't allowed to visit.

It had been the last time he saw her. She hadn't turned to wave, or given him a hug or kiss goodbye. He understood, now, that she was lost in her thoughts and that her thoughts were racing and racing and it was like being a passenger on a runaway train and there was no way to stop or control it.

And then in a burst of shame and horror, Achille suddenly remembered Gilbert. He had given the boy no dinner and nothing soft to sleep on. He had chained the boy to the bolt in the floor and then forgotten all about him.

He mumbled something to Valerie and hurried off.

Valerie heard him running to the barn and wondered what was going on. I don't have much time, she thought. He'll try again, and next time I might not be so lucky.

And then she saw something that she hadn't seen in seven years. At first she couldn't believe it. Had Achille really, after all these vigilant years with never a mistake, just left the root cellar without locking it behind him?

Slowly she crept towards the door. It was not even latched properly, and an inch, a whole inch of sunlight was pouring through the crack between the door and the sill. She stared at it.

Valerie listened. A rooster crowed in the distance, the cows mooed in the west pasture, birds were singing their hearts out in the May sunshine. She hesitated. She thought she could hear talking but that too was unimaginable and she wondered if all of it—the open door, the sound of talking, the birds—was a hallu-cination.

Long moments slipped by in the damp root cellar as she stood looking at the cracked-open door and the light coming in.

And then she gathered every bit of strength and hope that she had, put her hand on the door, and pushed it open. She looked around the farmyard but did not see Achille or Bourbon anywhere. But there was the tractor, its snout pointing towards the road, to freedom. She had never driven one before but she knew how to work a clutch. All she had to do was run and get on it and drive away, out of this nightmare and back into her life.

She ran as fast as she could though that was no longer very fast at all. Her legs were weak and shaky and her heart thumped. She swung up into the seat easily enough, almost choking with emotion. The key was in the ignition and she touched it with her fingers, then quickly settled her feet on the clutch and accelerator.

She turned the key.

The tractor sputtered to life and then died.

Valerie knew the sound would bring Achille running from wherever he was. She turned the key again, and again the engine caught. She eased up on the clutch and pressed the accelerator but too hard. It coughed twice and went dead.

"Come *ON!*" she said. She turned the key again and again, flooding the engine so that it no longer even sputtered.

When she looked up, Achille was already halfway across the farmyard, Bourbon at his heels. Valerie thought she heard someone shouting, someone inside the barn? But Achille never allowed anyone in the barn, not even the men he sold his milk to.

"What do you think you're doing?" he said to her, not sounding angry so much as wounded. "Where do you think you're going, Valerie? You know you belong here with me. With me always." He pried her fingers off the ignition key, wrapped one arm around her and lifted her off the seat like she was no heavier than a sack of feed.

In their seven years together, Achille had never touched Valerie except incidentally: brushing against her while moving around the small root cellar, or when she would stumble into him while on one of their walks. It had been one thing she could be grateful for. But now Achille put both his arms around her and hugged her. His head dropped onto her shoulder and she could feel him trembling, as though his insides were shaking and would not stop.

More than anything, Achille wanted control over his world. And now any semblance of that was splintering into a million pieces, and he felt nothing but dread. He would lose Valerie, Aimée, and Bourbon. His girls. He would lose them all.

They would come for him just as they had come for his mother.

He let out a cry of anguish and hugged Valerie more tightly before leading her back into the root cellar, and this time, he made sure the padlock was secure before he went away.

৽৶

MOLLY TOOK her time at the market that Saturday. She was feeling a little annoyed at Ben, thinking that he must know about Gilbert's disappearance but had not called to tell her about it or discuss whether it was connected to their investigation of Valerie. She knew she was being childish but she didn't want to call him first and hoped she might run into him at the market.

She had a long talk with Manette about her mother-in-law's latest ailments (which Manette was positive were more imagined than anything else), another long talk with Rémy about the problem of soil depletion and what needed to be done about it, and yet another with Raoul, the pig farmer, about the best way to roast pork, as well as the latest decisions of the government that were too atrocious to be borne.

The whole time she talked with her friends she was aware of an undercurrent of anxiety, felt not only by her but by the other villagers too. In the last week there had been a murder and then a child had disappeared. The illusion of safety felt irreparably torn and all the friendly conversations in the world weren't going to repair it, though they all persevered, because what else could they do?

After Molly had finished her marketing, she wandered in the direction of Pâtisserie Bujold, always figuring that in times of stress, an almond croissant was a whole lot better than nothing. "Bonjour Monsieur Nugent," she said, no longer even noticing the way his eyes lingered on her. "*Six croissants aux amandes, s'il te plaît.*"

He dropped the six golden crescents into a white paper bag. "Tell me," said Molly impulsively. "What do you think has happened to Gilbert Renaud?"

Monsieur Nugent's eyebrows rose so far up they nearly went over the top of his head; he was unused to Molly saying anything more to him than was absolutely necessary. "I cannot say, Madame Sutton," he said. "Perhaps he has run away. But a boy so young? His home life would have to be dire to take such dramatic action. And his mother—she may be strict, but she is not cruel. Always buys réligieuses on Sundays."

Molly nodded. She agreed that a mother who bought réligieuses every week did not sound like someone to run away from, even though her own experience with the woman had been awkward. She had the feeling Monsieur Nugent had been giving the case some thought. And why not? When your fellow villagers disappear at the rate they did in Castillac, who wouldn't be looking for explanations?

It was nine-thirty. Time to get back to La Baraque with these last croissants for her guests, and say goodbye to the De Groots and Wesley Addison, who was heading back to the States at long last. After lunch, Constance would arrive for their Saturday ritual of manic cleaning before the new guests arrived late that afternoon.

But Molly didn't feel like going home, not just yet. She nibbled on a croissant, for once barely tasting it, and wandered along the streets of her beloved village, thinking about Valerie and Gilbert and keeping an eye out for Dufort. She walked down the alley that privately she called Underwear Lane, and was not disappointed as the clothesline in the backyard of the La Perla house was crowded with sumptuously extravagant underthings, surely dry in an instant in the day's bright heat.

Will I ever meet the La Perla woman? she wondered. Or have I already?

She finished the croissant and ducked into a takeout place for a cup of coffee to sip as she walked. The image of Gilbert Renaud kept popping into her head. Please let him simply have gotten mad about something and run away, she thought. Please don't let anything terrible happen to that boy. I couldn't stand it.

Letting go of Oscar had taken much effort and a lot of tears, and Oscar was safely in Australia with his parents, happy and healthy, not in any danger. She barely knew Gilbert. A couple of short conversations, that was all. Nonetheless, she felt...not responsible for him, but connected to him somehow, the way it can be when you meet somebody and know you're going to hit it off. What had been going on that day when she visited the Renaud farm? Had he been trying to get her alone for some reason, or had she been imagining things? Was his mother...was it possible she had done something to him?

Was Madame Renaud just over-protective and suspicious of strangers, or something else? Something much worse?

Lapin had been useless so far in the search for Valerie. But surely there was some chance he knew Madame Renaud; maybe he had helped with the estate when her husband died. Enough of a chance to make Molly decide that the guests could wait a little longer for their morning croissants.

She circled back around to her scooter and secured her basket to the back, hopped on, and got to Lapin's shop in a matter of minutes.

The little bell tinkled as she came inside, but Lapin did not appear.

"Lapin!" she called.

No answer. It was perplexing that a proprietor would leave his shop unlocked and unmanned, and on a Saturday when the village was filled with people. Another reminder that she was not in Boston anymore, though she snickered at her naïveté at thinking Castillac was going to be all unicorns and rainbows without a criminal to be found.

"Lapin!" she called again.

Idly she looked at the jewelry on the front counter. She put on a bracelet and held out her arm to admire it. She ran her hand along the necklaces hanging on a stand.

And then, this time, she saw it. A silver necklace with a charm. A star charm.

Valerie's necklace.

Molly held her breath as she removed it from the stand. The file from the gendarmerie had been very specific: Valerie always, always wore this particular piece of jewelry. The necklace was silver with small links. The charm was also silver, the star had five points, and the points were long and narrow. About the size of a one-euro coin.

In every detail, exactly like this one.

"Lapin!" she called again, her voice strained. He must have picked up the necklace from someone's house, someone local. Why else would it be in his shop? He must have gotten it from the very house where Valerie was still prisoner.

Finally, finally a break! Once Lapin looked up in his records where the necklace came from, they'd have him. And her!

Molly heard someone at the door and whirled around. "Lapin!" she said to the big man. "Where the hell have you been? Listen, I—"

"Bonjour to you too," he said, with a half-smile. "Really, Molly, there is no need to always be in a rush."

"Just listen, Lapin. This necklace—" she said, holding it out, "where did it come from? It's important."

Lapin glanced at the necklace and shrugged. "Oh, now. I'm very good at my job, you know that, Molly. Didn't I get the furniture for your pigeonnier for you at a good price? And just the right pieces, weren't they, style-wise?"

"Lapin, *please*," Molly begged. "Just tell me where you got the necklace!"

"Record-keeping, I'm afraid...it is not my strength. If I get a genuine antique, I keep documentation, of course. Provenance makes profit, you understand? But a little trinket like that? Sorry, my dear. I couldn't tell you where that little thing came from if my life depended on it."

Chapter Forty-One

The boy hadn't said a word when Achille brought him a jug of milk and a blanket. A cement floor is cold even in May. But the boy had not said thank you or bonjour or anything at all, but just looked at him without expression.

Achille thought about the little frog he had kept in his room when he was a child, and how it had clung to the stick he had put in the jar and stared at him with its big eyes. In only a day the frog's color had gotten dusky and dull and even a child could see it was doing poorly.

Achille had let the frog go, even though it had taken all his will to do it. But the boy?

He knows about Valerie. And he will tell.

Achille had no doubt that the boy would tell, and no delusion that anything he could say or do would induce the boy to keep quiet. He was a talker, anyone could see that, even though once he was chained up, he had barely said a word.

Achille imagined that Gilbert had many friends, that he enjoyed playing and joking with them during *récréation*, that he could even talk to adults and strangers without fear.

He's not like me. He would tell.

Achille had been so distressed he had forgotten to eat anything. His belly ached. He kept imagining a whole flock of official cars turning into his driveway with sirens whooping and blaring, men jumping out with drawn weapons. Himself being led away. Away from his girls and Bourbon and the farm.

He paced around the dark kitchen, his thoughts jumbled and darting.

He would tell. She's my Valerie. Aimée is waiting for her cannelé. Cannelé, cannelé, cannelé, he thought, the words giving a beat to his pacing.

His mother's sagging shoulders in the green dress with little sprigs of flowers on it.

Finally Achille went outside and walked to the tool room of the barn. He picked up a length of rope and a hunting knife of his father's, a short and sharp knife his father had used to skin boars, a process that had sickened Achille.

His mouth was flooding with saliva.

A man must do what needs to be done.

As MUCH AS she wanted to stay at Lapin's shop and interrogate him to within an inch of his life, it was Saturday—Changeover Day—and Molly had too much to do that couldn't be put off any longer. She had guests to say goodbye to, cleaning to do, new guests to greet. She called Ben but got no answer. Reluctantly she told Lapin she'd be back when she could and sped off to La Baraque with the slightly wilted croissants strapped to the back of the scooter.

Molly drove right through the yard and through the meadow to the door of the pigeonnier. Bobo thought this was the most interesting thing she had seen in ages and bounded along beside her.

"Bonjour, Herman and Anika!" Molly called out, unhooking

the strap that held the bag of croissants on the back of the scooter. She was wondering just how quickly she could get things at La Baraque sorted and return to Lapin. "I have one last break-fast for you before you go!"

Silence.

She looked at her phone to check the time, then cocked her head, listening. Had they left already? Were they still in bed? Molly thought this must be the most successful honeymoon of all time; sightings of the couple had been as rare as ivory-billed woodpeckers.

"Hello?" she called. How does one say good morning in Dutch? "*Welkom!*" she called. No, she thought, that's not it....

She knocked on the door, waited another moment, and then lifted the latch. Someone was crying.

"Oh! Excuse me," she said softly, seeing Anika sitting on the edge of the sofa, her face buried in a handkerchief. "What is wrong?"

Anika cried harder. Molly stood just inside the door, feeling awkward. She had barely exchanged two words with this woman and had thought that the couple was having the most ecstatic time hidden away from the world in the magical pigeonnier.

Guess not.

"Anika? Is there something I can do? What's happened?"

"Herman...." she said, her voice breaking.

I figured as much, thought Molly.

"Is he upstairs?" she asked gently.

"No," said Anika. "He...he went into the village by himself this morning. He's been gone for hours. I've got us all packed and ready to go, and he's just disappeared."

"That's why you're upset? Don't you think he's probably just having a last look around?"

Anika burst into tears.

Molly knew she was the first one to see monsters in every closet, but this time she was pretty sure Anika was massively overreacting. "Look, I brought some croissants. You can make coffee in the coffeemaker if you haven't already, and by the time you finish eating, I bet Herman will be back. You've got another hour before I'll need to get in here to get ready for the new guests."

She put several croissants on a plate in the tiny kitchen, mumbled a few comforting words, and headed into the house to see about Wesley Addison.

Speaking of monsters in closets, there had been a moment when Molly had wondered if Wesley Addison had shoved his poor wife over the cliff at Beynac and then managed to do in Valerie Boutillier while he was at it. She blamed those suspicions on a lack of coffee, however, and thankfully they had not taken root.

When she came in through the terrace door, she found Addison standing in the living room with his packed bag beside him.

"Oh!" said Molly, always surprised to find someone in her house. "Bonjour! I'm sorry I'm late, I got delayed in the village—" She got a flash of Valerie's necklace then, and had to put on a fake expression to hide her agitation.

"Miss Sutton!" boomed Wesley.

"I'm sorry," she said, running a hand over her face. "I'm terribly distracted this morning. What were you saying?"

"I was saying that perhaps the next time I visit you might put a small refrigerator in the room? I do enjoy a cold beverage and it would have been quite convenient."

Molly smiled and nodded, having no intention of buying any small refrigerators.

"The taxi should be arriving at any moment, if he is a punctual sort," said Mr. Addison.

Molly walked out the front door with him, saying all the right things about how glad she was he had come and how much pleasure it would give her to see him in the future. Christophe appeared at the same moment as Constance, and Mr. Addison was bundled into the taxi and gone.

"A nutter, that one," said Constance, waving energetically as the taxi turned onto rue des Chênes.

"For sure," said Molly. "But a good heart. I can't believe I'm saying this, but I do hope he comes back. Now then, are you ready? The De Groots haven't left yet. Possibly trouble in paradise, I'm not sure. But while we wait we can at least attack the haunted room, and you can tell me the latest."

"I wish you wouldn't call it the haunted room," said Constance. "It's not a good idea to joke about stuff like that, Molls."

They gathered up the vacuum cleaner and the rest of the cleaning supplies and headed up the worn wooden stairs. She didn't think even the juiciest bit of gossip would distract her enough to get through the cleaning without losing her mind. After the haunted room, they still had the pigeonnier ahead of them, the new guests were due to arrive at four, and all she could think of was how on earth was she going to figure out where that necklace had come from?

Chapter Forty-Two

Molly and Constance did get through the cleaning, although not quite as thoroughly as Molly usually insisted on. Thomas had called Constance, there had been meetings, there had been kissing and abject apologies and grand promises made, but Molly had listened with only half an ear. She kept leaning the mop against a wall and calling Dufort, thinking about the necklace, about Valerie, about stupid Lapin who could have instantly led them straight to her if he hadn't been so lazy and sloppy with his record-keeping.

Herman De Groot had shown up and all was bliss again with the honeymooners, and blessedly, they were picked up on time. Molly and Constance cleaned the pigeonnier in short order, Constance biked off to meet Thomas, and the new guests, a South African family, were installed in the cottage. Fastest Changeover Day in history, Molly thought gratefully. She yelled at Bobo to stay and ran to the scooter. Before taking off, she tried Ben one more time. Still no answer.

Molly was a fast driver but usually not reckless, but on the short trip to Lapin's shop she nearly hit an old woman, nicked a car that was parked a little ways into the street, and ran a red light (after looking both ways). Quickly she parked outside the shop and banged on the door, then opened it and shouted for Lapin.

"Molly," he said, lumbering out from behind a tower of new boxes. "Calm yourself, and tell me what's so important about that necklace?" He gestured to a small bowl on the counter where she had put it carefully before she left.

Molly looked down at the necklace and then back at Lapin. "This necklace...." She paused, unsure how much to tell him. "Look, you probably already know this since there seem to be few secrets in Castillac, the way people talk. Dufort and I have been looking for Valerie Boutillier."

Lapin widened his eyes like a cartoon character.

Molly shook her head with a half-smile. "See, I figured you probably already knew. So listen, this necklace? It was *hers*. Valerie's. No, I'm not joking. You've got the key to her disappearance right here, Lapin. You've got to have records somewhere? You must make inventory lists when you take care of people's estates or whatever it is you do, you freaking vulture?"

Lapin smirked. "No need to get nasty, la bombe." He rubbed his chin with one hand and then shrugged. "I know I should keep better records. It's a failing, I admit that. I'm not a dot-your-i's-and-cross-your-t's kind of guy. More of an artist, really. Or at least an appreciator of art."

"This is not about who you are! You're saying you have *nothing?* No notes, nothing at all we can check? Obviously you got this necklace from somebody around here, right? Do you at least have a list of the places you've been, of who has hired you?"

"Um, yes, that I do have," he said, moving past her and turning sideways to get down the aisle jammed with antique toys. "Hold on, I'll get the notebook...."

Molly started to follow but the crowded back of the shop made her feel claustrophobic and she decided to stay put. She opened her hand and looked at the necklace again. The silver was tarnished. She wondered why Valerie had worn it so religiously that everyone remembered it. What did the necklace mean to her?

Come on, Lapin! she urged silently.

She heard something crash to the floor and Lapin muttering. He came back to the front of the shop down the other aisle, which was no less jammed.

"Well," he said, "not sure it will help, but I do have this. When I get a job, I write down the name and address because I might have to send an invoice or a check. So while I'm quite sure I never wrote down anything about that particular necklace, I can say that most likely it came from one of the names in here. Sometimes I might pick something up at a *vide-grenier* or flea market, if it catches my eye—but in all honesty, that necklace has no value. I only have it in the shop so that a young girl might be able to get something she'd think was fancy. It's nothing special."

"Oh, but it *is*," said Molly. "If we have any luck at all, it's going to lead us back to Valerie Boutillier at long, long last. Please tell me you have the names organized at least by year?"

"I'm not entirely incompetent," said Lapin, holding the notebook out. "Where should we start? Seven years ago?"

"Yes. Obviously earlier won't be any use. And I suppose you could have gotten the necklace at any point since then. Now open that notebook and let's have a look."

Lapin opened the notebook to 1999 and put it on the counter so they could both see.

"How come every single person in France has beautiful handwriting but you? Good Lord, Lapin, such scribbling," said Molly, using the English word for "scribbling" since in her excitement her French was getting shaky.

Lapin ignored the jab. "I'm not sure what looking at the list of names is going to accomplish anyway, if there's no record of which family sold me the necklace," he said. "And I am sorry for not keeping better records. But look at this place," he said, gesturing around the shop. "People collect *so* much stuff—sometimes I might collect hundreds of things just from one estate. And most of it's junk, just between you and me."

"You were all up in these people's business right after a death in the family—you saw them at a difficult time in their lives, a time when maybe their defenses weren't as strong as usual? Thinking back, did anyone—or anything—feel a little off? Come on, look at each name, and tell me if you remember anything at all."

Lapin nodded and chewed his lip, as Molly ran her fingers slowly down the first page of names.

"Are you looking, Lapin? And thinking?"

"Yes! Settle down, Molly. I have a bottle of pineau in my desk, would you like a nip?"

"No! I want you to focus on this list of names and tell me what you know. Why is it you seem to be the key to half the murders in Castillac, and so reluctant about it?"

Lapin grinned and shrugged a theatrical shrug, trying to hide his reaction to the reference to the Amy Bennett case, which was still painful to him.

"Wait a minute," said Molly slowly. "What year are we looking at, in this column?

Lapin leaned down to look more closely, then flipped back a page. "2004."

"Two years ago?"

Lapin nodded.

"These names," said Molly pointing to Jean-Pierre Labiche and Marie Labiche, route de Canard, Castillac.

"Yeah? Dairy farm just outside of the village. Um, nondescript farmhouse but a nice piece of land. Their son farms it now."

"And you were hired after they died?"

"Yes. An ordinary job, I believe, nothing there of much value. I did sell a few old farm implements to some Brits who used them as decorations in the yard."

"But so...Jean-Pierre and Marie, they were Achille's parents, and they died the same year, 2004?"

Lapin nodded. "If I remember correctly, I was hired in 2004 to sell some things that had been part of their estates. I believe they died awhile before that."

Molly said slowly, "I met the son. Achille. He told me his parents were alive."

Lapin and Molly looked searchingly at each other.

"I don't know why he would do that," said Lapin. "He's rather a shy sort. Harmless enough, I suppose. Doesn't like to come into the village much. Keeps to himself."

"Could you have gotten the necklace from him?"

"I told you—I'm about 99.9% sure it came from someone in the notebook...."

"What do you mean, 'rather a shy sort'?"

Lapin held up his palms. "I don't want to—"

"Oh my God," said Molly, slowly. "He lives...I'm right about this, aren't I? He lives right next door to Gilbert Renaud? The missing boy?"

❦

"THANK HEAVENS YOU PICKED UP," said Molly, having called Dufort for what felt like the millionth time. "Where have you been? At Rémy's?"

"No," said Dufort. "I was out for a walk, in La Double."

"I've got news," Molly said. "Ben, a *lead*. For real. Can you meet me at Lapin's shop right now?"

"On my way." It was something to love about him, how he didn't slow down to ask a lot of questions but understood she was serious and came immediately.

There was no room to move around inside the shop so she stepped out to the sidewalk and walked up and down, Lapin following. "Tell me everything you know about Labiche," said

Molly. "It was only two years ago that he hired you. How close together did his parents die? Did he seem, I don't know, capable of...of...."

"Of abducting Valerie? I couldn't answer that, Molly. How is anyone supposed to see that possibility in another person?" Lapin thought for a moment. "His parents had been dead for some time before Achille hired me, I'm pretty sure. Maybe four or five years earlier, something like that? It's not unusual for people to wait awhile after a death before hiring me. They want to keep reminders around, it helps them grieve, you understand? And then later on, they start thinking maybe they could make a little extra money if they sold some stuff they don't really want anyway, and that's when I get the call.

"Obviously if I had gotten the idea he was up to something I might have mentioned it to Dufort. But to be honest, I think you're barking up the wrong tree. So what if he lied? Maybe he likes to pretend his parents are still alive because he's lonely. It doesn't have to mean anything."

"Just tell me what you remember, Lapin. What sort of person is he?"

"Achille is...let me see...sort of placid. Like a cow. I remember thinking here was a man who had exactly the right job. Dairy farmer, you understand. The last person I would guess capable of violence, or something sick like abducting Valerie."

They heard a loud motorcycle and both of them startled and looked down the street to see who it was, but the street was empty. Molly was trying, mostly unsuccessfully, to think of reasonable explanations for Labiche to lie about his parents' being alive.

Sometimes people blurt out some stupid thing they don't mean, and then are too embarrassed to admit they said the wrong thing. Molly had certainly done so, although she was getting better at correcting herself.

That was believable. It fit with Labiche having some social difficulties, too. But...she did not think that was what happened.

She could remember his expression as he spoke, and it was not the flustered look of someone who has burst out with words he did not mean to say. It was...veiled hostility, she would call it. She imagined that he had liked the idea of his parents showing up and getting rid of this bothersome person—her—and none too gently either.

She thought Labiche needed his parents to manage for him, even at his age and in a situation as harmless as a woman he didn't know asking a few questions about geneology. His parents had been dead for years, and yet he still needed them that much, even for a simple social exchange, a few sentences back and forth.

"What else, Lapin? Give me more detail. Can you remember what you bought from him? Did he make a tidy sum?"

"Nah," said Lapin. "An antique plow, a wagon wheel, he didn't have much." Lapin paused. "Well, he's a bit odd, all right," he said finally. "But you know, growing up with a mother like that, it couldn't have been easy. He was terribly shy. Probably got made fun of at school. You know how it is."

"What do you mean, 'a mother like that'?"

"I don't know what her diagnosis was, but uh, *totalement loufoque. Dingue.* Off her rocker. She was taken off to the psychiatric hospital more than once." He waved at Dufort who was walking briskly down the street towards them.

Molly couldn't wait another second to tell him what she'd found. "Ben! Lapin has Valerie's necklace!" she shouted, holding it out for him to see. Ben hurried up to them.

"What? Let me see..."

"And Achille Labiche—he lied to me about his parents. Told me they were in the back pasture when I went to see him, and Lapin says they've been dead for years. Lied right to my face for no good reason. And—as I don't have to tell you—he lives *right next door* to the Renauds. He could have Gilbert as well." She delivered these last sentences as though they were the crowning glory of an airtight case against Labiche, but Dufort looked unimpressed.

"Molly, you've got to understand. Achille...he's had a pretty sad life. His mother wasn't well and I believe she died in the mental hospital a long while ago. He was lucky enough to have a good father, but still, as you can imagine, a thing like that is very tough for a boy. I don't think—"

"But Ben! The *necklace!*"

Dufort reached out his hand and Molly dropped it into his palm. He looked at it for a long moment, then held it up, but it was too tarnished to catch the light.

"Where did you get it?" he asked Lapin.

Lapin shrugged. "Just a bauble. Nothing anyone would pay much attention to."

"It is silver though, yes? Real silver?"

Lapin shrugged again. "The chain is. But not the charm, which is nickel. I told Molly that I only had it in the shop because it's something a little girl might like."

"Indeed. I remember her mother told me that Valerie wore it because her older brother gave it to her when she was young. She was devoted to him. He had a heart condition no one knew about and died in his sleep out of the blue when he was at university."

"How horrible," said Molly under her breath.

"Yes. Well, finding the necklace is a start, Molly. Good work." He smiled at her and lifted his arm as though to put it around her shoulders but then let it drop.

"But...you're not going to do anything? What about the lie Labiche told? You don't think that's strange? It was like he wanted to scare me off, like he was saying the grownups were coming and I'd better get going."

Dufort looked at Molly. "The way it is here, in Castillac," he said slowly. "We try our best to take care of our weaker members. Community means everything. So what if Achille has trouble talking to people and keeps to himself," he shrugged. "It's no reason to jump to the conclusion that the necklace came from his farm. Not unless Lapin says it did."

Molly desperately wanted to stamp her feet and yell but she contained herself. "The problem is," she said, her face turning red, "that you grew up here, and you have this loyalty to everyone in the village that's so deep you can't really accept that someone is capable of something evil. You have no *objectivity*."

Dufort looked stung. It did not help that lack of objectivity was exactly the reason the gendamerie did not want officers serving the communities where they had grown up, and he had cajoled them into allowing him to work in Castillac anyway.

Molly saw that she had hit a nerve, and with a softer tone said, "Shouldn't we at least go out there and poke around, ask some questions?"

"We've got nothing to tie him to the necklace or to Gilbert," said Dufort. "And today's Saturday—isn't this your big work day of the week, moving guests in and out?"

"Yes," said Molly crossly. "It's all taken care of—it's nearly dinnertime, Ben. I think we should hurry out to that farm, I really, really do. Can't we just pay him a friendly visit?"

Dufort looked off down the street. "Well, I'm not official anymore, now that I've quit the gendarmerie."

"Exactly! And you know Labiche, right? It's not like you'd be showing up to a stranger's house. Come on, let's go!"

"I wouldn't say I *know* him, Molly. But all right. You'll promise not to do anything that will make him want to call Maron? That would be awkward," he said, with a small smile. "No running past him to get a look in the attic, no accusations?"

Molly threw her arms around him. "What do you take me for? I'll behave."

Dufort nodded and put the necklace in his pocket. "I'm doubtful about this, Molly. Just because the man doesn't fit in with everyone else doesn't mean he's capable of snatching girls off the street." In spite of his words, for a moment he allowed the possibility to enter his mind that the case was actually on the point of being solved. But he couldn't allow it for more than a second before his defenses against disappointment flew up, solid as ever.

"And if I'm wrong and Valerie *is* there, well, no one will be happier than I, believe me. I'll jog back to my apartment and get my car. Meet you at the south intersection just before the village."

Molly nodded, gunned the engine, and took off. Lapin and Dufort watched Molly zip down rue Saterne on her muddy scooter.

"She's really something," said Lapin.

"Yes," said Dufort, blushing. "She certainly is."

Chapter Forty-Three

I t was cool in the barn. There was a window in the room where Gilbert was chained to the floor, and he could see the warm sun shining but not feel it. He spread the blanket Achille had given him on the floor, and curled up on his side.

He was so afraid.

Most of the time he could push thoughts of his mother out of his head. He knew she was doing everything she could to find him —she was not one of those people who get hysterical and just run in circles or give up. No, she would be hysterical and calling up the gendarmes every other minute, and out searching the woods herself until she was about to drop from exhaustion. He tried to think of Dufort coming to the rescue, and taking Labiche away in handcuffs, but the image felt made up and didn't make him feel any better.

Plus he couldn't forget that no one had found Valerie in all those years, when she had been practically right under their noses.

No one had listened when he tried to tell them. And now... Gilbert worried he would never have the chance to explain.

Gilbert sat up and inspected the chain again. It was linked to a loop on the thick leather belt Monsieur Labiche had cinched around him. If only he could get the belt off! He sucked in his stomach to loosen it just a little, and tried to pry the little piece of metal out of the hole in the leather, but he couldn't move it even a tiny bit. He kept trying, over and over, but got nowhere, the tips of his fingers now raw.

Is Valerie chained up somewhere too, nearby? he wondered.

He wasn't hungry. Monsieur Labiche had given him some milk that morning, and toast. Since the morning milking, all had been quiet.

He was afraid, but finally Gilbert decided to risk making some bird calls. At first he did them quietly, but when Monsieur Labiche did not appear, he made them louder and then louder still. He didn't know what he expected to happen as a result, only that he felt better for having made some noise. Maybe Valerie, if she was still alive, would hear, and know she wasn't alone.

He didn't actually know any bird calls, not technically. But he made bird-like sounds, tweeting and whistling and cawing, disrupting the calm quiet of the farmyard. He paused from time to time to listen, but heard nothing in response.

Monsieur Labiche had kept Valerie for all this time, all these years...but Gilbert understood that it was not the same for him. Labiche had not chosen him.

There was no good way to think about that.

Some rustling out in the farmyard. A yip from the dog, and then he heard Labiche's footsteps on the concrete floor of the barn, coming towards him.

Chapter Forty-Four

Molly kept the scooter running while she waited anxiously for Dufort to show up at the south intersection. Where on earth is Ben, she thought, pulling out her phone but resisting the urge to call. She craned her neck to see down both streets that led out of the village, hoping to see his dented green Renault appear.

Waiting was agony. She was dying to get to the farm and have a look around. Maybe Labiche would be busy and she could sneak off and have a real look around. She didn't remember noticing on her first visit, but probably the farm had numerous outbuildings, the perfect place to keep someone hidden.

Molly felt supercharged, as though she needed to move, needed speed. Her mind flicked quickly through various scenarios and images like a slide projector on steroids. Oscar. Saying goodbye to Wesley Addison. Bobo jumping joyfully through the meadow after a vole. The warm, sturdy feeling of Ben's hand when he had held hers on the walk with Boney.

Valerie. Gilbert. The necklace. The note.

Eventually the green Renault came into view. Molly waved, Dufort waved back and then pulled ahead of her, turning onto

Route de Canard. The Labiche farm was only a few kilometers away.

Molly glanced at the Renaud farmhouse as she passed it, wondering if Madame Renaud was home or if maybe Gilbert had turned up, but then her attention was back to Labiche and Valerie.

Dufort had parked just a short ways down the driveway, far from the house, and Molly hopped off the scooter and used the kickstand. The farmyard was quiet. They saw no chickens, no dogs, not even any cows. To Molly the place felt ageless, the old stone buildings (except for the new barn) looking as though they must always have been there.

"No car, but I'm not sure whether he owns one," murmured Dufort.

Molly was swiveling her head around, scanning for anything that seemed out of order, just as she had when doing her phony survey. *Maybe I'm just no good at finding something when I don't know what I'm looking for*, she thought. She walked slightly behind Ben, reminding herself to let him take the lead if Labiche turned out to be home.

"Monsieur Labiche!" called Dufort, in what Molly thought of as his gendarme-friendly voice. He rapped on the door of the farmhouse.

No answer.

"Maybe we should check the barn?" Molly said, hoping to get a good look around in there.

Dufort rapped again. "Labiche!" he said. They waited, then began walking towards the barn.

Ben and Molly had just gotten around the side of the house when they saw the dog. A border collie, running in that smooth, workmanlike way of collies when they have a job to do.

"Hello, dog!" said Molly, reaching out her hand. But the dog wasn't interested in that. She yipped and nudged Dufort on the back of one calf, urging him in the direction of the barn.

"She's herding you," said Molly.

"Labiche!" Dufort called again.

The dog nipped at Molly's leg. "Ow! Look, I'll go where you want, just lead the way!" The dog made a wide circle and ran behind them, back and forth, barking, as they got closer and closer to the barn. Once they got to the end where the wide opening was, the dog ran past them and into a room off the side, towards the back.

Dufort looked at Molly. "It's trespassing, if we go in there."

"Ben," said Molly, "just follow the dog!"

As they entered the shade of the barn, they could hear their footsteps on the gritty concrete with a bit of an echo, and then, faintly, another sound. Moaning? Sobbing? The sound of anguish. Ben and Molly ran towards it. They got to the doorway where the dog had gone in, and saw Achille Labiche sitting on the concrete floor with his arms around Gilbert Renaud.

Gilbert's eyes widened with surprise and then joy.

"You came!" he said to Dufort, who pulled him away from Labiche, and pushed him into Molly's arms.

"Achille," he said, sadly.

"I didn't know what else to do," Achille answered. "It's not like I wanted him here," he said, choking on tears. "Take him! I never wanted him, I swear I didn't."

Molly worked at the belt to get Gilbert free. It was such a shock to find the boy here when she was so certain it was going to be Valerie, that she couldn't quite catch up to what was happening.

"Achille, why is Gilbert here?" Dufort said. His voice was gentle but Molly heard much complication in his tone—she heard his excitement, his apprehension, his worry that even now, what he had worked for for so long would once again not have any resolution.

"I'm not talking about it," said Achille, getting to his feet. "You have him now, go on to Madame Renaud's. She'll be worried sick." He brushed his hands together as though the whole business was concluded and then tucked them into the bib of his overalls. "I've got to have supper and then do the evening milking. My girls are depending on me. That's my routine. That's what I have to do next."

He walked quickly out of the room and down the center of the barn, and quickly Dufort went after him. "Call Maron!" he shouted over his shoulder.

"Should I come—" asked Molly.

"No! Just see to the boy and call Maron!"

Molly felt a hot flash of worry. Ben shouldn't be alone with that man, she thought, biting her lip.

"I'm so glad you're safe!" said Molly to Gilbert. "Just hold on while I call the gendarmes."

Gilbert nodded, his eyes never straying from Molly.

"Thérèse? It's Molly. Can you call Maron and get to the Labiche farm? We've got Gilbert." She looked gratefully at the boy, who was fiddling with the belt, not giving up.

"Yes. No. No, we just got here. Haven't had a chance yet to search for Valerie."

"She's here!" Gilbert piped up, stunned that once again he had forgotten to speak up the minute Madame Sutton and Chief Dufort had shown up.

"Wait, what?" said Molly.

"It's—I've seen her. She's here at the farm! Labiche has had her all this time!"

Molly was frozen for a moment, taking that in. Then she told Perrault, and told them to hurry because Ben was somewhere alone with Labiche, and who knew what he was capable of? He needed backup, and fast.

The phrase "cornered rat" kept popping into her mind.

"All right, let's get you out of this horrible contraption," she said to Gilbert, "and why don't you tell me everything you know about Valerie Boutillier."

Chapter Forty-Five

And then, like a house of cards that had somehow managed to remain standing far longer than physics would suggest possible, then all at once exploded into the air: the world of Achille Labiche, precariously intact for seven years, came tumbling down.

Maron and Perrault arrived in minutes, siren blaring just as Labiche had feared. Dufort was making him a cup of tea in the kitchen, hoping to calm him down. The farmer was sitting on a stool muttering to himself, twisting his hands, and staring at the floor.

Molly had gotten the belt off Gilbert though it had been no easy job. The instant he was free, the boy insisted they look for Valerie, and Molly had shaken his hand and agreed. First they looked all around the bottom floor of the barn since that's where they happened to be.

"She's not going to be in here, I don't think," said Gilbert. "At least, I think she would have called out. I was making noise," he said, not wanting to admit that much of that noise had been crying.

"What about outbuildings?" said Molly.

They ran outside and looked around. It was time for the evening milking and the cows were crowded up along the fence, jostling each other and mooing.

There was a small garage attached to the farmhouse that was open to the outside. It was crowded with barrels, a lawn mower, and boxes. Molly saw no other outbuildings, except for the padlocked door that seemed to lead right into the side of a small hill, between the house and the barn.

"What's that?" asked Molly, pointing to the root cellar.

"Valerie!" called Gilbert, lifting his face to feel the sun. "Valerie, we're coming!"

But they had no key and the lock was firm. Molly knocked on the wooden door. "Is anyone in there?"

"Yes," said a voice. "Please. It's me. I'm your Valerie."

Chapter Forty-Six

That night, after Valerie had been seen by a doctor and then taken to her family, and Achille was behind bars at the station, Molly and Dufort had dinner at Chez Papa. They knew everyone would be bursting with questions and figured it was best just to see their friends all at once. As seemed to be a common thing in Castillac—when a bolt of good news hit, villagers instinctively wanted to be together—to talk it over, and most of all, to celebrate.

The chef made the sautéed mushrooms Molly loved, along with a potato and onion dish that was full of cream and a kind of cheese she had never tasted before that she found utterly magnificent. Lawrence was drinking Negronis of course, and Frances sat at the end of the bar accepting kisses from Nico whenever he had an extra moment. Manette had come in from her house in the hills with one of her daughters. Dufort's herbalist was there. Even Madame Gervais put in an appearance, though she did not stay long.

"I just can't get over it," said Manette. "Achille Labiche, all this time? I've known him my whole life," she said wonderingly.

"Exactly what's so troubling," said Lawrence. "We go along

from day to day, thinking we know people. But," he added, after a deep sip of Negroni, "we're all unknowable, that's the uncomfortable truth of it."

"I'm not going that far," said Molly. "Sure, all right, maybe some people have a dark side that's hidden from the rest of us. But no one here can claim they really knew Labiche. They only saw him at the market, and that was rare. He was just part of the background, you know? A person on a tractor, a house you drove by sometimes. That's not actually knowing him, no matter how familiar he was."

"Point taken," said Lawrence, raising his glass to toast her.

Dufort said, "I'd add that the situation was very strange, too. Perhaps if he had been defiling his victim, as usually happens in these cases, it may not have gone on so long. People who had any dealings with him might have picked up on something. Or at least he'd have been known as someone with a dominating personality, or a scary need to control everything...."

"Or maybe that's another fiction we tell ourselves," said Lawrence. "that if someone is really unbalanced and capable of extreme cruelty, we'd be able to tell somehow."

"You're just the voice of sunshine tonight!" said Molly, clapping him on the back and kissing his cheek. She was feeling a little guilty for not seeing Lawrence more often, especially since she had the feeling he was not yet over his broken heart.

"So it's true that Labiche never touched her?" asked Manette.

"Yes," said Molly. "I'm sure Valerie will have much more to say about it, if she decides to tell the whole story publicly. But when we got her out of that root cellar, she told me he had only kept her prisoner, but never hurt her. She said he learned to cook her favorite dishes, which just seems so...bizarre."

"It was like she was a kind of pet," said Dufort. "He wanted her to stay with him always, be devoted to him, always available to him...."

He did not need to remind the other villagers of the fate of

Madame Labiche, who had been taken away so many times during Achille's childhood. It was the kind of story everyone knew, but whose effects no one could predict.

"Oh, Ben," said Molly, "that reminds me. I wanted to ask you —who is Aimée?"

Dufort said to the others, " as Achille was being taken away, he was mumbling apologies to Aimée. I have no idea who he was talking about, and can't even think of an Aimée in Castillac."

The crowd was quiet, thinking this over.

"Perrault did a thorough search of the property but I suppose there's a chance he has someone else hidden away somewhere. We'll keep looking. And keep talking to Achille as well. He may have more to tell us than he was willing to tonight. Maron is checking the Missing Persons list for the wider area," said Dufort, feeling a pang of wishing he were still in uniform, sweeping up the last details that remained of the case, now closed, of the disappearance of Valerie Boutillier.

"I never thought we'd see her again," said Nico. "And honestly? I really never thought we'd find her alive. So—hurray to the two of you, for not giving up!"

Nico had spoken loudly and everyone in the place burst into applause.

"It was the bravery of Gilbert Renaud that led us to her," said Molly, kneeling on her stool and speaking loud enough for everyone to hear, and the crowd clapped louder.

Dufort slipped his arm around Molly as she hopped off the stool. "Gilbert got us started," he said. "But finding her—and him —that's all down to you, Molly Sutton." And then he leaned his face close to hers, and there in front of almost everyone they knew in the entire village, he kissed her right on the mouth.

And she kissed back.

Epilogue

Asense of unrestrained joy descended on Castillac after the end of the Boutillier case. There was Valerie again, getting her strength back, joking with Michel at the Presse, teasing Pascal at the Café de la Place, spotted all over everywhere in her desire to see her old friends. Gilbert was home safe with his mother, although she was threatening to lock up his bike indefinitely and never let him leave the farm unsupervised until it was time to go to university.

Aimée did not tell her parents that Achille had been giving her cannelés, but she delighted in telling her friends how close she had come to disappearing and becoming part of Labiche's menagerie.

Achille was awaiting trial and being interviewed by a panel of psychiatrists. It was in one of these sessions, his voice trembling but with a note of defiance, that Labiche admitted he had killed Erwan Caradec, thoroughly surprising (and relieving) Maron and Perrault.

Molly emailed Wesley Addison to let him know that Valerie was back with her family, and he made a reservation for the month of June the following summer, if he could stay in the same room at La Baraque.

The talk around the village was no longer about abductions or mental illness or what constituted evil. Now it was about Dufort and Sutton, who had left Chez Papa that night holding hands, and no one had seen them for several days after.

Also by Nell Goddin

Glossary

Chapter 1:
    gîte..................a furnished vacation lodging, usually on the inexpensive side
    La Baraque...........shed, hut. (slang: dump)
    pigeonnier...........structure for raising pigeons. Dovecote.
    pâtisserie.............pastry shop

Chapter 2:
    gendarmerie.............police force (military arm)
    salut......................hey, hi
    bon......................good, fine

Chapter 3:
    potager...................vegetable garden
    rue des Chênes...........Oak Street

Chapter 4:
    la bombe.................good-looking woman (slang)
    à bientôt.................see you soon
    foie gras..................goose liver

GLOSSARY

Chapter 6:

coeur à la crème..........a creamy, cheesy dessert. Literally, heart of cream

soupçon...................a very small amount. Literally, a suspicion

Chapter 9:

croissant aux amandes...almond croissant

département..............region in France

Chapter 10:

épicerie...................small grocery store

mairie.....................town hall

Chapter 11:

oui.........................yes

Chapter 14:

Milice......................paramilitary force created by the Vichy government in France (during World War 2) to fight against the French Resistance

Chapter 16:

apéro......................short for apéritif. Cocktail.

verklempt.................too emotional to speak, overcome with feeling (Yiddish)

Chapter 17:

crêperie...................shop selling crêpes

Chapter 18:

bonsoir...................good evening

chérie.....................dear

Chapter 26:

absolument.................absolutely

Castillaçois..................people of Castillac

Chapter 27:

fauteuil à la Reine............Queen's armchair. An antique, open-sided, upholstered armchair.

ébéniste.......................cabinetmaker

Chapter 30:

cantine.......................cafeteria

primaire.......................primary school

Chapter 31:

boulangerie..................bakery

Chapter 40:

s'il te plaît...................please

Chapter 41:

récréation...................recess

Chapter 42:

vide-grenier.................tag sale, garage sale. Literally, empty-attic

totalement loufoque.......totally crazy

dingue.......................insane, nuts, crazy

Acknowledgments

A hearty shout-out to Elizabeth Cogar Batty and Nancy Kelley for their helpful critiques and encouragement. Thank you!

About the Author

Nell Goddin has been a mystery fan since reading Agatha Christie with her best friend on long summer days. She's a lover of all things French and has two children, two cats, and two dogs (both mutts with no sense of dignity whatsoever).

Drop by for a visit!
www.nellgoddin.com
nell@nellgoddin.com

Made in the USA
Las Vegas, NV
28 June 2023

74006135R00184